T0265564

THE MUNICH LIST

Alton Brunswick

THE MUNICH LIST

Addison & Highsmith

Addison & Highsmith Publishers

Las Vegas ◊ Chicago ◊ Palm Beach

Published in the United States of America by
Histria Books, a division of Histria LLC
7181 N. Hualapai Way, Ste. 130-86
Las Vegas, NV 89166 USA
HistriaBooks.com

Addison & Highsmith is an imprint of Histria Books. Titles published under the imprints of Histria Books are distributed worldwide.

All rights reserved. No part of this book may be reprinted or reproduced or utilized in any form or by any electronic, mechanical or other means, now known or hereafter invented, including photocopying and recording, or in any information storage or retrieval system, without the permission in writing from the Publisher.

Library of Congress Control Number: 2022943057

ISBN 978-1-59211-179-4 (hardcover)
ISBN 978-1-59211-239-5 (eBook)

Copyright © 2022 by Alton Brunswick

CHAPTER ONE

San Diego, California.

"Beautiful city, isn't it?" the bearded middle-aged man said as he dragged on his pipe, "I sometimes feel we still have a lot to offer this world. What do you think, pal?"

He looked out the window of the Bentley and exhaled.

The man next to him in the rear seat said nothing. He was much older, with sharp eyes set deep into their sockets. He was blond with beetle brows and small lips. His attention was on the golf course, studying players as they got down from their expensive cars, exquisite girls, obviously not their wives, following. He had been watching them with keen interest as they started arriving. The scene reminded him of his early years in the US when he could have as many as four women a day. He went to bed with any woman he wished. He had money and didn't have to work for them or the women. He shook his head and gave a smile.

"I know you still want Baxter," the smoking man said, nudging the older man.

This time he got his attention.

"Baxter? Why do you say that?"

"C'mon, pal. I'm no fool. I know what he has done to your business and his interest in buying the supermarket chain owned by the Patels. Don't bullshit me. I wasn't born yesterday."

"I understand your statement and know where you are coming from, but you are wrong about my intentions. On the contrary, I could have whatever I wanted in this country. He is no match for me in any way. As a matter of fact, I don't even think about him."

"Who are you? That's not true, and you know it. I know what you are planning. I hear things."

"I don't know what you have heard about me, but I suggest you check the source of information you have about me. You can easily get deceived."

The younger man pressed a button by his seat, a small compartment opened between the men, revealing a tiny compartment that served as a fridge. He reached for a pint bottle of liquor which he uncapped and sipped. The older man shut the fridge and looked at his colleague.

"What happened to your wife?"

"I killed her," replied the younger man.

"I thought so. I like honest men. Hopefully, you are not planning on killing me, are you?"

"Hell no."

"I better get to the course now. The fun is about to begin. As the champion, every player will like to beat me, and most importantly, my business is to make sure I stay on top till I retire. I want to retire as an undefeated champion."

"I know. I admire you not only in business but in golf as well. Unfortunately, I still haven't received payment for the work I did for you, Daddy."

The blond man twitched a brow as he gazed at his companion, "What work are you talking about?"

"We don't have to go over this shit again. You owe me, and you know it. I need my money now."

"I don't owe you anything. As far as I recall, you haven't done any work for me."

"If you don't pay me, I'll make you regret."

The older man opened the door while he looked at his friend.

"Threatening me? You'll make me regret? Regret what?"

"C'mon, man, it's an awful lot of money you owe me. You can't deny it. I will not let you go without paying for my services."

"If you can tell the police what specific work you did for me and show evidence, I will definitely pay you. Don't forget you killed your wife and framed somebody else for it. Our conversation is recorded, so you can't change your story."

The older man burst into laughter as he stepped out of the Bentley with a cap in his hand, which he donned and pulled up the lapel of his jacket. Meanwhile, the man in the car had his gun out and was fixing a silencer to it. As the older man shut the door and started towards the players, the younger man aimed his gun at him. Suddenly, the window by him shattered, his head exploding before he could pull the trigger. The gun fell off his hand as he hunched forward against the rear of the driver's seat. A man in a tuxedo hurried to take the wheel of the Bentley and drove away immediately. Ten minutes later, another Bentley of the same color pulled to a halt at the same spot. The driver got out and walked to a shed where two carts stood. He scanned the course occasionally with binoculars.

As the game progressed, the ball went towards the end of the course, boarded by scrubland. The older man went after it. He did that to alert his competitors that he was still strong enough to run—he didn't need anybody's assistance. The few spectators cheered anytime he did that. He liked that. He enjoyed the accolades of his peers and the media. He had received a message that his colleague in the Bentley was dead, and he knew exactly why. While he searched for the ball, he heard a sound behind him and whirled. A masked man stood in front of him, with one hand in his long coat, the other behind him. The blond man knew the man was armed, but he didn't know who he was and why he was there. The masked man smiled as his cheeks bulged. The blond man was aware that the man knew him.

"Who are?" he asked as he focused on the face he couldn't see.

"You killed him, didn't you?"

"I killed who? I don't know what you're talking about."

"I saw what happened to him. Your men shot him in the rear seat of your car minutes ago."

"Look, I came here to play golf, and that's what I'm doing. If you witnessed something unlawful or criminal, I suggest you go to the cops with your evidence."

The older man turned to leave. The masked man cocked his gun, causing him to freeze.

"If you make one wrong move, you're finished. Don't forget I know who you are."

The older man turned to face him. The statement appeared to have jolted him.

"What did you say, young man?"

"I said I know who you are. Not only here in California, but ..." he pointed the gun at the older man's face, "...you know what I'm talking about, don't you?"

"Who are you? And what are you talking about?"

"I don't have to tell you who I am, but I believe you know exactly what I'm talking about. I know what you have done. I know where you are headed, but more importantly, I want you to remember what you have done to me and my business. You are doing well now, and the world hails you, but what about me and my family? The world sees you as a hero, but what about the lives you have affected negatively to become who you are today?"

The masked man neared him and punched his face, sending him to the ground. The older man sat against the trunk of a tree while he tried to figure out who might be behind the mask. The man had attacked without warning, and he had a hard time trying to remember any discussion or transaction that might have moved him to attack.

"The name Fanny mean anything to you?" asked the masked man.

"No. Hey pal, I think you've got the wrong man here. I don't know you. Why don't you show your face so I can see you? Then I can recognize you if I know you."

"That ..." he kicked the older man in the chest, "... is privileged."

The older man held his chest and coughed a couple of times.

"I don't know what you're talking about. Go ahead and kill me if that's why you came and stop harassing me."

"You are not worth it, but I want you to know that as long as I live, you will not know peace."

"I don't care what you do. I don't know anybody by the name you mentioned."

The masked man put his gun to the head of his victim.

"I will expose you and make sure you go to jail. You have changed your name, so no one will know who you are or link you to anything. The world sees you as a hero, as a savior, but I don't. You disgust me. I will make sure you go down and never have the opportunity to rise again. That's a promise."

Suddenly, there were bursts of gunfire around them. The masked man spun around instantly but saw nothing. He took off towards the end of the scrubland while he returned fire at where he thought the shots had come from. Two armed men helped their boss to his feet and took him back to the course while three pursued the fleeing masked man.

A bullet grazed the ear of the running man while another ripped through his coat. He ran very fast, knowing more than one shooter was behind him. He lifted his gun over his head and returned fire without looking back. Up ahead, a sedan was fast approaching him. He kept firing on the run while he darted in a zigzag manner to avoid the bullets aimed at him. His weapon ran out of ammo. He dumped it and took out a rifle as he lunged into the rear seat of the moving sedan through the rolled-down window. A bullet caught the driver's arm as the attackers closed in on them with a volley. A Ford sedan screeched to a halt by the attackers; they got in quickly and charged after the fleeing sedan. They continued firing until the rear tire of the sedan in front of them burst, and a barrage hit the side of the sedan, killing the driver instantly. The car skidded and smashed into a lone tree. As the masked man and two of his men got out of the car, another volley sent his men to the ground, one clutching his throat. The masked man was out of ammo again. All his shots had hit nothing.

The attackers were fast closing in on him. He crawled towards the gun of his dead colleague, using him as a shield. When he tried it, it was no use. Two more bullets hit the mangled sedan and exploded the gas tank. The car exploded with a bang, as a third bullet caught him in the arm. He knew death was near. He had to do something to stay alive. He had to improvise if he was to outwit the armed men within thirty yards of him. He collected blood from the stomach wound of his colleague and smeared it on his face. Then he sprawled on the ground next to the burning tire, feigning death. The attackers reached him and studied him briefly.

"I think he's dead," one said.

"They are all dead. Let's get out of here," another suggested.

The masked man was relieved his plan had worked. One of the men reached for his radio and relayed a message to the older man that their mission was accomplished and there was no cause for alarm. They began for their Ford sedan. Forty yards from the tree, a truck stood. The masked man had arrived in it. He knew the men could return to make sure he was really dead. He stole a glance at the receding men. Then he heard a faint voice on the radio asking them to ensure all the enemies were dead. His heart pounded within his chest. He got up quickly and ran towards the truck. One of the men saw him and opened fire, his colleagues firing moments later. The masked man started the truck while taking a rifle from beneath his seat. While the truck rumbled away, he fired back at the attackers. They got in their car and took after him. After a brief gunfight that got both fighters running out of ammo, the masked man lost his pursuers at a highway crossing when a traffic cop spotted the speeding Ford sedan and took after it on his motorbike. The excited masked man reached for a cigarette from his breast pocket and lit it. He was grateful for the intervention of the traffic cop. He had seen his bike parked by a fire hydrant and raced the truck across it, hoping that the cop would see the sedan when it showed up. Fortunately, it had worked, and he was glad to have gotten away with his life.

Meanwhile, the sedan suddenly branched off the highway onto a side street and barreled out of sight, leaving the pursuing cop stranded at the congested exit. The angry cop, who had dismounted to restore order, returned to his bike, braying furiously into his radio. Finally, he mounted the bike and returned to his post.

CHAPTER TWO

Munich, Germany

The airport was as busy as it had been all year. Men and women in expensive suits and dresses, clutched briefcases, some sipping coffee, steamed in and out of it like diners in a restaurant. These were businessmen and women rushing to catch local flights for important meetings or connecting for international flights. Local and foreign tourists arrived and departed the beautiful city through the airport at the same rate. A few took photographs of the airport, a situation that excited the airport manager. He liked to see tourists happy whenever they arrived in Germany through Munich. A young man from Africa ranted bitterly at the treatment meted out by two immigration officers who suspected he might be carrying drugs. He showed his documents to the manager that showed he was there to do postgraduate studies at Technische Universität München. It took the apology of a female immigration officer to calm him down.

Outside the airport, the street teemed with shoppers, passengers, and motorists. Street lights, lights from office blocks, expensive shops and the airport provided illumination. Arranged buses conveyed tourists to and from the parking while cabs did brisk business.

A black man in a suit, of athletic build, with an afro hairdo, carrying two suitcases, emerged through the exit door onto the street and hailed a cab. The cab moved forward to a halt in front of him, the driver getting down instantly. He stashed the suitcases in the cab's trunk while the passenger sat down in the rear seat. The driver took the wheel and moved the cab on.

Five minutes later, a second black man emerged from the airport. He had the same features as the first, except he had one suitcase and wore jeans and a polo shirt. He got in a cab and moved on.

A third black man with a big sports bag barged out of the exit doors seven minutes later. His hair was shaved, and he wore khaki shorts and a T-shirt. His brown boots and red socks suggested a professional footballer arriving in town for the first time. He departed in a tourist bus, taking a window seat from where his attention was constantly on the streets, people, structures and life in Munich in the evening. He avoided the faces around him. Occasionally, he received a text message on his phone that told him to be alert for a particular stop. At the right place, he alerted the driver. He got off the bus and entered a waiting cab which took off immediately.

It was getting dark. Randolph and Calvin waited in front of a posh townhouse with their luggage while studying the surroundings. The house was tucked in the midst of a row of similar structures. The only exception was a condo at the end of the lane, which had been turned into a grocery store. They admired the row of well-tended flowers and narrow strip of manicured lawn that lined the walkway to the front door. The men hadn't bothered to look up the two-storied house for signs of humans. Instead, they chatted and smiled as they observed the cars that passed occasionally. The few pedestrians, who strolled past, sometimes with their dogs, looked upon them as tenants leaving for holidays. A cab dropped Roger. He clutched his sports bag as he paid the driver. The cab moved on as he joined his colleagues. They surveyed the façade of the house for a while and then started past the row of flower pots towards the front door.

"I like this place," Roger said.

"It sure is a fine house. Whoever owns it must be well-heeled. A German entrepreneur, I understand. Was involved in some shit, got busted, and is now behind bars," Randolph informed.

"At least he has a house. When he comes out, he will have a place to put his head," Calvin contributed.

"Apparently, the German police have no idea what the man is really worth. They have no idea what the man owns. Smart move, wouldn't you say?"

"Very smart."

They reached the front door, made of steel and painted white. A small door knocker tucked up the door looked frail, giving the impression that whoever lived in the property wasn't concerned about it. The men hoped they were at the right house. As Roger reached for the knocker, the door opened suddenly, revealing a slender woman with both hands behind her. She smiled a welcome, to which the men nodded while they shared a look. When her right hand shot forward, it clutched a brown envelope which she handed to Roger. He passed it on to Randolph instantly without looking at the address or intended recipient. The woman looked on expectantly. Randolph felt the envelope, made a sign with his hand. The woman responded firmly with her left hand. Satisfied, he reached for a small white envelope in his pocket and gave it to her. She opened it immediately, checked the contents, and pursed her lips. The men looked on as she flipped shut the envelope, folded it, and tucked it in the pocket of her trousers. She smiled broadly, her hands clasped behind her. The men remained calm.

"Olga. Gracias," she said.

"It's nice to meet you, Olga. We will get in touch if we need you," alerted Randolph.

She walked past them briskly down the walkway and departed the house. Calvin observed her until she located a bike behind a flower pot and disappeared. He then followed his colleagues who had moved their luggage into the house, shutting the door behind him.

The furnishing in the lounge and dining was modern and decent. So was that in the kitchen. A TV played at low volume by the window that overlooked the frontage. Calvin grabbed the remote control on the center table and switched it off as the other two checked the rear door and windows, which overlooked a similar property where a woman was teaching her small son how to ride a horse.

"What a time to teach horse riding," Calvin asked softly.

Moments later, they were convinced the ground floor was safe. At the command of Randolph, the two colleagues hurried up the stairs to the second floor and searched every room, paying attention to signs of taps or hidden cameras. They repeated the exercise on the first floor and then descended to the ground floor to rejoin their boss.

"Clean everywhere," Roger assured.

"Good.

Roger opened the fridge in the corner of the dining. It was filled with assorted drinks. He took three canned sodas and shut it while Calvin set their luggage on the center table. They shared the drinks. Randolph pointed to the dining table; they looked back and shared smiles.

"We have to be careful though, guys," Calvin advised.

They moved to the table and took off the covering napkin. Food was served. Also on the table were wine, apple juice, and whisky.

"She was ready for us," Randolph said as he pulled a chair and sat down.

His colleagues did the same, grabbing cutlery at the same time.

"A toast first before we eat," Roger reminded.

"Good call, brother."

They lifted their soda.

"To good life and success in whatever we do."

"To good life and success in whatever we do," chorused the other two.

"No one should touch alcohol. We will deal with that later. Now though we eat," Randolph said.

"I think we need to know what is going on in Germany."

"Right," Calvin agreed as he rose.

He moved to the center table, took the remote control, and put the TV back on. He took time searching for a channel that broadcast in English but couldn't find one. Finally, however, there was one that did sports for thirty minutes. They preferred it. At least they knew what was discussed.

"I'm sure there is a channel that does business in English to cater to the numerous English-speaking people in Germany. The problem is I'm hungry and can't afford to spend all the time searching through over a hundred channels. You know how bad the food served on the flight was. Let me eat first and then I can take my time and get us the right channel."

"Don't worry about it. We are fine with what we see on the screen," Randolph replied.

"Hmm, the food is good. It's been a while since I ate in a restaurant," admitted Calvin.

"I like Spanish food. It tastes like what my grandma used to prepare for us when I was in junior high," Roger praised.

"Shut up, soldier. You don't even know your grandma. This slop isn't Spanish. It's German," Randolph corrected.

"I will not accept that word from you, boss. The food is good, but Olga said gracias."

"I know. She uses the Spanish language to cover her ass."

"No accent. She must be a pro," admitted Calvin.

"You can't be in this business if you are not a pro. You must know languages. They travel at short notice on different passports and names. Wherever they find themselves, they blend in nicely. A Russian woman was caught in Ethiopia selling guns underground. She spoke fluent Cushitic, Amharic, and Swahili."

"My word!"

"And guess what? She had wampum around her waist and was dancing a local dance to a group of Yupik tourists. She did it so well that people thought she had been in town for thirty years. It turned out she had studied it back in Russia and had only been in town for two months."

"I'm impressed."

They had more soda from the fridge.

"I wouldn't be surprised if she is back here with us in this house as we speak."

"You mean somewhere in the house?" Calvin asked.

"That's what I mean. These are very intelligent and cunning creatures who can sneak into the White House and take photos of the president eating nuts and disappear before the wind blows."

"I see what you mean."

"Eat fast, gentlemen, because we have work to do. We leave as soon as we are done."

"We obey."

Randolph retrieved the brown envelope Olga had given them and placed it on the end of the table.

Later, when eating was over, and the table cleared, they stood around the dining table, studying a set of drawings. There were four architectural and structural drawings that showed a museum's ground floor and basement designs—one with details of the chimney and shafts, the last showing the roof. Randolph's hand was on the ground floor drawing.

"So, how do we get in?" Roger asked.

"We go up the sewer pipe to the roof. And then down the duct or shaft and crawl space," replied Randolph as he pointed to the roof and chimney pot.

"Sounds good to me, but what about security? Surely a place as important as this museum will be heavily guarded with all kinds of security networks," Calvin wanted to know.

The men shared looks, Randolph smiling.

"Whatever security arrangement they have there will be breached tonight. Whoever is in charge should be prepared for a pleasant surprise. Any opposition will be eliminated without fail. We are not here to be Boy Scouts. We are here for a mission, and we must approach it with all the seriousness it deserves and finish it well. Why else will somebody spend money to fly us in here when he could have spent it on holidays in Seychelles with Asian blondes?"

Laughter.

"I like that talk, boss. Whether they like it or not, here we come. And we are coming like a mighty rushing wind. We will take them by surprise."

"It's been a while since I put somebody down. The last was in Iraq," Roger boasted.

"You too?" Calvin asked, looking at Roger.

"Oh, yeah. I hope the drawings we have are the right ones, though, boss?"

Randolph shared a look with his men, knowing he hadn't considered the possibility the details could be wrong.

"Hopefully, we have the right ones. If it turns out Olga gave us the wrong information, we will pursue her and take her out before leaving the country through Switzerland. We will not spare her lest we get trapped. We may be ex-soldiers, but this country has one of the best armies in the world. If we get caught, we are on our own. No one will come to our aid."

They discussed the drawings as Randolph made a call to alert somebody a car would be needed in ten minutes. He hung up and consulted a coded message on one of the drawings.

He hurried to the kitchen, where he pressed a tiny button in the wall behind a cabinet. A little door opened, revealing a fridge. He reached into it and took out the item in it. A small box. He shut the door and rejoined his colleagues. Roger had made sketches of the most needed details from the drawings. After that, he folded the drawings into the sofa. Randolph laid the box on the dining table and opened it. It contained a thumb and an index finger. He shut the box quickly so the contents didn't warm up, then replaced it in the hidden fridge.

Back with his colleagues, he made another call and hung up. This time he gave a coded message to remind somebody that his services would be needed in twenty minutes.

The weather was warm with slight winds at times. Three minutes later, a black sedan pulled in front of the house. Randolph signaled to Roger to check out who was there. He nodded, moved quickly to the window, parted the curtain slightly, and peeked out. He watched as the driver stepped out of the sedan as a motorbike screeched to a halt behind it. Without saying a word or looking up at the house, the driver sat behind the biker and zoomed out of sight with a big roar of the engine.

"Who was there?" Randolph asked.

"Our cruise ship is here. The motorbike has taken the driver away."

"Good. Gentlemen?"

Calvin and Roger looked at him.

"This is it. This is what we came for. We may not have done this kind of thing before, but our employer has so much confidence in us that he paid a lot to get us in here. We are used to close-quarter combat, urban and jungle warfare, but we have to do ourselves and our employer proud. We may not return to this house as anything could happen in this mission. Therefore, we can't leave traces that we ever came here. Let's get rid of anything that is connected to us. If we succeed, we can get back whatever we destroy in this house."

"Good call. You are the boss, Randolph," Calvin acknowledged.

Six minutes later, the three men stepped out of the house clad in black combat fatigues, each wearing black gloves and goggles. Calvin held a black kit bag. They locked the house door, got in the sedan, and departed in haste.

CHAPTER THREE

The museum had been a tourist attraction for years. Even locals patronized it as if it had just been opened. Folks, especially grandparents, loved it and liked telling their grandchildren about it. Each year, it received over a million and a half visitors. This year the figure had shot up when news spread that two vampire bats mysteriously flew in through the wall, moved over a pitcher containing water seven times, and disappeared the way they flew in. Three days later, a blind woman had her sight restored when her granddaughter mischievously fetched the water for her to drink when she complained of thirst. The museum had received three times the number it had seen all year in just three months. The Chancellor, his family, and party stalwarts had been there to check on the blind woman's claims. Even the Vatican had sent a delegation to authenticate the claim. Its cupola had subsequently been painted in gold to make it easier for tourists and visitors to locate it even from afar. The structure was an old two-storied edifice, judging by the long capitals supporting the entablature. A heavy iron door with huge padlocks guarded the entrance while the sensor-grilled windows flashed lights at regular intervals. The street in front of it was very quiet. Except for the few cars that raced past occasionally, there were no pedestrians in sight. It would get busy during the day when tourists arrived.

Seventy-five yards or so from the frontage of the museum, the sedan stood in front of a clothing shop located at the turn at the junction. The masked men waited while Randolph consulted with the time on his watch every now and then. Calvin monitored the side of the museum using binoculars. There was no guard outside the structure though he knew there might be some in the museum or tucked invisibly somewhere around.

"What the hell is keeping him?" Roger asked.

"Easy, man. What he is doing is meant only for experts, so I guess we just have to be patient and wait for his signal. That's what he does for a living. He wouldn't be put in charge if he wasn't good at it," Randolph answered.

They sank out of sight as a police car raced past, turned left at the junction and barreled out of sight.

"Even then, he is taking too long to pull it off."

"Roger, take it easy. We will be fine. I can tell you are edgy. Relax man. We will get it over and done with, get on the next available ship from Italy and disappear," Calvin advised.

Randolph checked the time again.

"Get ready, gents. Our moment is at hand. Make sure all weapons are cocked and ready for action," Randolph informed.

Suddenly, all the street lights in front of the museum and lights in shops and nearby offices went out. The three men got out of the sedan instantly with the kit bag and dashed to the façade of the museum. They crouched to the edge, careful to avoid the windows that flashed lights regularly.

With little fuss, they located the steel pipe that ran from the concrete drain to the roof gutter. With astonishing rapidity, they climbed up the pipe onto the roof. Almost immediately, dark figures rushed out of the museum with flashlights. The three men observed quietly as the lights came back on. They noted the men were security officers. One shone his torch at the roof, forcing the three men to withdraw quickly. Two others checked the padlocks on the entrance door and windows for signs of a breach. Satisfied, they converged, consulting in German.

"Everything is intact. I don't see anything," one security officer claimed.

"The windows are fine," proclaimed another.

"It's good to know. I don't see anything or anybody on the roof. I think we are fine. Back to your posts, then friends, but keep your eyes open. Anything is possible." the leader commanded.

His men agreed as they barged into the museum.

Meanwhile, Randolph worked the chimney pot while his colleagues stood guard on the circular concrete slab around the dome with their guns poised. Unfortunately, there was no access ladder from the roof to the lower floors. Therefore, any repair work on the roof would have to be carried out using a long ladder from the ground. Nevertheless, Randolph succeeded in removing the pot, put back the tools he used in the kit bag, and took a look in the chimney.

The lead security officer sat behind a row of TV screens that monitored activities in and around the museum. His full six-foot-four height, muscled upper body and slightly protruding stomach struggled to fit into his chair. He ran his hand through his closely cropped hair as he ate muffins and drank coffee. A small radio by him played German pop music at low volume. A sachet of nuts stood next to the cup of coffee. Occasionally, he fetched a few in his hand and shoved them in his mouth one at a time. While he studied the monitors, he jerked his head slightly back and forth to the music. As he dug into a muffin, the landline phone rang. He scooted across the floor in his swivel chair to reach the phone. With his mouth still stuffed with food, he took time chewing and swallowing before he lifted the handset.

"Hello?"

While he waited for the caller to respond, he took a bite of another muffin.

On one of the screens, the three men descended into a crawl space. Randolph opened a control panel quickly and disconnected two wires, then closed the panel instantly.

"Hello? Helloooo? Anybody there? Anybody on the line? Please speak because if you don't, I will have you arrested for making a prank call," the security officer said softly in German.

Hearing nothing, he set the handset down on the phone, returned to his seat and continued eating. He set the volume on the radio slightly higher as a favorite song played.

The men in the crawl space made their way to the end of the shaft and turned the corner. They had crawled as quickly as possible while the man took the ghost call. Everything was perfectly timed and executed to perfection. Randolph reached the midpoint of that section of the shaft, where he located a branch that led to a room. He worked it quickly, allowing them to slip into a dark room with little noise. Their special shoes made sure they made very little noise only highly trained ears could detect. Roger reached for a small flashlight in his pocket and put it on quickly, directing it at a door. Calvin placed his ear gently against it. There was no noise or voice behind it. He gave Randolph a thumbs up, indicating it was safe to make their next move.

"Two and a half minutes are all we have," Randolph reminded undertones.

"Where are we?" Roger asked.

"Ground floor. C'mon Roger. Focus. I thought you made a sketch of the museum? Why are you asking loose questions? The security alarm on the door is disabled. We assemble here immediately after the operation and move out as we came in. Don't drop your guard at any time. Don't get distracted by anything. We are here for a mission, and that's what we will accomplish."

His colleagues nodded as he retrieved a magnetic-stripped card and inserted it into a card reader by the door. Moments later, a green dot glowed, indicating clearance. The door opened slowly as Randolph stuck his head out and looked out briefly. He waved his men on as they stepped out of the dark room into a corridor. While he led the way, Roger followed with his gun pointing alternately to both sides to tackle any surprises. Calvin brought up the rear with his back to them. His task was to guard them against anybody who showed up in the corridor behind them. They reached the end and rounded a corner onto a short corridor where they found a short staircase. It led to the basement. They descended quickly to a heavy metal door. Randolph raised a fist, alerting them to halt.

"This door is stress sensor lined...." Randolph informed the others as he shared a look with his men, "...that means we can't stress or put pressure on it."

At his signal, his men turned towards the staircase, each pointing his gun to the corridor. The short floor in front of the door dead-ended against walls. Randolph studied the sensor and panel in the wall by the door. He reached for an atomizer in his fatigue and directed a fine spray around the edges of the door. He entered a code on the panel and awaited a response while reaching for the box in the kit bag. He opened it quickly, took out the thumb and index finger. A light flashed on the panel's display, followed by a sentence in German. Randolph didn't bother with that.

"Please print your thumb and index finger," demanded the auto-response in German.

Randolph placed them on the sensor. Suddenly, the face of a male appeared on the sensor, the door sliding open immediately. He set the finger and thumb back in the box and handed it to Roger, charging him to stand guard at the door. He nodded and set the box down as the two hurried through the door that was already beginning to shut.

The lead security officer read a pornographic magazine, smiling to himself as he leafed through the pages. Another sachet of nuts was open on the desk in front of him. On his left was another porn magazine. He lifted the mag close to his face, scrutinizing a woman's pose. He worked nights mainly and felt lonely and bored monitoring screens. The museum and its environs were usually quiet at night. With very little to do on duty, he preoccupied himself with porn mags.

Meanwhile, all the screens showed the same picture:

It portrayed the main museum hall, showing paintings, historical and scientific materials and artifacts.

Randolph scanned the walls of the windowless room for cameras or any other surveillance device while Calvin paid attention to the ceiling and floor. There were alphabetically labeled cabinets along all four walls of the room. Randolph consulted a paper in his hand and moved to the cabinet marked 'S.' He entered a code, and the steel door opened, revealing many drawers labeled with names starting with the letter. He ran his finger along quickly and located one that ended with 'Z.' He entered another code that opened it, revealing a black envelope. He took it and studied it briefly. Satisfied, he had the right envelope, he tucked it in his fatigues, the drawer shutting by itself. The door to the cabinet also closed automatically. The two men dashed back to the door and rapped on it. Roger repeated the exercise on the panel, opening the door moments later. The three scurried out of the basement back into the dark room. Randolph was pleased with the performance of his men. He gave them thumbs up, to which they responded excitedly.

With his legs up on the desk, the lead security officer studied the screens. Nothing struck him initially as he still reminisced the photos he had seen in the mag. He kept looking at the screens. Moments later, he noted something wasn't right with them. All showed the same picture. He squinted a couple of times, thinking it was a dream. He rose and moved closer to the monitors to take a good look. He was right. All the screens couldn't show the same picture. He reached for the landline phone instantly and dialed.

"What?" queried the recipient in angry German.

"Security at the museum has been breached! We have company! Somebody or people are in the building!"

"Ok. Calm down. I will alert the police. Hold the fort in the meantime. We are coming in."

He hung up and hurried to a tiny locker in the wall, which he opened. He worked two wires quickly, restoring normal transmission to some of the screens. He moved back to the monitors and noted on one, moments later, that three dots were in line. He rushed back to the phone and dialed again. He was right about the intrusion.

"They are headed for the roof! Three of them! The roof! Get there now!"

"Three? I'm going to bust their skulls to death! Who will be bold and stupid enough to break into this museum?"

The lead officer scrambled the handset in its cradle, yanked out a gun and departed the room.

On the ground outside, four armed security officers were at the front, looking up the roof. Three had their guns pointing to it while the fourth brayed furiously into a walkie-talkie. While he spoke, he waved for the three to spread out and wait for the intruders. They obliged.

The three masked men crawled very fast in the shaft, rounded a corner and got into the chimney breast. They worked their way up and emerged from the pot. Roger was the first to reach the pipe that took them up the roof. He peered at the ground but saw nothing. He gripped it and began to climb down while his rifle hung around his neck. Suddenly, gunshots were fired at him, forcing Randolph and Calvin to retreat initially. Two bullets caught Roger in the nape and spine. He lost his grip on the pipe and fell to the ground with a thud. Calvin took a quick peek at the ground and showed four fingers to indicate there were four shooters. Randolph nodded as they looked for a way out. They couldn't return fire as they didn't know how many more officers waited for them, even if they succeeded in dealing with the four. While they checked the roof for a way of escape, Randolph considered going back into the chimney to escape through one of the windows on the ground floor. Suddenly, an escape hatch opened, revealing the lead security officer. Randolph spotted him and gunned him down before the man could react. The man slumped back into the hatch and tumbled down a steel ladder to the floor. Randolph looked at Calvin and signaled to the ground.

"It's the only way out," he said.

Calvin acknowledged as the two men took positions on the roof. The two engaged the ground men in a gunfight in unison. While the fight raged, a chopper appeared suddenly overhead, its headlight exposing the two on the roof. A hailstorm of bullets from the chopper ricocheted off the dome, forcing the two to duck for cover. Randolph turned and returned fire, blowing out the lights of the chopper. At the same time, Calvin aimed at the pilot and fired two shots in quick succession. A bullet shattered the side window, the second hitting the pilot in the head. He hunched on the control panel, losing control of the chopper. It yawed menacingly, spun a couple of times, hit one side of the roof, and fell towards the ground. The security officers fled the scene before it fell to the ground. The two masked men seized the opportunity and came down the pipe as quickly as possible as they fired on the fleeing officers. They fired back a volley at the two, forcing them to let go of the pipe. They fell to the ground, still clutching their guns, the kit bag hanging around Randolph's neck. He returned fire and scattered the officers who were beginning to regroup and charge them.

Calvin's fire hit two officers in the leg and felled them. A third was repelled by a shot to his left shoulder. Calvin spotted Roger's body on the ground under the chopper, his head severed. While the fourth officer contemplated what to do, the two masked men hurried into their sedan and took off. As it barreled past a parked truck in front of a store, three police cars spun out of the intersection after them. Randolph didn't look back as he needed to get them to safety. Calvin checked his gun for rounds. It had only one. He reached for another rifle in the kit bag and cocked it while Randolph rocketed past night diners having beers and food. They had to lose their pursuers if they were to stay alive.

As the sedan swerved off to the right onto a side street, another police car blocked the end of the street. Randolph stepped on the brakes instantly, stopping the sedan with a screech. At the same time, Calvin fired shots at the advancing cars behind them. The sedan backed up and took an exit behind the backyard of a row of condos, clearing waste bins and flowerpots. Dogs began to bark behind them. Calvin leaned in the passenger window and fired a well-aimed shot that hit the front tire of the first car. It careened off its track, ran through a wooden fence and smashed into the rear of a condo, knocking down a door. A second aimed shot caught the shooter's shoulder in the second police car. The officer retreated from the window, but another officer in the rear seat fired a shot out of his window that hit Calvin's head. He dropped his rifle and hunched in the window with his arms flailing.

"Calvin? Why have you stopped shooting? Calvin? Calvin, talk to me!" Randolph yelled.

Suspecting Calvin had been shot, he held his fatigues and pulled him. Calvin's head scrambled against the window frame, blood oozing.

"Shit!" Randolph exclaimed as he flattened the accelerator.

Shots riddled the rear screen, another whipping past his ear as the sedan reached the end of the condos and plunged into the slow-moving night traffic. Now the police were gaining on him, almost overtaking the sedan. He swerved onto the sidewalk, frightening a couple out of its way. A squad truck Randolph didn't know had joined in the chase impacted the rear of the sedan. A second impact sideswiped the sedan.

Further crashes and pounding sent the car spinning, somersaulting and crashing into a parked RV. Randolph got out of the car and took off immediately, still holding the kit bag and his rifle. The squad truck behind it smashed into the side of the sedan and caught fire, sending both vehicles up in the air. The second police car screeched to a halt behind the squad truck. The officer in the front looked around and spotted a fleeing man. He pointed to the fleeing man. The driver turned the car into the direction of Randolph and pursued him, the third following. He turned into a narrow lane.

A red sedan with two men in it raced to a halt at one end of the lane. Its driver rolled down his window and watched Randolph as he gunned for the other end. When the two police cars approached, the sedan reversed from the entrance, its occupants sinking in their seats to avoid being seen by the police. The two vehicles reached the edge of the lane, the driver in the first pointing to Randolph, but the lane was too narrow for the cars. One parked as two officers got down and pursued Randolph on foot. At the same time, he barked orders into his radio. The masked man could hear the pursuing officer as he commanded somebody to bind the suspect. Randolph didn't understand the language, but he knew damn well what a pursuing officer would do if he couldn't catch a suspect. He would ask for reinforcements and also somebody to block the direction of the suspect. The pursuing officer fired a shot at him and missed. Another bullet grazed his elbow. Randolph turned, returned fire and continued running. The officer ducked to the floor. As the Randolph neared the end of the lane, a shot from the officer caught his leg. He fell but recovered quickly, knowing what was coming after him. He limped across the street, leaped over a fence and headed off, though he didn't know where it led to. He rounded the house, panting and sweating. A dog was alerted, prompting barks that informed the pursuing officer. He fired two shots immediately and missed. Down the street, behind the house, were the neon lights of a mall. The red sedan kept pace, the occupants monitoring proceedings.

The officer knocked down the fence and produced his best run in ages, admitting his suspect was good. Randolph was almost at the mall entrance, the officer not far behind. The red sedan zoomed to the car park as one of the police cars approached. The officer aimed to fire a shot, but two shoppers edged out with their shopping trolley at the same time. He lowered the weapon, pursing his lips in frustration. They got out of the masked man's way as he barged into the mall. Three other shoppers exited, dropped their shopping and swerved to the side to allow him to pass. A fourth pulled her small daughter close to her.

Meanwhile, the two men in the sedan got out of their car and hurried after Randolph.

Randolph limped past a startled female stocker to the doll aisle. She was so scared at the sight of the masked, armed man she tripped on a toy left on the floor and fell against the shelf. Her head took the punishment. Randolph fell and rose as he struggled to maintain his balance. His pace had been greatly reduced by the wound to his leg. Another frightened stocker reached for her phone and was about to dial. He pointed his gun at her face, shaking his head. The woman knew what the message was and put the device back in her pocket. He allowed himself a thin smile as she was forced to sink onto the couch behind her. He looked around him and found toys. He snatched a teddy bear and collapsed to the floor. The two men following him spotted him and opened fire, sending shoppers screaming at the top of their voices. The shots missed him but alerted the police officer, who hurried to the scene and readied to attack. He came under fire instantly.

One shooter's bullet caught his thigh. His return fire got the shooter in the chest, knocking him down. The second shooter who had been hiding behind a shelf fired a barrage at the officer, killing him instantly. When the shooter turned, Randolph's gun was pointing at him. Not fazed, the shooter made a move to shoot, but the masked man made no mistake at all. His shot hit the man's head, and he fell on the woman on the couch, who screamed as she shoved him aside and took off. Randolph got up and started limping away from the scene. The first shooter, still holding his chest, aimed his gun and fired a shot at the masked man. The bullet hit close to his spine. Randolph fell to the floor, dropping the teddy bear. He pulled himself to a sitting position and glanced at the shooter on the floor. He wondered who the two shooters were since they weren't police officers. He didn't rule out the possibility they could be plainclothes officers, but he had killed the police officer. Both men were pointing their guns at each other now, but the man on the floor seemed to be getting to the end of his journey. His chest still spewed out blood. He pulled the trigger but found out to his shock that he was out of ammo. Randolph wished he could get near him and threaten him to find out who he and his fallen colleague worked for, but he didn't have that luxury. He didn't have the strength and time to pull that off. He had to get out of the mall.

With the man still in shock after running out of ammo, a bullet caught his forehead. His head fell to the floor, a puddle of blood forming around it. Randolph rose again, falling almost immediately. He concealed his weapon in his fatigues and crawled to the exit door, incoming shoppers stepping aside to avoid him. A woman asked why no one called for help for the masked man. A stocker beckoned her to keep quiet. Randolph staggered to his feet and hobbled out of the mall towards the car park. He noticed that shoppers and employees alike were making phone calls. The police would swarm the mall in the next minutes.

A blue Mercedes with a young lady behind the wheel pulled into the only parking space available in the car park. Sirens blared in the distance. Randolph knew he had to get out of the vicinity immediately, but he was in no position to drive. His back ached, as did his leg. He looked back as he scooted away from the mall. The police cars were still not in sight, but the sirens were louder. In a matter of minutes, they would appear. He hoped traffic would slow them down so he could get away before they arrived. Beyond the car park, the tiny strip of lawn sloped towards a ditch. He hurried towards it as the driver of the Mercedes checked her face in the mirror. She wore khaki trousers and black anorak and was in her early 20s. She grabbed her small handbag and checked how much money she had, having rushed to the mall on impulse. She did that sometimes when she had access to her cousin's Mercedes. She had visited a friend half a mile away and decided to impulse shop once she was in the vicinity of the mall.

As she readied to open the door, the passenger door suddenly opened, revealing Randolph's face. He had removed the mask so he couldn't be identified by his pursuers. Startled, she reached over the seat to shut the door. Then she saw that he was in pain. She withdrew her hand as he hauled himself into the seat with some difficulty and slammed the door. She was still at a loss as to why this strange man had suddenly appeared in her car. She flinched as he looked at her with a grin that didn't look friendly. She knew he was a convict or being pursued by somebody. He reached into the pocket of his fatigues. Her face changed instantly, thinking he was getting a gun. Then he produced the envelope in his shaky hand and glanced at her face.

"Do you speak English?" he asked in a low tone.

She nodded gently.

"Good. Take this."

He offered the envelope to her, but she refused to take it.

"Go ahead and take it. It won't kill you. There is no bomb in it."

She looked at him briefly and reached for it hesitantly.

"I want you to hold on to it with everything inside you. I mean, guard it with all that you have."

She wasn't comfortable with the envelope in her hand, especially when it came from a wounded stranger who might be dangerous. As she moved to give it back to him, his hand went into his fatigues again, freezing her.

"Can you make it to the US?"

"Yes. Why ask? Who are you anyway?"

"That's not important at this point. They will do anything to prevent you from leaving this country and entering the US."

He coughed as an ambulance screeched to a halt in front of the mall. He was relieved the police had still not arrived. She scrutinized the envelope again, wondering what it contained. She didn't know anything about the stranger but was sure he was on the run. That meant the envelope contained valuable material or information. She tried to open the door to raise the alarm, but he pointed a pistol at her face, shaking his head gently.

"Will you stop scaring me? I don't know who you are. I came here to shop and get back to my cousin as soon as possible. This car belongs to her, and she is waiting for it. Usually, at this time, she goes on a trip to the country with her boyfriend. I have to write my final exam. That means I have to report to the academy on time. Will you put the weapon away?"

"Exam?"

"Yes. Exam. My future and life depend on it."

"What are you studying?" ·

"I'm in military school. One month more and I become a military officer. Now you understand why your presence in my car is a nuisance? Can you please take the gun out of my face?"

"So, you are a cadet?"

"Officer cadet."

"That's cute. I'm gonna mention three names. Make sure you don't forget them."

She studied his face.

"Go ahead because you are wasting my time. I have to get back to my cousin before she gets mad at me."

"Randolph Sith, Calvin Travers, and Roger Palmer. Long Beach. California."

"What about them?"

"After this shit is over, find their relatives and help them if you can."

She twitched a brow and moved closer to him.

"Who do you think you are talking to, man? You get into my car uninvited, refuse to mention your name and what you have gotten yourself into, and now you want me to go after people I don't know to help them? Who in his right senses will do that? I still don't know you, and what help are you talking about anyway?"

"You talk too much for a cadet. I don't know your name either, so we are even."

"My name is Steffie Shroeder. Happy?" she queried angrily, flinging her hands in his face. "You are confusing me with all these responsibilities. I don't understand anything."

He gave a short smile.

"Don't talk like that."

"Why not? Why the hell not? What would you do in my shoes?"

"Cadets don't get confused. Hold yourself up and pay attention. Call the post code plus four ones."

"Post code? What post code?"

"Yes. I will give you a card bearing the post code. COMB ASS when prompted. You will receive a US passport."

Her mouth hung open in shock.

"What the hell is going on? Why are you not telling me anything? I can't handle whatever you want me to do. I have an exam to write. Please get out of my car and leave me alone."

He laughed.

"Welcome to the party. Don't trust anybody. She will take you to my apartment. Toilet. Ceiling. $15,000…" he wiped the rivulet of blood from his nose and sniffed, "…you have to fight with everything, whatever you have learned in military school. Whether you like it or not, you are among sharks and lions. They will not give up for as long as you have the envelope."

She opened the door and attempted to get out, but she felt something against her groin. When she looked down, a hunter's knife was thrusting against her.

"Don't do anything stupid, young lady. You have no idea how many lives you are going to save and the good you will be doing to the world by taking the envelope to California. I suggest you sit still and listen carefully."

"Ok, so who am I now? What name do I write in future?"

"Good question. Catching up very fast, huh? Valery Hunter. You were born on December 12, 1988."

A siren blared furiously. This time it was the police. Randolph lowered his head gently to avoid them. No one in the mall could identify him since they didn't see his face. He had given the impression he was headed for the ditch behind the parking lot but had maneuvered behind the parked cars to the Mercedes.

"Are they here for you?" she asked, looking back at the two police cars.

He nodded. Steffie knew it was her opportunity to get away from the man. She didn't want her name soiled and her photos in every newspaper for the wrong reasons. She looked at him, wondering if what she was about to do was right. The man could be innocent, for which reason he must be protected, but she didn't have proof and had to protect her image. On second thought, she decided to go for it. She opened the door suddenly and placed one foot out on the pavement. All of a sudden, a barrage of gunfire ripped through the rear door, forcing her to move her foot back into the car. She glanced back quickly at the shooter, wondering whether she was the target or the man in her car or if they were stray bullets. She could see three men were firing at her.

"Move out of here now! If they get you, your life will be miserable. You won't like this world again. You won't like Germany again. They are not the police. Phone calls have been made; the police have been frustrated from getting here on time so these guys could come in and do what they have been tasked to do."

"What the hell have you gotten me into?" She fumed as she started the car, "Who are they anyway? Do you know them?"

She shifted the gear into reverse and backed up, hitting the rear of a slowly moving truck. She wheeled the Mercedes onto the street and took off with a loud screech. Her door was still open. She reached out, grabbed it, and shut it.

"They are working for somebody I don't know, but I know they came to kill."

The shooters fired a couple of shots but missed the target. They got in their car and set to give chase but found themselves surrounded by police officers. They got out of the car with their hands in the air.

"Did you get the registration number?" one shooter asked in an undertone.

"Yes," replied a colleague.

"Good. We shall be out soon, and the owner of that Mercedes is toast. I don't even know why these guys bothered to come here."

"Why arrest us when we can't be prosecuted?"

The shooters shared a smile.

The officers cuffed them and took them away in their cars.

CHAPTER FOUR

Two police officers spoke to the head security officer at the museum about the break-in. A black car arrived at the front door; the curator, a plump man, got down and hurried to join the officers. They walked to the ground floor corridor that led to the basement stairs. The head security officer looked at him balefully, wondering why it had taken so long for the man to respond to his call. They trotted down the stairs to the basement. The curator went through the necessary protocols and got the door open. They dashed in.

The security officer began to search the steel drawers from one end while the curator checked from the other end. The police officers followed them, looking on. Finally, the curator reached the 'S' Cabinet, opened the drawer, and found the black envelope missing from the one that ended with 'Z.'

"Shit!" he exclaimed, looking at the security officer.

Heads turned instantly. The others joined him as he pointed to the drawer. The security officer knew what had happened.

"Oh my God!" exclaimed the security officer.

"I can see the drawer is empty but what specifically is missing?" asked the senior police officer.

"A black envelope," replied the curator.

"What is in it?"

"I'm not allowed to disclose its contents."

The police officers shared an anxious look that changed to curiosity.

"Our job is to protect life and property. How do we do that if you don't help us?" queried the younger police officer

The curator considered his question briefly as he closed the drawer. The officer repeated his question.

"A letter. That's all I can say. It's all I know, actually. That is what is listed in our database."

"What else has gone wrong here?"

"Everything else is intact, I presume."

"Thank you. We will get in touch if the need arises."

They exited the room, the two officers in the lead.

The curator lit a cigar and took a drag. The security officer, angered by his smoking habit, shot him an angry glance.

"You are really something; you know that?"

"No, I am not. You are lousy. I think you slept on the job and allowed the intruders into the building. I wouldn't be surprised if you had something to do with the break-in," the curator replied.

"What the hell are you trying to suggest?" he asked as he grabbed the curator by his shirt front, "It took you hours to arrive here. What the hell took you?"

"I was having sex with my wife. Did you expect me to stop in the middle of such an important exercise? Now let go of my shirt before I report you to the police. I will make sure you get fired for incompetence."

The man still held his colleague's shirt.

"Let go of me, I said. I want to get back to my wife and continue having fun."

The curator broke his grip and barreled out of the museum.

Steffie studied Randolph as she revved the Mercedes past everything in its lane. The man hunched towards the glove compartment. He was obviously in great pain but didn't seem alarmed. He must be an assassin or some professional, she thought. She noticed the blood on his leg and the back of his fatigues. She kept speeding. He looked back at the highway and tapped her arm gently.

"I think you should slow down. I know we are not being followed. I don't think we are still in danger. We don't have to attract the attention of the police," he advised.

"I know we are being followed, but this is my city. They know where we are headed and can use other routes to get us. They may be waiting for us somewhere ahead. Let's get to safety first."

The Mercedes still barreled along without regard for motorists and pedestrians. It rounded a corner, past a row of apartment blocks into a poorly lit alley, and halted, jolting her passenger. She took the envelope and studied it briefly. Randolph still looked down at the floor as she glanced at him. He groaned slightly and writhed in pain. He angled his head and gazed at her face. He sat upright and leaned gently towards her, wiping blood off his lips. She was certain the man wouldn't survive the next few minutes.

"Talk to me."

"There are seven names on the paper in that envelope. They are all dead, but some of their descendants are still alive. Open it and check for yourself."

She opened the envelope and took out the folded paper.

GERHARD REUTER, ULRICH MOLLER, MICHAEL STROMBERGER, LARS HASS, ERIKA KINSKY, OTTO VAN MEKEL, HELMUT PFISTER.

"What about them?"

He smiled to give the impression he was fine. However, Steffie noticed he was getting weaker.

"I have to get you to the hospital."

He wagged his head slowly.

"Ok. So what do I do with the list?"

"Part of Hitler's execution team. They were doctors. Reuter killed Jews. He and his nephew, Jeurgen."

She watched him, the hand holding the gun falling slowly to his side.

"I'm listening."

"When Germany fell, Jeurgen murdered Gerhard and his family in the cacophony that followed."

He began to shiver, pain stretching his face. He hunched forward suddenly, his head hitting the dashboard.

She grabbed his back and yanked him back to an upright position.

"Please don't die on me."

He shot her a pleasant look, smiling thinly.

"I won't die on you. Who says I'm gonna die anyway?"

He laughed

"So, after Germany fell, what happened next?

"Glad you are following. He ran to the US with his ill-gotten wealth. I mean jewelry he stole from his uncle. Then he established companies in the US. He is now a respected man, donating to universities, charities, and churches. I mean, he is big in the United States. People adore him. He is worshipped in certain quarters."

He slumped forward and crashed onto the dashboard again, his gaze still on her. She helped him to sit upright.

"He's done everything to cover his ass till now. My task is to send this list to the US."

"Why should I believe you?"

"You don't have to. Get this envelope to Johann Steinberg in California. He's the only one who can ID him. And then the rest will be done by him."

"Is this some kind of vendetta for something this Jeurgen might have done?"

"I'm not authorized to discuss that, but I said earlier that lives will be saved, and the world will be a better place. If you can make it, you will become a hero overnight."

He reached into his pocket, took out a business card bearing Johann's contact details and gave it to her.

"My name is on the back. Show this card to him. He knows what to do."

She flipped the card, studied the scribbling at the back and tucked it into her jacket.

"Who hired you? Who are you working for?"

"That information is privileged. Just tell Johann I'm sorry. I thought I could pull this mission off and see him again, but it didn't happen. I'm sure he will be happy that I got him what he asked for..." he stared at her face, "...you can't go back to your apartment. It is too dangerous. And if there is somebody in your apartment, that person's life is already in danger."

"Why?"

"The shooters saw your registration. You're a target now. You and anybody connected to you will be hunted wherever you go in this world."

A wave of fear swept across her face.

"The world? What have you gotten me into? I was having a happy quiet life until you stormed my car, and now I have to run for my life for God knows how long."

"I know. I'm sorry, but I had to give it to somebody, and you happened to be the right person at the right time. Any inconvenience caused is regretted. I'm also sorry to let you know that the army is over for you. Rejoice—no more exams. Don't trust anybody or anything. Not even your panty or tampon."

She smiled for the first time, prompting him to laugh.

"You have a nice smile."

"Thank you, but I'm worried not only for my life but for that of my cousin."

"I know. You have to dispose of this car. Avoid public places."

He retrieved a credit card and a chip from his fatigues and gave them to her.

"The code is the reverse of Johann's postcode without the middle number. It is all yours."

"What happens to me after all this? Assuming I make it to California?"

"Have faith. You'll make it. Stay in the US; Johann will fix you. No friends, no contact from now on. Your life will change from then on."

They shared a look.

"He'll enroll you back in university. A-any u-uni. Good lu-lu..."

Suddenly, his voice dropped to a whisper. He shivered violently and leaned against the door, hands flailing. Steffie reached over and felt for his pulse. There was nothing. He was gone. Dead. She tucked the envelope into her jacket and pulled him back into his seat, but he slumped back against the door. The engine of the Mercedes roared as she shifted into gear, backed up to the main road and sped off. She understood now how precarious it would be to show herself in public places. Her preoccupation was to get home on time to save her cousin. She hoped the people after her wouldn't find her before she did. It would be a painful experience if anything terrible happened to her. She had a date with her boyfriend and had agreed to lend Steffie the Mercedes for her shopping. Unfortunately, what used to be a routine had turned out to be a chilling outing with a strange dead man in her car. She had suddenly been given a mission she wasn't sure could be achieved. She thought of her mates in military school and what they would say about her, especially if a camera had captured her number plate. She shook her head in disbelief.

The car rocketed and took an exit off the highway onto a cart track. It traveled for a few minutes through farms and turned onto a dirt track that wove through groves of trees. She had made sure not to look at the faces of farmers as she drove. The Mercedes halted by a tree. She got down and rounded the bonnet to open the passenger door. Randolph's body fell towards her. She held him and studied his face for a while, hoping he had told her the truth and not a nicely-rehearsed story to get her involved in somebody's dirty war. She pulled the body out gently and shoved it down an embankment. She checked her jacket to ensure the envelope was intact as she removed her valuables from the glove compartment. She could no longer use the car as he had advised. It would be very difficult to explain to her cousin why the Mercedes could no longer be used. On second thought, she decided it would be helpful if she removed the registration plate and got a new one, so the car wasn't lost, as she didn't have the money to replace it. She opened the trunk and took a tool kit from which she got a screwdriver and spanner. She removed both plates, scratched off the letters and numbers and mangled the plates. She locked the trunk and got in the car, started it, and left the grove of trees.

CHAPTER FIVE

When the Mercedes reached the highway, it was almost 2300 hours. She parked it in a gas station, got out and locked the doors. She walked back to the highway with the hood of her anorak pulled over her head. The sunglasses that covered her face got motorists wondering if she was a hooker. She had dumped the mangled license plates in a drain before she turned the car into the highway. The few cars that passed slowed down, some drivers whistling at her. She ignored them while she watched for a cab. She was still in a state of shock and couldn't believe her military career was over all of a sudden. She had worked so hard to enroll in the school, and now everything had gone to waste. She cursed Randolph for barging into her car. Her world had suddenly been turned upside down. She didn't know how to explain to friends and loved ones why she had to abandon her training when she had just a month to graduation. Folks knew she was about to become an officer and were preparing to attend her graduation ceremony. What would she tell them now?

A truck slowed down and honked. The driver asked if she wanted a lift. She waggled her hand and looked away. She didn't need a lift. A cab showed in the distance. She flagged it down and got in. Looking out the window, she told the driver where to take her. The driver nodded and moved the cab on without any attempt to look at her face. Except for a few clubbers and late diners in town, many places were quiet, and traffic was almost nonexistent. Steffie still thought of the mission ahead of her. Her world was about to change, and she didn't know how to explain it to her cousin. The Mercedes was at a safe place where no one would bother to check. All that was needed was getting a new registration. Thankfully, it wasn't registered in Steffie's name.

The cab dropped her in front of an off-license and moved on. She stood briefly as if checking the contents of her handbag while she stole a glance at the receding cab. When it was gone, she hurried past a house and appeared at the rear of a condo. She stopped and looked back carefully. No one followed her. She walked briskly to the front door and rapped on it, looking around her to be sure she was alone. She knocked again, mentioning a code in an undertone. Moments later, a girl answered the door; Steffie entered quickly and shut the door behind her. A light came on in the lounge. Steffie checked all the windows to make sure they were locked. She checked the rear door and then rejoined her cousin. She changed her khaki trousers into black jeans but kept her anorak.

"Care to tell me what this is about? What the hell is wrong with you? Look at the time? I told you I had a date with my boyfriend and you said you would be gone for thirty minutes. And how many hours have you spent shopping?"

"I know, and I'm sorry. Unfortunately, I don't have time to explain everything to you. I don't even think you would believe me if I told you. I want you to go for your car at the gas station by the highway just opposite the hardware store. The registration plates were stolen. Don't ask me who did it because I don't have an answer to that question. You have to get a new registration. Don't get the old one."

Her cousin held Steffie by the hand.

"What did you say? Have you gotten into trouble? I want to know before it's too late."

Steffie was picking the things she would need from their room. Her cousin followed her, repeating the question.

"I told you there is no time to explain things. Please, I have to leave and when I do make sure all the doors and windows are shut. Don't answer any questions about me. Don't tell anybody we are related; otherwise…."

"Otherwise, what? What Steffie? What have you done that has put my life in danger?"

"Nothing. Just do as I have told you, and you will be fine."

"Your behavior is strange, Steffie. Talk to me."

"Yeah. Strange things happen sometimes."

Moments later, a motorbike arrived at the spot where the cab had dropped Steffie. The rider dismounted and walked past the house to the cobblestoned lane that ran across the five condos. He stopped, and braced by a wooden storehouse, took out a monocular, and started observing the condos. All had lights in one or two rooms. The first one had a woman giving a child milk from a feeding bottle. The man moved to the second one, where a man was having sex with his wife on a couch. He stood watching for a while until his phone rang, alerting him to keep going. Finally, at the third condo, he spotted Steffie and her cousin. He retrieved his gun immediately and called the caller back on his phone. He dialed again and got through.

"Talk to me," came the response.

"I see two girls in the third condo.

"Good. Go!"

He ended the call, tucked the phone in his pocket and started for the condo.

The girls were still talking.

"Look, I took your car, but it is not lost. You know where to find it, so why are you bugging me? I made a mistake, and I have apologized. What more do you want?"

"I want to know the truth. You haven't told me everything."

Suddenly, a hailstorm of gunfire hit the condo, shattering the windows. Steffie dashed to the floor behind the couch, dragging her cousin with her. However, she wasn't as fast as Steffie and took a bullet in her thigh. She opened her mouth to scream, Steffie covered it with her hand. She knew her cousin would scream the moment she took her hand off her mouth. She had to contain the situation she had created. If her cousin died, she wouldn't forgive herself.

"Shh. Shh. Please don't make any noise. I will take care of business."

She didn't hear a response but knew her advice would be adhered to. She released her grip, picked up the remote control and hurled it at the light, knocking it out and throwing the room into darkness. She rose quickly and crawled to the kitchen, where she grabbed a knife and hurried back to the door. She could sense the shooter was still there. As she ducked to peep under the door, she noticed the man's head move past the window. She opened the door quietly and stepped out behind him. As he peeked into the kitchen, she stabbed his ear with the knife and yanked it out. He fell and dropped the gun, which she scooped up. Leaving him wincing and moaning on the ground, she hurried into the condo and lifted her cousin onto the couch.

"I'm sorry, but give me the chance to correct things, Ok?"

Steffie could hear her weeping.

"Ok."

"Let me get your belongings. We are getting out right now."

Steffie hurried into the room and got her cousin's belongings, collected her and got out through the rear door. They dashed away into the dark. She carried her cousin on her back, so she didn't slow them down. She had seen the motorbike leaning against the wall by the front door, but she suspected the wounded man might still be armed. If they went out front to use the bike, they could both get killed.

"We can't stay together, cousin," Steffie said.

"Hey, what the hell is wrong with you, Steffie? You got me shot, and now you are abandoning me?"

"I'm not abandoning you. The shooter isn't dead, and he knows we are two. He will call for reinforcements and get his people to look out for two girls. Understand now? Unless he is working alone, that is what is going to happen. I will get you into a cab. You can get to a clinic away from here and get your thigh fixed. The bullet didn't penetrate your flesh; it just grazed it. Tell the nurses it was an accident. Don't go back to the condo for anything, please. Be wise. Don't mention my name anywhere."

"So, how do I manage with one leg?"

"I know what you mean and how you feel. You will be fine."

"Fine? Fine? Is that all you have to say to me?"

"Just understand. And we all will be fine."

Meanwhile, the shooter had recovered, though blood still oozed from his ear. He burst in through the window, still wearing his helmet, another gun in his hand. He searched the rooms for signs of the two girls but didn't find any. He exited, making a call on his phone.

Steffie was running along the periphery of the park as fast as she could, her footsteps attracting barks from several dogs. She would be safer walking, but she had to get away as quickly as possible. If the people after her knew where she lived, they would come after her. Randolph's advice rang in her mind. She had hailed a cab and gotten her cousin into it, hoping it would take her to safety. She felt for the envelope in her jacket. It was the most important thing in her life now. As she rounded the edge of the park, a motorbike roared suddenly behind her. She looked back while still on the run. The attacker was coming after her.

"These guys don't give up," she said as she increased her speed.

The bike gained on her. She did her best to get towards the nearby bushes bordering the park so she could hide. She tripped on a branch and fell. A shot rang behind her, informing her that death was near. The man was still armed, as she suspected. Her hand hit a plank on the ground. She had a gun but didn't know if it still contained bullets. She rose quickly, clutching the plank. She lunged into the bush instantly, a shot just missing her left arm.

The man stopped at the edge of the park and studied it. He flashed a torch across the front. Seeing no sign of Steffie, he fixed a light to his helmet and moved the bike on after her. As he revved past her, she rose suddenly and whacked the back of the man's head with the plank. He fell off the bike onto the ground and rolled a couple of times, then was stopped by a tree. The light on his helmet was smashed. He had lost his gun. He tried to rise with the help of the tree but fell again. She knew the man was dazed as she had hit him hard. She walked to him, helped him to his feet, and kicked him in the groin. He held his groin and winced. She hit his chest with the plank. The man fell again, holding his chest. Now his chest, ear and groin ached. He rose in a sheer show of defiance, but she could hear his groans. Another powerful strike to his chest broke the plank and sent him flying off his feet. The man landed on the ground with a thud. Illumination was poor, but she wanted to know how the man was. She picked up his gun and walked to him, removing his helmet. A pockmarked face was revealed. As he lifted his eyes to look at her face, she stomped his face so hard he screamed. He held his face with both hands as she squatted by him.

"Hopefully, you speak German? I know you can hear me. Who are you? Who sent you? And why are you pursuing me?"

In the moonlight, she could see the man's blood-streaked cheeks widen in a smile.

"Which one do you want me to answer first? You forgot to ask my marital status," he asked defiantly.

She couldn't believe what she had just heard.

"Your life is in my hands, and you dare to mock me?"

She kicked his face. He screamed and flinched away from her.

"I know, but you don't have the balls to do it."

"Oh, yes, I do and will do it."

Suddenly, she punched his face, cracking his lips and nose. He groaned again and held his nose, protesting with a lifted hand. She reached into his pocket and yanked out his phone.

"The phone is yours. Keep it, but please don't kill me."

"My questions are still not answered."

She pocketed the phone and clenched her fist, about to strike his face again. A tiny dancing red dot suddenly appeared on his forehead.

"Ok! Ok! I don't work with names, but they are powerful. They are very powerful. One is a wom…"

The man's head suddenly exploded in her face. She turned instantly and saw three figures holding guns with laser sights bearing down on her on foot. She donned the man's helmet, dashed to the bike and lifted it to an upright position. The men began to fire at her as she started the engine. The engine roared to life right away. She revved it and barreled out of sight, a bullet narrowly missing her neck. One of the attackers got on his phone immediately, telling the listener the target had gotten away.

Headlights appeared behind the men. A car screeched to a stop by them; they jumped in as the vehicle zoomed after her.

CHAPTER SIX

Steffie walked into a small store tucked under a storied house. She had had a close shave with the attackers who knew where she was headed and used another route to lay an ambush for her. While they fired at her, an armed man, who she suspected might be a police or security officer, thought the shots were aimed at him and had returned fire. That had allowed her to escape on the bike. She needed food and items for the next few days. Her usual shop was the mall where she could get all she needed, but this small one would be just fine for now. Not many people shopped here. She went to the soft drinks shelf before she remembered she hadn't taken a basket. Still wearing her helmet, she rushed to grab one and started shopping, picking soft drinks, toothpaste and cookies. Passing the hardware aisle, she picked scissors, hair dye, a mirror, and glue. As she moved towards the end of the shelf, she spotted some ponchos and stopped briefly, contemplating. She snatched up a green one and headed towards the till. She remembered to pick a small flashlight before she reached the till and paid with cash from her purse, which also contained the card given to her by Randolph.

"Anything else I can help you with, Miss?" the cashier asked as she placed her shopping in a plastic bag.

"No. Thanks for asking anyway," Steffie replied as she felt for the envelope in her anorak.

Steffie gave a brief smile and departed the store.

The bike was still in place. She tied her shopping firmly to the carrier and took time checking the bike thoroughly for a tracking device. Then, satisfied, she mounted it and zoomed out of sight.

The ride on the highway felt good. She felt human again. She had stopped by a payphone two minutes after leaving the store to call three clinics to enquire about her cousin. She had been careful not to mention her name but just say a relative. The night nurse at the third clinic had confirmed she had been there and that her situation was firmly under control. There was no cause for alarm. Relieved, she had raced the bike through alleys and back streets to avoid her pursuers. Finally, she was out of danger, at least for now. The bike ran through an intersection without stopping, halting by a shop that was open 24/7. She got off the bike and ran to a nearby drain to urinate. The shop was empty save night stockers busy filling shelves for the next day. The cashier read newspapers while a security officer dozed at the entrance. Two vehicles were parked in the parking lot. As she finished and headed back to the bike, she spotted two people in one of the parked cars and became suspicious. They weren't there when she arrived. As she mounted the bike and started it, two quick shots rang out, aimed at her. At the same time, the car started and charged after her. She took off immediately, hoping another person would come to her aid. She didn't want to get involved in fights where she had been seen. The cashier in the store, for instance, could identify her and alert the police. Even with the helmet and sunglasses on, her face could still be seen by intelligent people. While on the highway, she careened the bike to avoid the shots coming at her. At the next intersection, a cab waited for the green light. She reached it and alerted the driver to block the lane of the car pursuing her. She told him they had robbed the store she had shopped at. The driver believed her and swerved his cab instantly across the lane as the bike crossed the intersection to the other side. The oncoming car swerved wildly to the side to avoid the cab, and in the process, the driver lost control of the wheel. The car smashed through the barrier, went over the drain and crashed into a tree. Steffie gave the cab driver a thumbs up as he stepped out of the cab with a phone to his ear. He was calling the police. She smiled and took off, hoping the men didn't kill the cab driver. A kilometer away from the scene, she took an exit into the swamps. She had gone camping in this part of Munich a couple of times and was familiar with the geography of the place. The bike went through coppices, crossed a cart track, and skirted a hill. She stopped by a pond and checked her shopping, purse, and envelope. Everything was intact. She looked back for signs of her pursuers. The men knew every move she made and waited for her or arranged for men to come after her. She hoped the cab driver wouldn't inform the police she went past the intersection. If he did, the police would come after her in the brush where she hoped to seek refuge for the night. She continued, plunging into the dense brush, into the dark.

It was early in the morning. The three shooters at the mall sat in the tiny room at the police station. They had been held through the night and had been denied the right to make phone calls to their families. That angered them.

"Officer, I want you to tell me what my crime is! I came under attack and had to defend myself. What was my mistake in protecting my life and that of shoppers? What did I do wrong in defending innocent German citizens? Tell me!" one fumed.

"Calm down. We are here to establish your claims about the incident," replied the officer.

"You are all useless! A waste of taxpayers' money!" another chanted in Turkish.

"I warn you. If you insult me in a language that I don't understand, your case will worsen. Every word you say is recorded, and there are thousands of people who speak many languages in the force who will interpret what you just said. I suggest you mind your language."

The third suspect smashed the desk with his fist and said the same words as his friend, startling the officer.

"Is it because we are poor that you always pick on us or what? I mean, what are the criteria for arresting us? Would you have done the same if any of us were your relative? C'mon now, officer," he said.

The two other officers in the room looked on with their guns at the ready. While the officer questioned the men, the door suddenly opened, revealing a stout black-suited man. Heads turned to look at him, the officers most surprised. They hadn't been told of the man's visit and didn't know who he was. The questioning officer rose immediately to challenge him, but when the man flashed a badge in his face, the officer acknowledged him with a smile and departed the room instantly, snapping his finger at his colleagues. The other officers followed him, wondering why their senior colleague didn't take time to scrutinize the badge. Something isn't right, one thought, looking back at the man. He shut the door anyway.

The man sat across from the men who were excited to see him. They had expected him to show up last night when they were arrested at the mall.

"How are you doing, gentlemen?" he asked gently.

"Mercedes. Registration number..."

"Wait a minute." The man cut him off with a raised hand. He reached into the pocket of his suit and handed a piece of paper and pen to the shooter. "Please write it down for me. I work better with written information."

He scribbled the information on it. The man snatched it and, without looking at it, tucked it into his pocket.

"Thank you," he said as he rose.

He pocketed the pen and started towards the door, leaving the men surprised. They shared worried looks.

"What? Are you leaving us here?" one shooter asked disappointingly.

"Yes. Don't worry that you are here. You will be released later today."

"What assurances do we have? I just gave you valuable information. You haven't given us anything, and you tell me we will be released? Is that all you can offer us?"

"Yes. That's what you need. Kill me if what I said doesn't happen. You have my word. Believe me, keep hope alive and live."

He opened the door and left the room. The men looked on, sharing cautious optimism. They had to believe him. They didn't know him but knew where he had come from.

"Do you believe him, brothers?" one asked.

"What options do we have? Let us give him the benefit of the doubt," replied another.

The interrogating officer popped back in and took his seat, the two others following. He had received a message to release the men on orders from above. Names had been mentioned. Names the officer dared not challenge. He told them what the suited man had told them. They were excited as they slapped hands. They had the assurance they needed now.

Birds chirped and trilled in the brush while ducks quacked in the distance. A rabbit dashed behind a cat and climbed a tree before the cat became aware. It had been crawling slowly in the grass towards a pigeon. The rabbit's sudden movement scared the bird away. Against the base of one of the trees, the bike leaned. Up in the tree, Steffie slept in a hammock between two branches. Her hands were over the backpack on her chest. Her eyelids moved slightly, her eyes opening moments later. She squinted a couple of times and yawned, her eyes darting around the branches. She could still hear the birds. The quacks informed her people lived nearby, or the ducks were near a water body. She hadn't slept well, but it was enough to ensure she went through the day without needing sleep. A high level of alertness was needed wherever she found herself. She leaned over and took a look down the tree. Her bike was there. That was refreshing. She reached into the backpack and retrieved the gun. She checked the magazine for rounds. It contained six bullets. It would keep her going for a while. She snapped it back in and returned it to the backpack. She took the cell phone, fixed Randolph's chip in, and dialed. It rang a couple of times, but there was no response. She tried again. At the third attempt, she got through.

"Hello, my name is…."

"Ass?" a female voice cut her.

"Comb."

"What happened to him?"

"He didn't make it. He died outside the museum."

"You mean all three of them?"

"Yes."

"Meet me under the bridge in thirty minutes. Red scarf, red shirt and white skirt."

The call ended. Steffie took out the scissors and mirror and started cutting her hair quickly. Two minutes later, she got all her stuff back in the backpack, strapped it on her back and climbed down the tree. She removed the registration plate on the bike, mounted it and departed in a hurry. She was aware that the people after her were still searching for her and had to be ready for them. The envelope was still intact, and anybody who knew what it contained would come after her. Even her cousin could betray her for money if she knew what she was carrying. The thought of her cousin reminded her to call her cell phone to check on her. She would do that after meeting the woman under the bridge.

The bike ran well in the brush and dirt track. It had enough gas to last for a while. She enjoyed the ride better when the bike hit the highway. It wasn't clear if she could trust the woman she was going to meet, given that Randolph was dead. She would know the envelope had been passed onto Steffie. It explained why she had to get a new passport and get out of the country. Everybody would like to become a hero if Randolph's story was believable. She didn't have grounds to doubt him, given what had prevailed so far. She had seen the list, the seven names. What was still not clear was what would happen in California if she was able to make it there. What if she made it, and the reason for acquiring the list differed from what she had been made to believe? What if Randolph saw an opportunity, was using her for his dirty work and took it?

Martina Jeremies, mid-50s, was a slender woman with sharp Asian features. The product of a German nurse and an Asian mine worker, she had worked as a science teacher for ten years after leaving university. She had done it on the orders of her mother, whom she loved so much and wouldn't do anything against her will. Her father had died when she was two, and she had known only her mother all her life. They didn't have links to the Philippines, where he hailed from. Her mother had made frantic attempts to get in touch with his family, but they would have none of it. Eventually, she gave up and focused on her life. Martina had had a modest but decent life since graduating from university, even though her relationship with men had largely been chaotic. She had surrounded herself with some pretty good friends.

Two years later, they had attended a birthday party of a couple who happened to have the same birthday but different years. One of her good friends had died under mysterious circumstances after the party, and the police failed to make a single arrest. Peeved by this development, she had enrolled in law and international security in the same university she had had her baccalaureate. Now she was in charge of German Intelligence, having worked in various capacities for years and had risen through the ranks. She watched a football match on TV in the lounge of her three-bed storied house while she sipped coffee. She was crazy about soccer and never missed any match Bayern München played at home whenever she had time and would go to see the games live. Her phone rang. She continued watching the match as the phone continued ringing. She glanced at the phone, wondering who might be calling when she was having fun. She set the mug of coffee down in the saucer on the coffee table by her, stretched her hand and pulled the landline phone towards her. A quick look at the caller ID revealed where the call was coming from—it was from the black-suited man who was in the police station to see the three arrested men. This line was secure. She lifted the handset to her ear.

"Speak," she said.

"Mercedes sedan. It was driven by Steffie Shroeder, an Army cadet. My checks haven't revealed who actually owns it, but I'm still working to establish that."

"The envelope is what I want and not her life. If she resists, however, kill her without fail."

"Got it. Will keep you posted."

She hung up and resumed drinking. Then her cell phone rang. She snatched it from the coffee table, not bothering to check who was calling. This number was called by important people—people authorized to call at any time. She flipped it open and listened.

"Talk to me. I have been expecting your call since last night. Since you haven't called, I have taken the liberty to call instead," the caller said.

"We have a little problem," Martina replied.

"That's why I have called you. I have heard of disturbances in the museum."

"We have a suspect on the run, but she won't get far."

"A she? Your suspect is a she? That's a new one."

"Yes…" she laughed quietly, "… as I said, she will not get far. Details at this point are still sketchy, but it is a minor incident. It's the reason I didn't bother to disturb your peace with it."

"I believe you. Remember to keep me posted."

"I hear you and will comply."

The call ended. She dropped the phone and stepped out to the balcony with the mug of coffee in her hand. She wondered who told the caller about the incident in the museum.

She looked down at the streets that fronted her house and the one to the left and smiled to herself. The house was beautifully set in the middle of a manicured lawn, a narrow walkway leading to the canopied entrance that separated two fountains. A semicircular driveway bounded the fountains while a high iron gate seamed the high fence that bordered the property. An armed, uniformed guard manned the gate for twelve hours, after which another relieved him. She leaned on the baluster and admired traffic at the intersection while her dog licked her feet. She liked her house. A property she had bought from a retired factory worker who wanted to go back to Stuttgart to spend time with his family. She had paid fifteen percent less than the asking price for it, having driven a hard bargain. The seller was desperate to leave Munich and go home.

"What the hell is going on here, officer? We just finished answering your questions. So why have you started again?" one suspect asked angrily.

The interrogating officer ignored his ranting and shifted his attention to the next suspect. They were still in cuffs. Suddenly, another man in a blue suit barged in with a similar badge as the previous man. The officer was surprised to see him. He rose immediately and bounded him. An armed officer pointed his weapon at the suspects while the other focused on the suited man.

"How may I help you? How did you get in here?" asked the officer.

The man didn't answer but handed the badge to him and stretched his neck to look at the suspects. The suspects looked at each other, shocked at the man's behavior and why he was interested in them. They wondered who the first man had been if this was the real person to secure their release. The man snatched the badge from the officer and pocketed it.

"Will you excuse me, please? I'll be done in two minutes. I promise you," the suited man said.

The interrogating officer looked at him and then at his colleagues, realizing he'd made a mistake with the first man. He hadn't bothered to check his badge correctly. It had looked genuine to him.

"This is ridiculous! How many of you do I have to indulge?"

"Hey, I'm performing my official duty. What is the fuss about? If you have any issues, please talk to my boss."

"One man has already been here to interview us," one suspect informed him.

The man stared at him.

"He was dressed like you and had a badge like yours," protested another suspect.

The man's gaze fell on the interrogating officer.

"What? Somebody has been here already? What did he ask? Why didn't you check his badge? You should have reported it to headquarters. You always have to check with us to ensure the right people are allowed to talk to suspects. How the hell did you allow this to happen? I demand an explanation now, officer! Now! I mean now!" the man fumed, slamming the tabletop.

"I'm backing out of this case. I can't take this shit. Men in suits just show up and show badges to have access to suspects? How the hell am I supposed to know who is real and who is not? What would you have done in my situation? Huh? Tell me."

The officer stormed out of the room. Moments later, the police chief hurried in and forced the suited man to leave, telling him he wasn't afraid to lose his job once he did the right thing. The suspects were visibly worried now. They knew they could be behind bars a while longer.

CHAPTER SEVEN

The parade square had the aura of a graduation. Soldiers had painted the square and surrounding structures. Even the air smelled of paint. The drill instructor in his well-pressed camouflage uniform stood in front of a squad of seventy-five cadets in military uniforms. Their hair was closely shaved. As they stood at attention in four rows of nineteen, the instructor began to inspect their turnout. They had had morning physicals already and prepared for lectures. Standing before that was drill which many didn't like. When he reached the end of the last row, he noticed one cadet was missing. Surprised, he marched back briskly and took his place in front of them.

"Officer Cadets! The last time I met you, there were seventy-six of you. Today I see one is missing. Can anybody explain to me why that is so?"

The cadets looked around them to see who was missing. A cadet next to the empty position knew Steffie's movements. She contemplated whether to speak or not. The instructor repeated his question. He knew someone knew the whereabouts of the missing cadet.

"She went home yesterday but didn't return. I can't tell you why," replied the cadet.

"I know she went home yesterday because I granted her a pass to go. Her cousin, whom I know very well, isn't feeling well, so I allowed her to go visit her. Who else knows something other than what we've heard?"

"I know a friend of hers; maybe we can check with her to see if we can glean something new," another cadet suggested.

Other cadets gave their take on Steffie's absence, one saying she was the last to see her leave. Many laughed, the instructor alerting him if something went wrong with her, he would be in trouble. The cadet covered his mouth in astonishment.

Suddenly, a green sedan swerved onto the square and came to a halt by the instructor. Two men in black suits and wearing sunglasses got out of the car and strode to the instructor. One of the men had a photo in his hand, which he showed to the instructor. It was Steffie's picture.

"Do you know her?" one of the men asked.

"Who are you?" the instructor asked, studying the faces of the men.

The man showed him a badge which he studied briefly and parried off his face. The men were shocked at his behavior. The instructor had no respect for them, one thought.

"She is supposed to be part of this squad. I just discovered she isn't here. Don't ask me where she is because I don't have an answer to that question."

"She was involved in an incident at a mall last night. Suspects died."

The cadets heard him and began to discuss among themselves. Some were surprised to hear it, but others felt otherwise. One said she had long known Steffie was onto something sinister. Another added it explained why she didn't really talk much with her colleagues.

"One of the men who died was seen in her Mercedes as she fled the scene. Do you or any of your cadets have any idea where we might find her?"

"What are you saying? That she is a criminal or in cahoots with criminals?"

"My question is not answered."

"I told you I don't have a response to that. Well, the answer is no."

"She's a suspect, a threat to national security," warned the second man.

The instructor remained silent. For a moment, he didn't know whether or not to believe the men. He had known Steffie since she was twelve and couldn't believe what he had just been told. Finally, the man handed him a business card.

"Please alert us as soon as you have information about her that might help us find her."

"Ok, but I hope you have the right suspect? She is a good cadet and wouldn't get into anything dirty. I just hope you know what you are doing?"

"That's what people say whenever they hear of loved ones getting involved in shitty games. So yes, is the answer to your concern. We know exactly what we are doing."

"Right. I'll let my superiors know."

"No need. We've notified them already. She's been declared AWOL. There are orders for her to be shot on sight."

"Hey! You can't do that to her. What proof do you have that she was part of what you are alleging? It could be a case of mistaken identity. I suggest you take a second look at your facts and evidence. You could be very wrong, and I sincerely believe that's what is happening in this case."

"Thanks for your long lecture. You are a soldier and a trainer. Do your job while we do what we are paid to do. We are experts in what we do just, as you are when running in the brush with guns under the pretext of defending this nation."

The men burst into a silent laugh.

"This isn't funny. The young cadet's life is on the line."

"Have a good day, soldier."

The instructor looked on as the men got back in their car and left. The bewildered instructor turned to look at the cadets.

"Drill is over! Fall out!"

The cadets fell out, still discussing the issue among themselves. Some departed quickly while Steffie's detractors stood on the square, mocking her. The instructor knew where to find Steffie's cousin. He had been to the condo a couple of times. He still didn't believe Steffie knew anything about the incident alluded to by the two men. He would send a soldier to check it out and also consult with the police to see what would come out of it. He liked his cadets and wouldn't want to lose any of them to crime, death or accident. He had always advised them against bad friends, drinking alcohol, and smoking. He wasn't religious but felt one habit led to the other and sometimes got people into situations they couldn't extricate themselves from. The successful completion of the training and graduation was an indication that he was a good instructor. He wasn't the only person training the cadets, but it showed how competent the entire training team was. He reached the door to his office. He would call the condo first to check if somebody was home. He opened the door and walked in.

The bike arrived at the first pair of piers. Steffie dismounted and propped it against one of the piers. She strolled away from it while she looked for the woman. The weather was windy and cold. Still in her helmet and sunglasses, she wrapped the poncho around her and leaned on one of the piers. The woman wasn't there yet, but Steffie would wait for her. Her hand was on the gun while she carefully looked around. A dove flew over her head, attracting her attention. Her eyes followed it as it flew to a nest on the side of the overhead carriageway. She heard a cough behind her and spun around instantly, the gun ready to shoot, though the poncho was still around her. Olga stood in front of her, sternly staring at Steffie. Her dress was as per the description on the phone. For a moment, they stared at each other askance. Olga wondered how Randolph met the girl in front of her and what made him choose her for the mission. Steffie wondered if the right woman stood in front of her.

"Call my number," Olga demanded.

Steffie did; Olga's cell phone rang. The two continued staring at each other.

"You just failed as a pro. When you are on a mission, you don't stand looking at monkeys!"

"Hey! Don't talk to me like that. Look, I'm sorry. I've had enough hell already."

"I caught you looking at that pigeon."

"I said I'm sorry."

"Do you have it?"

"Have what?"

"What he came for, of course. The man who gave my number to you came for something. Do you have it?"

"No, but he told me where to get it. He said it's in a café in town. He said you should take me to his apartment."

"Follow me."

Olga turned around and moved on. Steffie got her stuff from the bike and followed her. They walked past a couple of piers to a cab.

"Get in!"

Steffie got in the back of the cab as Olga took the wheel. The cab moved off, Steffie still studying Olga's face. She, in turn, stole a glance at her passenger occasionally, wondering if Randolph was truly dead. If so, could her passenger have killed him to have access to the envelope? She had heard one of the three died in the shootout at the museum. Whether the other two were really dead and how they died, she didn't know. Olga glanced at Steffie in the rearview mirror and smiled. Steffie's gaze was on her, while her hand rested on her gun.

"So, what do you do for a living?" asked Olga.

"I'm not working as of now."

Olga shook her head and laughed.

"You expect me to believe you? Ha!"

Steffie studied Olga's face, wondering what her statement meant.

"You're a runaway cadet. You have been declared AWOL. You are a deserter. Did you know that?"

"How do you know that? Who told you that?"

Olga took a rolled-up poster and threw it over her shoulder at her.

"Check it out!"

Steffie caught it and unrolled it quickly. To her surprise, she found her portrait staring at her. Underneath and above the photo was the inscription: WANTED.

Steffie was devastated by the development. She was on a collision course with the law. That meant she couldn't go out as she would have wanted to. Her life was in shambles now, especially if she couldn't make it to California. She felt the urge to get her passport and get out of the country as quickly as possible. Pretty soon, the police and security officers would be coming after her. Olga knew her and what she was up to and could easily betray her. The ports, train stations and airports would be watched closely.

The cab swerved into an alley and made a sudden turn towards an open gate in the wall. The gate closed immediately after them.

Some cars were parked inside, some being sprayed while others waited for minor bodywork. Two huge overhead lamps illuminated the garage. They remained in the cab. Olga was calm, but Steffie looked around for what could be a trap. She wasn't sure why she had been brought here. Randolph said she would be taken to his house, and now she found herself in a garage. A lady in grey coveralls was spraying a car at the end of the working floor. She stopped as soon as she spotted the cab and headed towards a room. The occupants of the cab climbed down and followed her, Steffie taking a quick inventory of the garage. She still looked around for surprises. With the helmet off, her hair was exposed. It was white and closely shaven. As Olga reached the door, Steffie took hold of her arm, getting her attention.

"Why are we here?" Steffie asked.

"You should have asked this question the moment I turned the car into the garage. You should have challenged me. If I came here to kill you, I've got you, haven't I? You are simply not on top of your game. And by the way, your disguise isn't good enough. Once I can identify you, so can anyone with a good eye. Are you sure you didn't kill the man who gave my contact details to you?"

Steffie let go of Olga's arm, knowing the woman was right about her attitude and reactions to events.

"Don't talk to me like that. I didn't kill him. He got into my car when I was going to shop. I had to abandon my plan just to get him out of danger. Unfortunately, he died in my car on the way to the clinic."

Olga shot her a look, "I thought you said they all died at the museum? Now I'm hearing something different."

"Look, you have got to believe me. I didn't know anything and didn't have anything to do with whatever they came to do. I just happened to be at the mall's parking lot, and he got into my car. So when I said all three died, I meant that was what he said to me."

"Whatever."

They walked into the room. The only furniture was a table. They stood by the table, waiting to see what would happen next. Steffie was worried as her question wasn't answered.

Spanners, screwdrivers, and car tools crammed one end of the floor. A white cloth hung on the ceiling batten above them. The woman who'd been spraying looked at them. They stared back at her. She flipped on the light so they could see each other's faces. The sprayer flung both hands at them, inviting Steffie to speak. She knew Olga and didn't need to know her mission. Steffie was the visitor and must make her mission known.

"I believe you know why I'm here. I don't have to say much. Just get on with it," Steffie said.

"No. I don't know why you are here, so tell me why and don't waste my time," replied the sprayer.

Steffie looked at Olga, whose eyes were fixated on the sprayer.

"Comb Ass," Olga alerted.

The sprayer remembered with a smile. Olga shook her head, still unsure whether Steffie was up to the task ahead of her. She didn't know what Steffie's mission was specifically, but usually, the people she helped were smart. So far, she hadn't seen that in Steffie.

"Name and DOB?" the sprayer asked.

She stooped and peeled back one end of the floor carpet while she looked at Steffie.

"Valery Hunter. 12 12 88," answered Steffie.

The sprayer removed a small square board in the floor, revealing a hatch leading into a basement. She descended into the basement and popped back up with a blank copy of a US passport, a camera and a small box. She pulled a white cloth from the box and hung it on the wall, waving Steffie to stand in front of it. Steffie put down her luggage and obliged. The woman marked a line on the floor and asked her to stand there as two shots of her face were taken.

"My charge is $3000. I don't accept cash."

"No problem."

Steffie reached for the card Randolph had given her and gave it to her. The sprayer opened the box and took out a handheld machine. She swiped the card in a slot and handed it back to Steffie, waiting for validation. The transaction went through.

"The card is valid. Thanks. It will only take five minutes. Please wait outside."

"Ok."

Steffie lifted her luggage and stepped out, Olga following.

"What is your name?" Steffie asked, looking at Olga.

"Why ask?"

"I just think I deserve to know."

"You don't have genuine reasons for asking that question, and for that reason, I decline to respond to it."

While they chatted, the sprayer rejoined them with the passport and handed it to Steffie.

"Thank you."

"The pleasure is mine. Be bold. Death stares at you."

"I know."

The sprayer removed the covering on the windshield and windows on the re-painted car and gave the key to Olga. She and Steffie discarded the cab, climbed into the car, and made a left out of the garage as the gate shut behind them. It led into an alley, then on to a street that led to a part of Munich populated by low-income residents.

CHAPTER EIGHT

Olga dropped Steffie in front of the posh townhouse where Randolph and his colleagues had stayed; then, she honked to get Steffie's attention. Steffie hurried to the passenger window, and Olga threw the key to the house to her.

"Remember, no friends. Someone will pick you up in five minutes. Stay alert at all times."

"Ok. Thank you.

The car moved on as Steffie headed for the front door. She had to hurry and be ready within five minutes. She felt for the gun in her anorak. It was still there. So was the envelope. She unlocked the front door and opened it. After taking a quick peek around the house, she barged in and shut the door behind her.

Olga had her phone to her ear as she drove past a truck.

"I just dropped her. Don't kill her. I repeat, don't kill her. Get the envelope. I repeat, get the envelope. She has it or will lead you to it. Wherever it is, you have to get it for me. Understand?"

She ended the call and swerved the car into the heavy traffic.

Steffie took the gun in one hand and a can of soda in the other. She was hungry and hadn't had anything to eat since morning. She remembered the door wasn't locked and went back to lock it. While she did, she looked out for pedestrians and motorists. The street was quiet. She hurried to the kitchen as she gulped the soda, her backpack still on her back. She checked the kitchen, bathroom, and all the rooms to ensure the house was safe. Then she dashed to the toilet, stood on the bowl, and pushed open a hatch in the ceiling. She reached in and groped the opening. Her hand hit something. She clutched it and took it out. It was a small plastic bag. She opened it quickly and found the cash in it. It was intact, as Randolph had said. She closed the hatch, tucked the cash in her trouser pocket and went back to the lounge. She reached into her backpack and took out two cookies from the packet, which she ate quickly. She drank another soda and dumped the can on the dining table. It was time to move. She unlocked the front door and stepped out, looking for the car promised her by Olga.

She surveyed the surroundings carefully and locked the door.

While she waited in front of the door, she heard a vehicle approaching. Quickly, she dashed behind the flowers at the front of the house. She watched as a white van raced to a halt in front of the house. A man in a baseball cap and blue overalls got out holding a pizza box. He walked briskly to the front door and knocked. While he waited, his hand went into his pocket and brought out a pistol. He held it behind him. He rapped on the door again while he took a quick look around him for signs of activity. No one was in sight. While he continued knocking, Steffie dashed silently to the van and inspected it. No one was inside, so she slipped into the back of it while she observed the man at the door.

The man looked around him again, set the pizza box on the ground, took out a small tool, and picked the lock. He walked in and ran to the various places he thought Steffie could be hiding. Moments later, he barged out angrily, stepping on the pizza box on the ground. He hurried into the van and shut the door. As he readied to start the van, Steffie pressed her gun into his nape. He froze instantly behind the wheel. She thrust her left hand into his jacket and took his gun. He looked at her face in the rearview mirror. The helmet and sunglasses made it difficult for him to see her face.

"Relax and don't panic. Who sent you?" Steffie snarled.

"What are you talking about?"

She fired a shot into the man's thigh. He moaned and held his leg. Another shot found the other thigh. He screamed.

"If you don't speak, I will shoot your shoulders and make sure you suffer before you die. Don't make me say that again."

"Ok. She sent me."

"Who is she?"

"The woman who just dropped you sent me."

"Mission?"

The man frowned while he shuddered. She noticed he was scared of death.

"She asked me to get the envelope."

"Well, when you go back, tell her I'm now going to get it from the cafe. I haven't gotten it yet."

"Ok."

"Don't you forget that, huh?"

He nodded, knowing she would let him get out with his life. However, she fired a shot into each knee, shoved him out of the van and took the wheel. She shifted into gear, made a U-turn and departed.

A soldier was posting photos of Steffie on every notice board in the military school. Officers, instructors and cadets gathered at every notice board to read. Two of her mates stood in front of a Humvee as they unloaded supplies from it into a store at the Mess. They watched the soldiers as they discussed the posters.

"I'm really surprised at this development," one cadet said.

"She was such a quiet girl. This whole saga is damn awful," lamented the other.

"She was this close..." his index finger almost touching his thumb, "...to graduating as an officer."

"Why sacrifice such an opportunity for drugs?"

"We don't know yet whether drugs were involved. Stop speculating."

"What else would make her do what she did? She must be very greedy. She wanted a quick way to riches."

"I hope what we are hearing isn't true. The instructor tasked me to check her out at her cousin's."

"Really? And what did you find?"

"Nothing. No one was there. Apparently, a soldier had already been sent before me. He also didn't find anything. So, we both found nothing."

"You know what I think?"

"No. And I don't want to know. I will wait for the instructor to come out of the Commandant's office and hear what transpired between them."

The cadets finished their work and hurried to join their mates.

The Commandant sat at his desk, looking at Steffie's picture in a newspaper as the instructor spoke. He didn't know Steffie, but his checks on her performance had revealed she was a good cadet. He had followed police reports and the media and was disappointed that one of his cadets was involved in such a mess. He had been in charge of the school for five years, and this was the first time such a situation had developed. He gazed at the instructor in front of him.

"Checks on her cousin and friends yielded nothing. Her house showed signs of struggle. Also, bullets were found in and around the condo, Sir," said the instructor.

The Commandant's smiling face changed instantly to grim. He held the instructor's gaze.

"What? Did I hear right? Bullets?"

"Yes, Sir. At this stage, we are not sure whether she had anything to do with it. It is possible she doesn't know anything about what we are reading in the media. Anything is possible."

"The police can't get it wrong. She was seen at the mall with one of the men in her car. Struggles in her house and bullets in her panty? And you tell me it may be speculation? No, I don't think so. How did we allow her into this school? We had a murderer among us and didn't know? Shit!"

"Sir, I think we ought to exercise restraint as of now till the investigations are over. Sad to say, she was the best cadet I've ever trained. Karate expert. Gymnast."

The commandant's eyebrows rose.

"I know that. Karate and gymnastics I didn't know about."

"She missed out on gold in the last Olympics."

"Thanks for telling me, but all that impeccable record is shit now."

"I hope not, Sir."

"Even if she appears and clears her name, I doubt if I can allow her to graduate. Dismiss!"

The instructor came to attention and saluted the officer.

"Sir!"

The Commandant ignored him, brushed the newspaper aside and set to work. The instructor turned about, stamped his foot, and marched out of the office. The officer grabbed his cell phone and made a call.

"I urge you to comb the area in which Steffie's cousin lived for signs of the stuff. She must have it. Go!" he said in a low tone and ended the call before his secretary walked in with a tray of tea and bagels.

Olga was frustrated by her inability to reach the man she had sent to get the envelope from Steffie. She hadn't been to the house to check for herself but was certain Steffie couldn't have harmed him. Equally unlikely was the possibility he might have gotten it from her and decided to keep it. She slammed on the wheel of the rented cab while a man with a rifle sat in the rear seat, watching her. The cab was parked at the end of the alley where the garage was located. She reached for her phone and made a call.

"Speak," a male voice declared in French.

She smiled, "Can you check on the target's house to see what happened to the man I sent there?"

"I asked somebody to do that, but there was no sign of him or his vehicle. However, blood was seen at the front of the house. I don't know who it belongs to. The house was empty."

"Thank you."

She dropped the phone in the pocket of her jacket and glanced back at the man in the rear seat. He fitted a silencer to his rifle. A police car turned into the alley and raced to a halt at the gate to the garage. Olga was shocked that the officers knew the gate existed in the wall. Two officers got down and waited in front of the gate, which parted slowly and allowed them in.

"I think you should go in now," Olga told the man in the back of the car.

He nodded and got out of the cab. At the other end of the alley, another police car waited.

While one officer spoke to the sprayer, his colleague strode around the garage. The cab brought in by Olga had been changed from green to blue.

"A lady matching the description you have given me brought that car for spraying," she pointed.

"Did she say when she will come for it?"

"She did but hasn't shown up yet."

"I see. Did she pay you, and was she alone?"

"She paid me."

"Will you be able to ID her if you saw her again?"

"Not quite because her hair was closely cropped."

"Hair color?"

"White."

Up on the steel roof truss, the man with the rifle opened a louver, took a position by the high window, and aimed at the sprayer. He adjusted the sights and caught her in the crosshairs of the weapon. He could hear their conversation.

"Is that all she requested of you? Just spray the cab?"

"Yes."

"Was she alone?"

The other officer rejoined them. The man on the truss took his eyes off the telescope on the weapon, gazed at him briefly, and focused on the sprayer.

"She came with a wom..."

Suddenly, her head exploded in front of them, spraying blood in their faces. She fell instantly while the officers turned round immediately, wiped the blood from their faces, and started looking for the killer. With their guns drawn, they searched under the vehicles and the room but found nothing.

"It must have come from the roof," one theorized.

They looked up the truss, but the shooter was gone. They charged towards the gate, one dashing towards the button that controlled it.

Meanwhile, the killer had concealed his weapon in his coat and let himself out from the roof. The cab was now in the alley close to the gate. Fortunately, the second police car had left in response to a distress call. He hurried into the rear seat of the moving cab as the officers burst out of the garage waving their guns. The cab was almost at the end of the alley. They spotted it, took after it while they opened fire at it, instantly smashing the rear window. The cab turned into the junction with a screech and disappeared. The officers hurried back into their car and took after it, one talking into his radio.

"Suspect on the run towards the circus! Cab! Red! Stop it and arrest the suspects!"

He kept the radio in its cradle as the car screeched menacingly past a woman walking her dog and took a sharp turn towards the street to the circus. It was the only way out of the place. Moments later, they spotted the cab ahead of them by three cars. The police car overtook two of the cars as its siren blared to alert motorists to get out of the way. The cab took a turn and barreled towards the highway. The car kept pace, honking as it meandered its way through, plunging into the speeding traffic as the cab scraped between two cars just before they passed each other at the middle of the intersection. The frightened drivers applied their brakes to avoid it, swerving and causing an accident. The turmoil that ensued brought the police pursuit to a halt. The officers got out of their car, looking on as the cab tore away from them. It turned at the next junction and vanished from sight. One officer got back on his radio to enquire why the second police team at the alley had been called off. He was told why. When he told the station the direction of the fleeing cab, he was told no cab had gone that way, so he knew the cab had used a secret route or stopped along the way, possibly to escape on foot or by other means.

"Shit!" he exclaimed as he smashed the radio on the pavement.

His colleague patted him on the back. He understood his frustration. Motorists were surprised the officers hadn't bothered to control the madness left in the wake of their chase after the cab but argued.

The white van pulled into the parking lot of the café. Steffie looked at her face in the mirror and liked what she saw. It wasn't the best disguise, but enough to get the job done. Olga knew her blonde locks could easily betray her to the police. She could also do it for anybody after her life if the price were good. She had arrived back at the posh house to get the man sent by Olga, but he was gone. She didn't have the time to clean up the blood on the floor. She knew it could create problems for her, even though the man couldn't be traced. A DNA test would undoubtedly tell he had been there if he died later. She got out quickly and headed for the entrance, looking down to avoid faces. Her hair was still white, but she was wearing a hat to hide it and was wearing her sunglasses. She would get her food and leave immediately. Her shoulder collided with the chest of a stout man as she approached the entrance. She said sorry and moved on. As she was about to enter the café, she looked at the wall by the entrance door and saw her 'Wanted' posters. Without showing any emotion, she dashed in and walked straight to the counter. The cashier attended to a customer, making her feel nervous. She didn't have time to spare. She stole a glance at the customers in the café and focused on the cashier. She placed her order and waited with her back to the diners. Another glance over her shoulder revealed a police car parked next to her van. It wasn't there when she parked it moments ago. She saw two officers get out of their car, one looking casually at the van. Her heart pounded within her chest. Her attention switched instantly to the sales assistant, wondering why her order wasn't ready. The sales assistant stared at her, expecting payment for her order. Steffie's focus was on the approaching officers, hoping they hadn't followed her. She noticed the sales assistant was still looking at her. Her stomach tightened as she looked away. Had the assistant identified her and possibly called the officers? She stretched out her hand. Then she got the message.

"Gosh. How much?" she asked.

"$5."

She slapped a fiver on the counter and glanced at the approaching officers, who were chatting excitedly about something that made them walk slowly. It was a great relief to Steffie, who didn't want them to see her at the counter. A waiter presented her with her order; she snatched it quickly and dashed into the restroom, located a couple of yards from the counter. Moments later, she opened the door a crack and took a peek at the counter. The officers were at the counter. She stepped out of the restroom boldly, walked briskly past the officers, and exited. She hurried into the van, still looking at them.

One of the officers showed a portrait of Steffie to the sales assistant.

"Seen her?" he asked while his colleague looked at the people eating in the café.

The sales assistant studied the photo briefly and remembered, smiling. The officers knew she knew something.

The van eased out of the car park slowly and disappeared from the vicinity.

"Yes," the sales assistant replied.

The officers looked at each other, excited.

"Yeah? Where do we find her?"

"She just left here."

"Holy cow! She just left here?"

She nodded.

"What was she wearing? Where did she go? Do you know?" the second officer asked.

"I think we should leave now," the first officer advised.

They departed the café immediately, one almost knocking down a man and his son.

They looked to both sides of the street but found nothing suspicious. It was business as usual as shoppers moved in and out of shops. Vehicles raced past in both directions. They observed each passerby and customer but didn't find her.

"Maybe we have to check the café again. She may still be in there," one suggested.

"Go and take a look while I radio for help."

"You can't radio when we don't know what she is wearing, which direction she went, and by what means of transport."

One checked the café while his colleague observed both sides of the street for signs of somebody walking fast or jogging away from the café. The officer returned from the café with negative news. He ran to the parking lot while the other checked the exit, located sixty yards away. After thoroughly checking the periphery and shoppers leaving the parking lot and finding nothing, they met in front of their car, one wondering why they failed to consider the possibility she might have been in the café.

"If she was in the café moments before we went in, then she must have seen us and outwitted us," one said.

"I agree. She saw us and slipped out when we were not watching her. Is it possible the sales assistant got it wrong? I mean, is it possible she mistook somebody else for our target?"

"I doubt it, but what baffles me is why she would bother to come here and buy food or for whatever reason when she knows she is wanted."

"She must be hiding around here somewhere. She can't have gone far."

"She can, actually, if she has a collaborator. I don't think she is operating alone if indeed she is who we have been made to believe she is."

A boy walked towards them. One officer showed the photo to him. He knew instantly what they wanted from him and pointed in a direction. As the excited officers moved towards their car, he changed his mind and pointed in the opposite direction. The confused officers ignored him and got in their car. As the car departed, the driver noticed the white van was gone.

"Where the hell are we supposed to search for this wench now?" the driver said.

"The white van. It's gone. It was there when we came in."

"Anybody at all could own a white van. I don't think that is a factor we should consider..." he looked at his colleague, "...wait a minute. Bingo!"

He reached for his radio immediately.

"Ocean One to Control."

"Go ahead, Ocean One."

"Suspect still in Area A, possibly in a white van."

"Copy. More men will be deployed in Area A. Out."

He dumped the device on the dashboard, lit a cigarette, and started smoking. His colleague looked away, swatting away the smoke as it assaulted his face.

"What is the matter with you, huh? You know how much I hate it when you do that stuff. Don't blow smoke in my face again."

The recalcitrant officer burst into laughter, blowing another cloud of smoke in his companion's face as the car raced past two big trucks parked on the same side of the highway. Tucked between them was the white van. Steffie lay across the front seats. They saw the trucks and van but made nothing of it due to the conversation about the smoke. Two minutes later, the driver's face changed when it occurred to him, they might have missed their target. He glanced at his colleague.

"I think we missed the van. We just passed it. Remember the two trucks?"

"Oh shit! We have failed to pay attention again. Let's go back to the trucks."

The driver stopped the car, wheeled around on the shoulder, and moved in the opposite direction towards the trucks at top speed. He made sure to stay on the shoulder so as not to affect traffic. When they arrived, the van was gone. A cursory look at where it stood showed tracks towards the shallow ditch to their right. They crossed it and saw tire marks in the bare ground towards the grass.

"The van went that way…" one pointed, "…towards the brush."

"I agree. That is where we have to go. Let us go after it. We will catch up with it soon."

They got back in their car, turned towards the ditch, and took after the tracks, beating up grass in the air. Then, a couple of yards into the grass, the car began to reduce in height. Initially, it appeared that it had plunged into a slope, but when the officers scrambled out of the vehicle through the windows, they realized they had driven into a pond.

One hundred yards ahead on the highway, Steffie observed from the van. She had driven the van in that direction, knowing they would come after her once they remembered seeing the van between the trucks. She had then turned the van around back onto the highway's shoulder and barreled past while the police car moved back to the trucks. But unfortunately, the officers had been so absorbed in reaching the trucks they hadn't bothered to check the vehicles in the traffic.

The van pulled up a couple of paces from a BMW coupe in a quiet street in front of a row of houses. A couple of cars were also parked on the street. She was tired and hungry. She reached for the food, opened the white paper bag, and took out her sandwich. She took a big bite that filled her mouth and made chewing difficult. She looked at her mouth in the mirror and gave a smile. Gradually, she chewed and swallowed while she monitored events around her in the side and rearview mirrors. She was surrounded by enemies. Olga had told her that her photos were everywhere, and Steffie had no cause to doubt her. She had seen it at the café. Men had been sent after her. Olga was also after her. Some were after the envelope, while others had been tasked to kill her. She remembered her cousin. The last call she made told her she had gone for the Mercedes and kept it in a friend's house. She had had to spray it a different color. Steffie was glad her cousin did well. Her boyfriend had forgiven her for the date blip. While she wolfed down her sandwich, a bike swerved onto the street from the main road towards the van.

She reached for her gun and waited. It scooted past without the rider looking in her direction. She put the radio on. Classical music was playing. She changed the dial to a station where a female newscaster was presenting news.

"This is the latest on the Steffie Shroeder case...."

She shoved the last piece of the sandwich in her mouth and listened to the radio avidly.

"She is suspected to be in Area A, possibly in a stolen white van. She is armed and dangerous...."

She rested her head on the wheel. It was surely over for her. Everybody would believe she was a criminal. Even those diehards who stood their ground for her, those who refused to believe the story, would change their minds now. Her instructor and colleagues in the school would be disappointed in her. She had tried to explain the issues to her cousin, but she knew it wasn't enough to convince her. The evidence against her was so strong that no amount of words could erase whatever she presented to her. Her cousin had accepted her explanation, but Steffie knew her story was doubted. She shook her head in disbelief as she rolled down the window and tossed out the food wrapper. She had to leave the country but how to get out was the problem. All the exit points were watched. She was on TV with her posters all over the place. The news continued on the radio. While she contemplated her next move, a street door opened, and a slender man came out and started towards the van. She spotted him and started the van. The man looked suspicious. He might be a good citizen who had heard of her and the white van and was coming to ensure he had the right target, she suspected.

"The public is advised to stay away from her. Finders are advised to alert the police immediately," the newscaster concluded.

The van made a U-turn and barreled out of sight. The suspicious man quickly yanked out his cell phone and made a call. She looked back at the man, hoping he didn't get in the coupe and take after her. She was sure now the man knew her and had come out to confront her. She would have had to deal with him to get away from him. That could have resulted in anything, even death. Unless it became absolutely imperative, there was no need to waste anybody.

CHAPTER NINE

The quaint shop was almost empty when Steffie walked in. It was her first time in this shop but the right one. She couldn't afford to shop in busy shops. She packed her stuff in a basket while scanning the shop for surprises. She placed her hand on her stomach anytime a shopper walked in. It gave her easy access to the gun. The knife and envelope were also in place. It was a routine she ran every now and then. She also paid attention to her van whenever a car pulled behind or by it. With her shopping basket by her on the floor, she grabbed a polo shirt and a pair of shorts and hurried to the till. The cashier began to run the register. Behind the cashier, a female employee was watching Steffie with keen interest. Steffie knew the employee had spotted her. A look behind the employee revealed a photo of her on the wall. Her knees buckled. The shop she thought would be a safe place to shop without fuss had turned out to be another nightmare. The employee turned towards an inner room. Steffie knew the employee was going to call the police or somebody, possibly the manager. The employee tripped and almost fell, but her grip on the wall kept her balanced.

When she raised her eyes, she saw Steffie's photo on the wall. Instantly, something moved in her, and she turned her head to look at Steffie. Even though Steffie still had her hat and sunglasses on, the employee could make her out. She had eyes for detail. Steffie focused on the display of the register, which proclaimed $19. At the same time, she stole a glance at the employee with her peripheral vision. She handed the credit card to the cashier, who swiped it and gave it back to her. Meanwhile, the employee wasn't sure if she had the right person in her sights as she kept comparing the image in the poster with Steffie. Finally, satisfied with her photo analysis, she focused on Steffie.

"It's her!" she screamed, pointing at Steffie.

Two shoppers turned to look at the employee, as did the cashier, who took a good look at the customer in front of her.

"What about her?" the cashier asked.

The employee pointed to the poster on the board while reaching for the landline phone on the wall. She began to dial a number they all knew was the police. Steffie snatched the receipt from the cashier, collected her shopping, and exited. The cashier didn't bother to move, and the two shoppers couldn't be bothered. Apparently, they hadn't heard about Steffie. The slender figure of the manager lunged out of the inner room. She was aware of the suspect and helped her employee by calling on her cell phone. Steffie heard the employee screaming into the phone as the manager stepped out after her. She hurried into the van and sped off, splashing dirty water on the woman.

While the van waited in the slow-moving traffic, two police cars wove their way through the traffic, blaring sirens. Finally, traffic began to part in front of them. Steffie turned off the radio in the van, looked back, and saw the parting cars. The big trucks prevented her from seeing what the sirens were about. Then the first police car appeared, the second following.

"Oh shit!" she exclaimed.

She swerved the van through the small space between two cars onto the shoulder and took off instantly. She cursed herself for not doing this earlier. She would have disappeared long before the arrival of the police. The employee in the shop had succeeded in alerting the police, yet Steffie hadn't heeded the threat and taken the proper precautions. She had committed another blunder she knew Olga would have killed her for. The police saw the van and took off after it, honking furiously. One car raced along the shoulder while the other stayed in the lane. The van was running low on gas, and Steffie hoped it would get her to safety before she ran out. And then she would figure out a way of refueling. There was always a way out in every situation. Another look behind told her the police car was gaining on the van. She didn't want a show down with the police and had to get away from them without spilling blood. Up ahead, an exit led to a side street she knew had shops and eateries. She swerved the van onto it and raced it down past coffee shops, shoppers and diners. Pedestrians frustrated her progress as they crossed the street at any time and any point. The van had to stop at times to allow the elderly and visually impaired to cross. They did it at an excruciatingly slow pace, much to Steffie's annoyance.

The police cars plunged diagonally onto the side street. The van swerved to the right onto the curb to avoid colliding with a milk van whose driver Steffie thought must be asleep behind the wheel, forcing shoppers to lunge out of the way. The milk van swerved suddenly to the right and crashed into one of two columns of a shop in an attempt also to avoid the van. The impact was so strong it shook the column and almost brought down the shop gallery that it supported, sending panic among the shoppers. Meanwhile, the cars following the van and milk van raced to prevent pedestrians from crossing the street and blocking traffic. They ended up colliding with each other as they tried to avoid hitting the rear of the milk van and van. The van managed to get out of the chaos but not the police cars. They had to get the van. Behind them, traffic was crazy. The two cars backed up towards the main street while they honked to ward off motorists who might want to also back up to the main street and use other routes. One hit the bumper of a car while the other sideswiped a sedan. Both turned in the main street, stabbed at the accelerators, and jerked the cars forward, tires screeching furiously. Their actions left chaos in their wake that motorists had to grapple with.

The van, meanwhile, had beaten them to the draw. Steffie knew what the police would do once traffic slowed on the side street. She had turned the corner and driven back on the next side street, gotten back into the main street, and driven off before the police remembered they could use that route. She lost them before they thought like professionals.

Moments later, the van was back on the highway. Steffie ate cookies as the vehicle sped along. She needed a new look and a new vehicle. The blonde hair and white van had served their purpose. It was time for a new appearance, a new finesse.

Steffie laughed to herself as she looked at her face in the mirror of the van. She had had another scare of two men on a bike and fired at them to ward them off. She was still alive, thanks to the gun she had. The van raced past an alley and stopped with a screech. She wasn't sure if she saw right. She contemplated briefly and reversed the van to the edge of the alley. She was right. Two girls stood by a black sports car. She turned the van into the alley and moved to a halt by them. One of the teen girls held a bottle of beer while the other smoked a cigarette. Steffie stepped down and approached them, wondering what they were doing there all by themselves. They stared at her as she approached them, the one smoking stepping in front of her. She took a long drag and exhaled into Steffie's face. She looked back at her friend and burst into laughter.

"Hello, my name is …."

"We don't need your name. Just tell us why you have come," one cut Steffie off.

She looked at the sports car and then at the girls. The smoking girl exhaled again into her face while her friend studied the van. Both were surprised that Steffie didn't flinch but smirked instead.

"You know, my dad gave me this van as a birthday gift," Steffie pointed.

"Lucky you. You know your dad, and he gave you a gift. I don't even know my dad," replied the smoking girl.

"My dad is in prison," the other girl informed.

"Oh, I'm so sorry to hear that. What sent him there?"

"He molested my twin brother and me. He had sex with both of us when we didn't know anything. He did it until the day he got drunk and told one of his friends what he had been doing to us. Then his friend reported the matter to the police, who moved in to arrest him. And guess what? When the police broke down the locked door, he was busy with me. Weird, isn't it?"

Steffie shook her head. She couldn't believe a father would do a thing like that to his own children.

"What do you say to my van plus a cool $500? I mean, in exchange for your car?"

The girls glanced at each other excitedly. They consulted briefly in undertones while they inspected the van. Steffie was impressed by the details they paid attention to. They knew a thing or two about automobiles. She had already refueled on her way towards the alley. A valet at a gas station had done it for her when she had lied and told him she wasn't feeling well. She had tipped him handsomely after he had bought cookies and soda and hair dye for her. Convinced the van was in good shape, the girls decided to accept the offer.

"Deal!" they exclaimed.

They slapped hands in the air, obviously happy about the deal. Steffie moved her stuff into the trunk of the sports car. She reached for $500 in her purse, which she was careful not to show, and then dropped the money in their hands.

"Thank you. To tell you the truth, we will sell the van and get another sports car. I am sure we can get one cheaper somewhere. I am glad you came along, sister."

Without wasting any more time, they finished smoking and drinking, got into the van, and drove off, honking and whistling. Steffie sat behind the wheel of the sports car and moved on. She needed a place to rest. She couldn't continue running around without rest. The task ahead of her was daunting, but she also needed to pay attention to her body lest she broke down and wasn't able to perform certain tasks when she had to.

Minutes later, the sports car hit the side street, moving in the opposite direction to the original direction of the van. She knew a motel on the outskirts of town that would serve her purpose. She needed a place her pursuers wouldn't bother to look for her. They wouldn't think she would be stupid enough to still dwell among people in motels, shop and eat or buy food at cafes. Those were places where she could easily be identified. They would think of places away from civilization. Her cousin was doing well, and grateful Steffie checked on her every now and then. She had told Steffie to stop calling her once her life was in danger. That news had excited Steffie, who had been living with guilt ever since they were attacked in their home. Now that her cousin had taken in the reality of the situation, Steffie would in good conscience be able to do what she had to. She still felt sorry for the pain she had caused her, but frankly, her cousin knew her better than anyone and knew Steffie wasn't a bad person.

The military came to mind as the car passed a military squad truck. She had dreamed of graduating as an officer and relished the day when she would be sent on an overseas mission. Iraq and Afghanistan had always been on her mind. She couldn't wait to have that experience. She had seen on TV as troops helped locals in those troubled countries and also stabilized them politically, although not all UN missions had been successful. Everything had been on course until the moment she found herself at the right place but at the wrong time. The day Randolph had bizarrely invaded her privacy and changed her world. Her dream for the military died instantly, along with the foreign mission fantasies. And now, all of a sudden, she was a wanted person hunted by the German police and security forces. She also knew it was possible that neighboring countries were on the alert for her. If that were the case, the whole of Europe would be looking out for her. She couldn't believe how her life had changed so drastically within a matter of days. She wasn't religious, but she recalled attending church service with her cousin, during which the preacher said anything was possible at any time. There was no turning back for her now. She had to make it to California alive and complete the task or get killed, or be arrested by the police. She had to make sure she didn't fall into the hands of the wrong people who might not hand her over to the police but keep her and torture her to death. The sports car barreled down the side street past two police cars Steffie knew were looking for her. She made sure not to look in their direction. Her hair was brown, the brown wig giving her the long hair that she liked. The car exited another side street, turned a corner to a motel, and pulled up in the car park.

She remained briefly behind the wheel, studying the motel, paying attention to the parked cars and people as they moved in and out of the motel. The number of vehicles in the parking lot told her the motel was quite busy. It was probably full of guests. She took one last careful look at the windows that overlooked the car park. Then, satisfied with her safety, she stepped out of the car, grabbed her stuff, and headed for the entrance of the motel. She wore shorts and a polo shirt, a hat covering her brown hair. She was careful not to look at anyone's face as she reached the door. The well-appointed lobby teemed with skiers with their skis. Another group of people she knew instantly were tourists listened as a male tour guide gave a lecture Steffie thought was boring, given the looks on the faces around the man. She moved to the reception and waited for her turn as the clerk attended to a guest. She didn't fidget or look at faces even though she considered the clerk and her surroundings. There was a landline phone on the reception desk, a desktop computer, and a sign-in book. A half-eaten candy apple lay in a small saucer to her left. A man coughed badly behind her, prompting her to look back. He read a newspaper while a girl she suspected might be his granddaughter fidgeted with a toy next to him. Two older folks chatted while a poorly-attended musical performance she thought was one of those boring festivals showed on the rather old TV on a table. Nobody bothered with it. Steffie inched forward to the clerk when the guest in front of her was served.

"How may I help you?" she asked.

"Bed," Steffie replied with a Danish accent.

"How many days?"

"One."

"$50. Cash or card works for me."

Steffie slapped the credit card on the counter. The clerk took it, swiped it in the register slot, and handed it back to her. Steffie took the receipt and turned her attention to the road maps on a stand behind the clerk. The clerk placed the key to her room on the counter.

"Room 5. Right. It's down the corridor…" she pointed, "…you can't miss it even if you were blind. Anything else I could help you with?"

Steffie cleared her throat and gave a brief smile.

"Actually, I'm new in town. I'm from Denmark."

"Bingo. I suspected the moment you first spoke. There is something about your accent that told me you are not from around here, but where did you learn to speak German?"

"In university. I studied languages, majoring in German."

The clerk smiled her welcome and handed a road map of Frankfurt to her. Steffie looked at it with a smile. The conversation was going well, but she was also wasting time.

"I'll like to see more of Germany for a book I'm writing. I'll move to Stuttgart tomorrow and then attend a wedding in Switzerland."

"Oh? You are attending a wedding in Switzerland, huh? I love weddings. God knows I do."

"Yes, I do too. One of my best friends in university is getting married to a circus clown."

The clerk's happy face changed suddenly.

"That's a low."

"Why do you say that? Circus clowns make a lot of money. The two love each other."

"I rest my case if you say so. I will never marry or allow my daughter to marry such a person."

The clerk yanked another road map off the stand and gave it to her. Steffie took another look around the lobby. There was no change since she last considered it.

"Munich. Munich to Austria, Munich to Poland, blah, blah, blah."

"Ok…" Steffie took the ones from Munich to Austria and Poland, "… thanks." She took the key and left. Her room was on the ground floor. She rounded a staircase, turned right, and found Room 5. She looked to both sides as she reached the door, unlocked it, and walked in, locking it behind her.

She looked at the room. A telephone stood on a desk sandwiched between a bureau and a wardrobe. The bed stood opposite the chair. She dropped her backpack and moved to the window that overlooked the parking lot. Her gun was still in place but out of ammo. She needed bullets. She returned to the bed, stooped, and checked under it. The wardrobe revealed hangers. The bureau drawers were empty. She went to the bathroom and toilet. The place was clean even though she couldn't discard the possibility of a bug or tap in the room. She lifted the mattress and checked it thoroughly but found nothing. The telephone was clean, as was the desk and the top of the wardrobe. She had to make a call, and the only phone she had could only call Olga. She glanced at the telephone on the desk, reached for the handset, lifted it, and dialed. She was fully aware of the risk associated with the call she was about to make, but it was necessary. She needed to make it.

"How may I help you, Room 5?"

"I need a connection to 762 593 4213."

"Done."

She returned the handset to the transmitter. Moments later, the phone rang. She picked up the receiver instantly.

"OD," a warped voice said.

She smiled at the acronym OD which meant order.

"BX. 6men. Ca. STANLEY. CPK. 180 clock."

"Ok. $2500."

She hung up, uncapped a drink, and sipped. She moved back to the window, drew back the curtain to survey the car park. She downed the drink and dumped the bottle out of the window to the ground to see if it attracted attention. The car park was quiet, with no car out of place. She needed one box of 6mm caliber bullets. In thirty minutes, the man she called would arrive at the car park. She heard men conversing in the corridor, prompting her to move to the door quickly to eavesdrop on them. She couldn't catch a word the men spoke. She released the security chain, opened the door a crack, and peered out. The men were receding towards the end of the corridor. She observed till they entered a room and shut the door behind them, and then she closed hers and locked it. She took the gun and checked for rounds. It had one in it. It was perhaps enough to fight off an attacker but not enough to take on a marksman or two or more attackers.

She sat on the bed and took out the maps from Reception. With the Munich map in her hand, she moved back to the window. There was a page for railway lines from Munich to Vienna. She took her time studying it as she marked points on it with a pen. Traveling by air was simply out of the question. The other modes of exiting the country were equally risky but worth exploring. If she could cross the border to any of the neighboring countries, she stood a chance of making it. The problem was, all the countries she had in mind were in a high state of alert. All information about her was by now available to the security forces and police in those countries. Perhaps Interpol was also in the know. She finished marking all the routes and checking the time involved in traveling from Munich to Vienna. She felt for the envelope. It was intact. She did that every thirty minutes or so to ensure she hadn't lost it. When she looked down at the parking lot, a man with bushy hair was riding a bicycle towards the motel. He stopped and dismounted with a box of chocolates, parking the bicycle by a trash container. She could make out the box because it was one of her favorites. She observed as he studied the motel. The man didn't attempt to get into the motel but instead chose to stand under a tree in front of the building. He was waiting for somebody. Steffie knew her man had arrived. She tucked the gun in the anorak over her polo shirt, left the room, and locked the door.

The corridor was quiet; conversations in low tones were audible as she passed the rooms. She walked leisurely past Reception as if she was taking a stroll outside. The security officer at the door was reading a newspaper. He paid attention only when guests came in, not when they left.

Steffie walked briskly towards the man who she now could see was wearing a wig. She looked to both sides of the motel and the parking lot as she approached him. Finally, she stopped with a yard between them, both studying each other's faces. This was not the time to smile or exchange pleasantries.

"Stan," she said.

"Ley."

She took the box from the man and inspected the contents. It was as per the order. Satisfied, she dug into her jacket, took out a small envelope, and handed it to him. The man opened it quickly, checked the money, and hurried to his bicycle. Without looking back, he mounted it and rode away. Pleased with what she had, she started back to the motel. The man in the wig looked back and saw her going back into the motel. He reached for his phone and made a call, saying he knew where Steffie was holed up.

Steffie had met a man three years ago at a nightclub during which there was a scuffle involving three men and two girls. The confusion had turned bloody when one pulled his gun and shot another in the chest. Then they took off with the girls leaving the man for dead. Steffie had gone to the man's rescue and called an ambulance. The man had a gun, but when he fired back, he discovered he was out of ammo. He had told Steffie where to get ammo whenever she needed it. She hadn't bothered with the card the man had given her though she had kept it since then. It had just come in handy. Now she was ready to take on any opposition. It wasn't her intention to kill, but when attacked and the intent to kill her was registered, she would have no other option than shoot to kill. She wouldn't shoot to defend herself. She quickly entered the motel, knowing she had to move as soon as possible. She still wasn't sure which route to use to get out of the country without being caught.

She walked past a couple at the desk, the clerk busy with an elderly couple. She was alert for guests who entered. When she saw Steffie, she forced a smile to which she got no response. Steffie rounded the stairs and disappeared to her room. The couple got their key and left the desk, the man struggling to pull the rather heavy luggage. The clerk wondered why they didn't just let the concierge help them. She had seen him approach the couple to help and been politely turned away when they alighted from a cab. She hoped they didn't have contraband in the two big suitcases. Two weeks ago, a woman from Thailand came to the motel with a suitcase containing a hundred young anacondas. She had also refused help from both the security officer and porter who worked part-time and studied at college. When her suitcase fell to the floor and accidentally opened, the creatures sprang out like prisoners who had broken out of jail, running in all directions and sending guests screaming and shrieking.

The guests in the lobby still chatted and gossiped. The coughing old man and his granddaughter still sat watching the TV. Nothing of importance was showing, but somehow they enjoyed it. The clerk wondered what they actually came to the motel for. Guests arrived for honeymoons, to celebrate birthdays and have parties, while others came to relax during holidays. It gave them a break from the hectic time in their various workplaces. This grandpa didn't seem to have anything in mind. The clerk wondered if the girl was actually his granddaughter. Suddenly, Steffie's mugshot appeared on the TV, the word 'WANTED' at the base of it. The clerk, who had been eating a sandwich, spotted the photo on the screen but made nothing of it. She continued eating while she unwrapped a lollipop. Then she heard the charges against the suspect and became interested, wondering why a beautiful girl like the suspect would engage in a crime like that. The suspect had been declared a threat to the security of not only Germany but also Europe. She shoved the last piece of sandwich in her mouth, rose, and walked to the TV to take a closer look at the photo. She scratched her head a couple of times, gazed at the ceiling, and then back at the image. Somehow the photo looked oddly familiar, but she couldn't place it. She scratched her chin a few times, and then she remembered seeing somebody who looked like the mugshot.

"Come on, girl. I have seen you before. Where? Where the hell did I see you? Come on, girl, try hard and remember," she mouthed.

While she walked back to the desk to attend to a guest, she remembered Steffie. With a broad smile on her face, she assisted the guest quickly, lifted the handset of the landline on her desk, and dialed.

Meanwhile, Steffie loaded both of her guns and inserted them in her anorak. She retrieved the envelope, checked the contents, and tucked it back in her polo shirt that was firmly tucked into her shorts. She hurried back to the window with the map of Munich in her hand. The street was quiet as it had been since she came to the motel. She went back to her backpack and made sure nothing was left in the room that could link police to her. It was time to leave. She had mapped out an escape. She would use the train to Austria and decide how to get out of that country. How she would get on the train without being seen was a challenge she didn't want to think about. Too much thinking didn't help in a situation like this. She had to take a risk; otherwise, she would forever remain in Germany. The longer she stayed, the slimmer her chances of escape got. She was ready to leave, but as a precaution, she took one last look out of the window to be absolutely certain it was safe to get out. The moment her face showed behind the curtain, bullets ripped through the window, shattering the pane. She ducked instantly to the floor. For a moment, the shooting ceased, allowing her to rise and carefully take a peek out. Four police officers were at the front of the motel. She pocketed the map, grabbed her backpack, and spun around to the door, slipping out of the room. She knew the officers were en route to her room. She braced on the wall by the door briefly, listening for conversation at the desk or voices from the advancing officers. She didn't want to walk into their trap. She lurched across the tiled floor and took refuge behind a column, her hand on one of her guns. Suddenly, a shot fired from behind her whipped past her ear and exploded in the column. She spun around while she ducked and returned fire, felling the officer instantly. She heard footsteps suddenly. They were fast approaching her, obviously following the shots. She lunged underneath the stairs that rose to the first floor and fired at the advancing feet. Two officers fell, holding their legs and wincing. She came out from beneath the stairs, looked back and front in quick succession while she kicked their weapons away from them. As she moved to round the stairs and head towards the desk, something impacted her back, knocking her to the floor. Pitched down on her face, she lost the gun. When she rolled over, an officer looked down at her. The fourth man and he was smiling at her. She ignored him, wondering why she hadn't suspected him from that angle. She could reach for the second gun, but if the officer read her intentions, she was dead.

"Bastard! Finally, I caught up with you. I have been looking for you for ages while you have been splashing cash around town. You have been using a credit card whose origin can't be traced. How ingenious! You have succeeded in downing my colleagues, but I have you, and what are you going to do next? How many more tricks do you have up your sleeve?"

She flinched and casually flung her hand slowly into her anorak. They heard footsteps.

"Have you found her? Pat, have you nabbed the bitch?" a colleague asked as he approached.

"Yeah! A beaut! A real beaut! You will love her!"

"Hold her! I'm gonna screw her so hard she'll scream!"

The officer smiled as he squatted by her, studying her face. Suddenly, her hands came out with a gun and fired a shot in the officer's shoulder. She shot the other instantly, forcing him to his knees. She kicked the gun out of his hand, rolled over instantly, and aimed her gun. As soon as the advancing officer's legs shot into view, she fired a shot and hit his leg. The officer fell, clutching his leg. He returned fire; she ducked, the bullet missing her. He fired again but discovered he was out of ammo. Surprised, he crawled towards Steffie's gun. Just as he was about to grab it, a foot stepped on his hand. He groaned as he tried to snatch his aching hand. He looked up and saw her.

"That's my gun you were trying to reach. Where is yours?" she asked.

She spun her foot on his hand, inflicting more harm. Then, while he winced, his hand stealthily moved slowly to his back, reaching for a sheathed hunter's knife.

"My gun is out of ammo."

"Interesting. So you were trying to get mine to kill me. Kill me with my own gun, huh?"

"I had to defend myself."

"How did you know I was here?"

"We had intelligence. You can't win."

"Who says I'm trying to win anything? I don't know why you are after me. Do you?"

"I do. We have information that you are a threat to national security."

"Have you bothered to check if the information you have is true?"

"Ouch!" he exclaimed as she pressed his hand with her foot.

Blood showed at the back of his hand.

"My question isn't answered."

"No. Know this, though. All the ports, airports, train stations are on alert. All institutions and cab drivers, hoteliers, and café managers are looking out for you. Even if the information we have about you isn't true, I have just witnessed how fast you are with guns. You are a good shot."

She smiled.

"Really? You flatter me."

"We just take orders and don't get to ask questions."

"So, what were the instructions?"

"Shoot to kill."

"I thought so."

She smiled thinly as she pointed her gun at his face. She lifted her foot and stomped on his hand again. Suddenly, he flung the knife at her foot. She stepped back immediately and stamped his face before he could recover. He dropped the knife and held his face, groaning.

She scooped up the gun and knife and aimed at his face. She had to move, but she felt pressed to know who informed them she was in the motel.

"Who told you I was here? I'm not gonna ask again."

"The... the cler ..."

Suddenly, two silenced shots hit his chest and killed him. Steffie turned around quickly and saw a window close. She ran to the window and looked out. A biker was fleeing. Steffie glanced at the face of the clerk retreating behind a column as she scurried past the reception area and departed the motel.

She reached her car, opened the door, and sat down, her hand in her jacket. As she closed the door, an officer appeared by the door, pointing a gun at her. She angled her head and looked at him, her hand on the gun. She had made yet another mistake by not checking for signs of more officers before stepping out. She could have been killed easily by anybody after her if the intent was to kill.

"You're not getting away. Step out of the car now, or I'll shoot you! Now!"

Feigning fear, she opened the door slowly as the officer stepped back, still pointing his gun at her. At the same time, she fired two quick shots into the arm that held the gun while still sitting. He danced and twisted, dropped his weapon, and leaned on the door, his wounded arm flailing in the car. She started the engine, backed up, turned, and moved on, dragging the officer along. He wasn't dead. She drove close to a trash container which caught the hanging officer and knocked him off to the pavement. She looked back to see if any other person was following her, wondering if the men were actually police officers or sent by the people after the envelope.

Moments after Steffie had left, Olga drove in a cab to the motel entrance. She got out immediately and went to the desk from where she had received a call that Steffie was there. She discovered to her shock from the clerk that Steffie was gone. She also saw the wounded officers still reeling and waiting for an ambulance. The clerk told her how good Steffie was with guns. Angered by the scene and comments, Olga returned to her cab and departed. She didn't have anything to lose now. She needed the envelope and would do anything to get it. If it meant killing Steffie herself, she would do it. She would handle matters by herself from now on. She couldn't trust anybody with this mission that was quickly getting out of control and becoming a nightmare.

CHAPTER TEN

"The last time we spoke, you said there was a little problem. Update me," the caller said.

"Yes, I did. We have still not been able to arrest her, but I assure you she won't get far," Martina replied.

"I suppose you know the implication of having her running around the streets of Germany with what she has? I mean, assuming she has it in the first place? You have to be on top of your game. We can't allow her to freely move about like she is doing now. I get the impression you are not doing something right."

"Give me time, and I will fix it. Even hardened criminals have been nabbed by my men and me. This shouldn't be a problem at all. Please don't panic. Everything is under control. There is absolutely no way out of the country for her. I assure you."

"Do you promise?"

"You have my word."

The call ended, leaving her thinking. She had posted men across the country based on information received from his informants, but none had led to the arrest of Steffie. That irritated her and made her look incompetent in the sight of the caller. She had handled top-notch criminals in the country, which had propelled her to her current position. She didn't understand why a mere cadet on the run couldn't be handled with all the networks and state machinery at her disposal. She thought of going after her to protect her image from her employer, who paid her handsomely. She had to keep her job and continue enjoying all the benefits that went with the job she did for him, but any attempt she made to handle the mission herself could put her reputation on the line. The German authorities she worked for didn't know the caller, and she preferred to keep it that way. She also knew the threat posed by her men, who could easily get greedy and desire the parcel for themselves and tell her nice stories. They could strike a deal with Steffie, for instance, for the right price. She grabbed her phone and made another call.

The Operations Room at the station was jammed with officers. A couple of TV screens were stashed in the wall. These monitors recorded activities within the city of Munich. Expert technicians manned a huge console. The police Chief and two officers looked on as an analyst watched a scene and scanned a tape. A map of Munich appeared on the screen in front of him.

"What do we have now?" the Chief asked as he wiped the sweat off his face.

"I can't tell where she is now. She's constantly on the move. It appears she has located the tracking device we placed under her car," replied the analyst.

"That means she has removed it…" an officer looked at the Chief, "… we are dealing with a professional. She wasn't just a cadet. She is more than that."

"Beats me how the military couldn't detect they had a deadly virus in their academy," the other officer said.

"She can't get far. It is just not possible for her to do that."

"She can't get out of the country. It's only a matter of time. I will resign and work as a pimp in the Bronx if she gets out of the country alive."

The officers laughed as a female officer walked in and pointed politely at the Chief.

"She just used the credit at a gas station. Area B," she informed.

The men shared a look as the Chief waved a hand.

"Go! Go! I want her face right before me in this office before I parade her before the media. Go!"

The two officers departed immediately.

"Thanks, Gemma," acknowledged the Chief.

The female officer nodded and walked out.

Four officers joined the two in a squad truck and zoomed out of sight, three police cars following.

The Chief lit a cigarette and took a pull, staring at an analyst struggling to fit his plump body into a chair. They both looked surprised at the news about Steffie.

"Do we stand a chance of arresting her?" The Chief asked.

"We do, but I admit she has far outsmarted us. I didn't give her a dog's chance. I thought of her as a cadet and not the smart assassin she has turned out to be. She seems to be one step ahead of us all the time, and that is where my worry is. We shouldn't lose sight of the fact that she has downed a couple of officers. The impression I get so far is that she doesn't want to kill people. Since our men are under the instruction to kill her, she is sometimes forced to shoot back to defend herself, and that is where I presume some of our men may have lost their lives."

"I agree with you. I will lose my job if she gets out of this country alive with whatever she is carrying. I want you to tell me how to prevent her from leaving the country."

The analyst stared his boss in the face for a while, knowing he had to come up with fast and workable answers.

"I will figure out a way, Chief. As soon as I do, I will let you know."

"I like that, but make sure that happens in the next two hours. Keep working, lads, and keep me posted on any new developments."

The Chief walked out.

The sports car raced to the car park of an apartment block. Steffie had met her cousin following an arranged meeting. She had done well and now believed Steffie was innocent. She had brought a cell phone for Steffie to use. Steffie had had a peaceful trip since leaving the motel, but she also knew she had to get rid of the black car. Whoever called the police from the motel must have seen it, and the pursuers would now be looking for it instead of the white van. If the girls were found driving the van and confronted, they would say they traded their car for it plus money. She studied the apartment briefly and the parking lot, paying attention to a particular window. The place was quiet.

Steffie took out the map and studied a road. She knew that roadblocks were on it but couldn't tell how many there were. So she marked another route, a detour from the road through the woods and farms that could also take her to her destination. She grabbed the phone her cousin had brought for her and dialed a number. Moments later, a young man emerged from the front door to the apartment and headed for the car park. Steffie saw him and smiled, waving a hand that caught his attention instantly. He trotted to the passenger door of her car, hunched over the window, and looked at her face. He was surprised.

"Am I dreaming or seeing clearer? You're a fucking phantom! You know that? I don't remember the last time I saw you, girl. I think I was still breastfeeding."

They laughed.

"Get in and stop joking. I don't have time to spare."

As he held the handle to open, he dropped a key, making sure it clanked so she could hear.

"Oops!"

"Please hurry up."

As he stooped to pick it up, he stuck a tracking device underneath the car, picked up the key, opened the door, and sat by her. The two stared at each other, not knowing what to say to each other. They hugged and kissed, staring into each other's eyes. He moved his hands along her smooth arms as their chests touched.

"What the hell is going on? You are everywhere. TV, newspapers, institutions, and what have you. I mean, your photos are everywhere."

"I'll fill you in at the appropriate time. Now is not the time to talk about it."

"Look at you. You look even more beautiful in a mess. Come here!"

She burst into laughter. He held her face and kissed her again, studying her face. He wished he could spend the rest of the day just holding and kissing her beautiful lips. Steffie had been his one and only girlfriend until she left for military training. She had promised him they would marry after her training. They chatted on the phone once in a while. He was so excited about it he told all his friends of the upcoming graduation ceremony. Then the unexpected happened, and now the graduation was off. Nonetheless, they were excited to see each other. Steffie had come to say goodbye even though she hadn't said it yet. It would be the last time they saw each other.

While they held on to each other, she saw a man in an SUV aiming a weapon at her. She wrenched from her man instantly, baffling him, and shifted into gear. She started the car. At the same time, the man in the SUV fired a shot. She backed up the car, the bullet hitting her man in the ear. He slumped forward as she swerved the car past a parked Porsche, over the curb onto the lawn that bordered the parking lot. The shooter was still firing as the car got away. The shooter started the SUV while he consulted a receiver in his hand. A moving dot indicated Steffie's location. He smiled to himself as he stabbed at the accelerator, jerking the vehicle forward. He didn't have to rush after Steffie since he knew where to find her.

"You're toast. Wherever you go, I will get you, bitch. The people who came after you didn't know what they were doing, and that's why you outsmarted them. You won, but I am no fool. I will get you. I will pursue you to the depths of hell if I have to," he boasted, beating his chest.

The SUV veered over the curb, plunged down the sloping lawn, and took after the sports car.

Steffie looked back as she drove down the bumpy slope towards a patch of grassland, hoping the shooter didn't have another team waiting for her somewhere ahead. The SUV still hadn't shown behind her. Either the shooter would use another route to get her or knew where she was headed and would lay an ambush for her. While she drove, the rear door windows shattered. She didn't stop but looked behind. Traffic was normal, with no sign of a gunman or the SUV. People minded their business. As the car jerked forward towards the junction, a shot missed her and hit the gas tank of a bus, causing spillage onto the pavement. She knew she was the target. The car slowed to a stop at the junction, awaiting the green light. She slipped out of the car and took cover behind a tire. As she lay on the pavement and looked out, four booted feet approached in unison. She raised her head slightly and saw them. They carried rifles and were bearing down on her car. She aimed at the legs and fired, catching one who began to limp. As his colleague readied to fire, a shot hit his hand, forcing him to switch the weapon to the other hand. She rose behind the car with her gun pointing to the man, shaking her head. The men understood her message and backed off onto a tiny path between stores, and disappeared. She got back into the car and moved on.

Traffic was heavy in the business district. Motorists avoided it and used a small bridge over a river. Steffie raced her car to a junction and stopped, trying to figure out the route that gave her a quicker way out of town. So far, the SUV hadn't shown up. She knew she was being followed, though. The car took a left turn and rocketed to the next junction, turning onto a major street that initially moved with traffic. A couple of yards from the junction, traffic suddenly slowed with many cars behind her. She didn't know why the situation that was promising only moments ago had changed all of a sudden. She looked ahead and then behind her but couldn't find a reason for it. The driver in the car in front of her asked another driver who was going in the opposite direction, and Steffie heard him tell the driver that there was heavy police and military presence with road blocks at both ends of the street. The man said the situation was even worse on the highway to which they were headed. Steffie looked in the rearview mirror. With road blocks at both sides, she couldn't use the street. She swerved out of her lane, detoured into an alley, raced at top speed to its end, crossed a street without paying attention to motorists, and continued into another alley. The SUV barreled past the junction of the alley and halted. It backed up to the junction and stopped.

Steffie's car was headed for the other exit. The shooter smiled as he watched the car, waiting to see what would happen. He took a rifle to which was fitted a silencer and telescope. He aimed at it and fired a shot that missed the car but hit the tire of a dumpster that passed across the alley. Although she didn't see the weapon, Steffie saw the SUV and the shooter in its window. She knew, however, she was the reason it was there and stepped on the accelerator towards the exit.

Suddenly, another SUV bounded out of the alley's exit, forcing her to slow down and eventually stop.

Both vehicles turned into the alley and halted, sandwiching the sports car. They had her, and she knew it. She didn't expect to be caught in a tight place like this alley. She grabbed her backpack, making sure all her valuables were intact. The vehicles started towards her, shots ringing out. She opened her door and ducked as the windows and windshield shattered. She lifted up her head and glanced at the walls on both sides. A barrage of shots riddled the open door, and then the shooting ceased. They knew she couldn't escape. Suddenly, she opened the passenger door and ran out with frightening speed towards the wall. The shooting began again, bullets just missing her legs. The vehicles closed in on her. She hurled the backpack over the wall and lunged for the top with both hands. She gripped it and, with incredible rapidity and strength, hauled herself over it into the property, bullets pitting the wall and spattering fragments of brick and mortar. The vehicles stopped by the car, and the men got out. One shooter stepped out of his SUV. It was the black-suited man from the police station. He stood on the car and looked into the property. He couldn't see Steffie but could see the other side of it. A street lay in front of it.

"The two of you go after her while they meet her on the other side," he pointed.

Two men neared the wall and leaped over while the rest got back in the vehicles and took off. Without a car, Steffie was limited in how far she could go. The suited man was sure of victory. He had combed everywhere for her, and finally, his efforts had paid off. Martina would be elated to hear that the target was cornered. He had been promised a hefty reward if he was able to get Steffie. And that feat was within reach now, but he wouldn't call Martina until he had total victory. He hoped his men on foot would do a good job and alert him where Steffie was.

The property was quiet, with a car parked out front in the driveway. Steffie hid behind it, still panting heavily. She had seen the two men come down the wall. On both sides of the house were wooden fences. She flung herself to the ground and observed as the two men advanced. One took his cell phone and dialed.

"What have you got?"

"We have checked the house and didn't find her."

"What? What the hell are you talking about? Don't give me that bullshit!"

"She must be somewhere on the property. We are still searching."

"Get her! Find her! Kill her! Don't let her get away; otherwise, you are both toast! You hear me? I said, get her before I get there!"

"Yes, sir!"

Steffie heard everything. They were to shoot and kill. She was the target, but she told herself she wouldn't make it easy for them. She smiled as the men approached the car, aiming her gun at their legs. She fired a shot and caught an ankle, sending the man down to the ground.

"Shit! I'm hit! She got me!" the man yelled.

While his colleague searched for Steffie, the man on the ground looked beneath the car and saw her, the gun pointing at his face. As he attempted to alert his colleague that the target was under the car, a bullet caught his arm. He dropped his gun and became silent. The other man spun around immediately, fear radiating from his every movement. His hand shook as he kept looking around him. It suddenly dawned on him to duck and look underneath the car. As soon as he did, his chest took a shot. He fell and released his gun. She looked at the wall from where they had come. It was quiet. Steffie rose, a barrage of bullets hit the car, riddling the doors and flattening two tires. The shots came from behind her. She looked back and saw the suited man with an automatic. The SUV was some distance behind him.

There were footsteps in the direction of the wall. She turned around again and spotted a man whom she had shot earlier. She ducked at the same time as shots from the automatic rang out. They missed her, but the man behind her fell to the ground. Meanwhile, Steffie had crawled under the car. It was the only hiding place available. She couldn't run into the house where some of the men could be waiting for him. She was cornered, but she wouldn't give in yet. The suited man smiled, knowing she couldn't make any more escape attempts. He reached the rear of the car.

"Helloooo? Are you there? Why are you hiding from me? I am unarmed. Come out and fight like a woman," he mocked.

As he was about to spin around the car, she hit his leg. He held his leg and staggered to the front of the car, where he thought she might want to escape from, but she was still underneath the car. He knew the danger of ducking to look under the car. With the tire providing cover for him, he lowered his gun and fired a barrage that he thought would definitely kill her. When he lifted his eyes, she was pointing her gun at him. She fired a shot into the shoulder that held the automatic, forcing him to drop it. As he struggled to come to terms with how she was able to escape his assault, another shot caught his other leg. Groaning and rolling on the ground, he looked under the car and saw her on the ground, pointing the gun at his face. This time she was closer. He had a second gun which his other hand reached, but it was late. His face was blown apart before he could move. She got out from under the car and walked to him. The man was gone. She dipped her hand into his suit and got a phone she knew would indicate who he might be working for or with. A quick look around her revealed the SUV was empty, but the second one wasn't there. So there were more men to expect. As she moved towards the vehicle, powerful hands suddenly grabbed her neck from behind, almost choking her. The driver of the second SUV hurled her onto the ground. She lost her gun and fell with a thud. As she tried to figure out who was attacking her, a powerful kick caught her ribs. She rolled a couple of times to the car tire and looked up. The man smiled down at her as she tried to rise. He kicked her again in the same area. She groaned and fell.

"Want to play tough? Get up and let's see how good you are," he said, looking in her face.

He punched her face as she held the tire and attempted to rise. She sat heavily on the ground. Another man emerged from the front of the car.

"Move it, cadet! Without your gun, what are you gonna do, huh?"

She had to do something to save herself from them. They broke into laughter as she struggled to steady herself. Finally, she rolled over and prostrated as if in severe pain, her hand in her anorak. One man admired her legs and nudged his friend, who whistled.

"Let's have fun with her. Surely the road has come to an end for her," one suggested.

"Good idea. What is the point in handing her over when we could have fun and still do our job? Let's do this."

One moved towards her, licking his lips while the other began to unzip his trousers. As they neared her, she rolled over suddenly and fired into the chest of the first man. The second man went for his gun, but a bullet caught his hand, and another hit his neck in quick succession. The first man took another to his cheek. Both danced, twisted, and crashed to the ground, their legs kicking in spasms. She rose quickly, still feeling the pain in her face and ribs. She searched their pockets, but neither had a phone or any document. She checked the house and found it empty, but there was a septic tank behind it. She dragged all the bodies into the tank and ran back to the car. Scooping up their guns, she ran to the SUV and searched it. It was empty. She looked underneath it. It didn't have a tracking device attached to it. She sat in and checked the glove compartment. She found nothing of importance. She started the vehicle, hoping men in the second SUV didn't come after her.

Moments later, the SUV was speeding along a cart track.

CHAPTER ELEVEN

Twenty minutes later, a stocky man holding a cell phone hurried to Martina in the lounge of her home. She was absorbed in a program on the TV and seemed oblivious to his presence. Finally, he coughed and got her attention.

"I have been calling for the past few minutes, but nobody is answering," the man said.

"Give it to me."

She took the phone from him and dialed. There was no response. She waved a hand; the man bowed and scurried out of sight. The driver of the second SUV had given her the impression that Steffie was cornered, and there was absolutely no way of her escaping. It was news that got her almost calling California to inform her employer. A second thought had restrained her. She didn't like the message received from her valet. She dialed another number but got no response. She rose and walked to the desk where another phone lay. She used it to dial a third number and got a response.

"Where the hell are they?" she asked angrily.

"They are all gone."

"What do you mean they are all gone?"

"I mean, they are all dead."

"What? What happened?"

"I don't know. I was tasked to remain in the second vehicle and communicate with you. When they failed to return in time, I drove to the place and found no bodies, but there was blood everywhere."

"How can you then conclude they are dead if you didn't find their bodies?"

"Where else could they be? They are not responding to my calls."

"Come now."

She ended the call and sat on the couch by the desk, wondering if the man had told her the truth. He could have killed them and fabricated a story. If they had the target, they could have gotten greedy and fought one another for the parcel. He could have killed them after they acquired the parcel, assuming they got the target. Anything was possible in a situation like this. She looked out of the window as if searching for something which didn't exist. A stroll to the balcony didn't help matters. She was restless, knowing a call would come in at any moment, and she must have something to tell her employer. She had given him her word and the impression that everything was under control. Now the situation seemed far from over. She didn't know where her men were and whether they were alive. People were missing; there was blood all over the place, and bodies couldn't be found. There was no sign of the target either. She had to come up with fast answers when the call came in. She could refuse to take the call and lie about her whereabouts while she got answers for him, but that could put her life in danger. The caller could hire assassins against her if he had cause to believe she was pulling a fast one on him or he was being shafted. She admitted Steffie was good if her men were indeed dead, and she was the one who killed them. The valet walked in again with another phone. This time she refused to take the call but asked who the caller was or what the message was. She learned that one of the SUVs had been spotted in the cart tracks of the Munich countryside. She rose and went out of the house to the front. The SUV was definitely running away from Munich or her. She had to find out who was driving that vehicle and where the person was headed. The parcel might be on that vehicle, or the driver might have answers.

San Diego

The old bearded man with grey hair sat in a wheelchair, smoking a pipe. He had had sleepless nights in the past three days. Usually, people in their seventies slept a lot and ate well. They played with their grandchildren and told them stories even if those stories weren't true. The kids liked to hear them, but it wasn't so with this old man. He had been expecting good news from Munich, but that hadn't come through, and that worried him. Business was good, and the US economy boomed. Housing developers were upbeat about the demand for housing across the country. There was general expansion in infrastructure development, which made him a very happy businessman. However, the thought of Steffie running around in Germany like a free electron bugged him. The man who had assaulted him at the golf course had said he knew him. All his efforts to get him had proved futile. Martina hadn't done a good job for him, and that irritated him when he considered the amount of money he had wired into her offshore account. He was a troubled man, having tried all the tricks he had deployed to perfection in the past and failed this time. There must surely be something he could do to contain the situation. He exhaled the smoke while he studied the lawn as if it contained the answers he desperately sought. The two suited men in front of him had been standing there for the past three minutes without him knowing. He took another long drag on the pipe, holding his chest and giving out dry coughs. He exhaled again and placed the pipe on the small table by him.

"Are you okay, sir?" One of the men asked, drawing his attention.

They knew he had issues. What specifically was the problem, they didn't know. He had summoned them for a reason. They had been with him for a while, and he didn't seem to notice. They understood him, considering his age and frailness. He stared at the faces before him and gave a smile that was largely enigmatic.

"I believe we know each other," he said in a croaky voice

"We do," replied one of the men.

"Good. It's a simple operation that requires a little tact and finesse."

"We are at your service. We are always glad to be of service to people."

The old man looked back at his house and continued talking.

"I run companies ranging from electronics, arms to pharmaceuticals. I'm in real estate too."

He scratched his head and focused on two puppies playing on the lawn. He wasn't sure whether what he was about to say was right. It was information he had held on to for decades. It had been his secret for years. Developments in the last few days had forced him to come out and say it. He wasn't even sure if the men before him were the right ones to hear it. He wished he could handle the mission himself. As he stared them in the face, the puppies ran to play around his feet, one licking them. He allowed himself a thin smile. The men focused on his face expectantly.

"I keep my important documents in Europe. I mean in Germany and England, to be specific. Please don't ask why I do that when I could keep them here because though I do have the answer, I'm not in the right frame of mind to tell you. You will know when you come back. I believe I will be fine then to tell you."

He retrieved a portrait of Steffie from the side of his wheelchair and passed it on to his colleagues. He studied it briefly and passed it on to his colleagues.

"We are listening, Sir."

"She stole my documents from a storage facility in Germany. A black envelope marked 'COMB ASS' is missing from my safe."

He lifted the pipe, took a drag, and exhaled. The men noticed his shaky hand, which almost dropped the pipe but for the intervention of the man near him. He steadied him in the wheelchair.

"I want it back. You won't have to kill her except in self-defense. I don't feel comfortable with blood and taking people's lives, but if you find that your lives could be in danger, then use your discretion."

The men looked at each other.

"Where specifically can we find her? I mean, in which city?"

"Munich. If she's moved elsewhere, I can't help you with that. However, I believe that with her photo, you can track her."

"That is right, but may I ask what's in the envelope? In case we find the envelope and the contents are gone, we should be able to track the contents. I don't see why we should travel all the way to Germany, get the target, and fail to get the parcel."

"You don't have to know that. Money is not an object. My checkbook is on the terrace. Get it for me."

"Sure."

As soon as the man left to get the checkbook, the old man glanced at his friend.

"Can I trust you with this op?" he asked.

"Yes, Conan," replied the man.

"Kill him when he gets it."

"Conan, Sir. Consider it done."

The man returned without the checkbook.

"I couldn't find it, sir. It wasn't there. You may have placed it somewhere and forgotten."

The old man groped the inner pockets of his jacket and pretentiously, remembered.

"Oh, dear! I had it in my pocket all along and didn't know. Age has a way of eroding one's memory."

"I understand, Sir."

He took it out and gave a short smile at the men.

"Old age, gentlemen. Whenever you hit a certain age, everything changes in your life. Can I have a pen, please?"

The other man handed him one, and he wrote them a check.

"This should do. Send me word when it's done. Avoid the German authorities. It will only complicate matters. Don't believe anybody who says I sent him. You are the only ones I'm sending."

"I did a gig there once. I'll check on my snitch if he is still alive. He may be able to get me something."

The old man nodded him a thank you. The men departed in a red sedan. The old man's wife, Angela, much younger than him, emerged from a room at the side of the elegant house and walked briskly to him. She kissed him and pushed the wheelchair up a ramp to the terrace.

"Can I have my pipe, please?" he asked.

"Sure," she replied.

She stowed him by the wall near the front door and hurried back to get his pipe from the table.

He reached for a small plastic container in his jacket, uncapped it, filled the pipe bowl with tobacco, and then lit it. She took the lighter and container of tobacco from him. She had been complaining about his smoking habits for years, but the stubborn old man had been adamant and refused to give up the habit.

"So, how did it go with them?"

"It went well. Very well, I must add."

"What are they supposed to do exactly?"

"Deliver a message."

"Don't insult my intelligence! Who do you think you are talking to? What's the point in hiding stuff from me? I have been with you for years. Do you think I'm naïve?"

He wheeled around and looked at her, surprised. She held his gaze in a show of defiance and boldness.

"I monitor all your calls to Germany. What are you running away from? Speak, or I'll go to the police! You think I don't see fear and worry in you anytime you call or hear from Germany? I know there is a problem somewhere, though I can't tell what it is exactly. There is something there that you are trying to protect or acquire, and until you get it, your worry will not cease."

"What the hell are you talking about?"

"I mean every word I say. You wouldn't send two men skilled in weaponry to deliver a message in Germany. If it was just a message, why didn't you send a letter or make a call? Or send an email? Does it make sense to you that a message is delivered by two men? I can't be married to a man full of secrets. You don't tell me anything. If something goes wrong, I wouldn't know what to say or do to defend myself. I virtually don't know anything about you. When I became suspicious of you and your activities, I began to monitor your calls. You are going to tell me, or I will have you arrested. Now!"

He looked around them. It was quiet. He wheeled into the lounge, Angela following. She repeated the call as she snatched the handset of a phone off the wall. She was about to make a call. He yanked a gun from underneath his seat and fired a muffled shot into her head. She dropped the handset and collapsed on him. Dead. He shoved her off him and hit the wall with the butt of the gun. Two men in white apparel came out from another side room and bowed before him.

"Get rid of her. I don't want any traces."

The men nodded and dragged her into a room and shut the door. One moved the body into an incinerator and began to cremate it. The old man wiped the blood stains from his hands and resumed smoking. One of the men came to mop the floor, applied antiseptic, bowed to him, and disappeared.

"Bitch," the old man said as he pulled on his pipe.

He had met her ten years ago at a party through a business partner who had known her since they were friends in high school. She was a saleswoman for a supermarket chain. Her beauty was so charming he had decided to marry her the following week, to the surprise of all his colleagues. Many had objected to the idea, but he ignored their comments and reservations and went ahead with the wedding, which some didn't attend. They had had a very good marriage, contrary to the expectation of the detractors. He had given her the world, and what did he ask in return? Loyalty and support. Instead, she had bugged his phone and monitored his conversation with a view to blackmailing him. He couldn't allow that to happen. She was a threat to his business and empire. He didn't entertain disloyalty and dissent. He thought of the two men he had sent, hoping they would succeed. He had to get in touch with Martina for an update. She might have something interesting for him. She might have something to cheer him up.

Munich

Martina fumed as she looked at the clock on the wall. She had driven to the last place the SUV was spotted but found no trace of it. As she refueled at a gas station, her vehicle had developed flat tires in the rear. While a valet fixed them, the engine began to smoke. She knew then that somebody was behind it. Amazingly, no one had seen anybody around her vehicle. Frustrated, she had had to abandon her mission and return home in a cab. She looked out from her balcony. The stocky man approached with a phone; she waved for him not to come near her. The man retreated and backed off. She could hear the phone ringing as she figured out what her next move would be. She reached for the gun in her jacket. Men could be sent after her anytime, and she had to be alert. The man appeared again, holding the phone. She glanced at him quizzically. The man pointed his hand to the phone, which was still ringing. She nodded as he moved closer and handed the device to her. She pressed the correct key on the phone and placed it to her hear

"I see you still haven't been able to contain the situation. You have also refused to talk to your employer. Talk to me," the voice said

"She can't get far. She is a wanted person now. It's a matter of when. I have every exit point covered. If she tries to escape the country, she will be nabbed. There is absolutely no way she can escape. As a matter of fact, I nearly had her cornered, but the police stepped in with a heavy presence, and I had to withdraw my men to avoid confusion and suspicion."

"If she slips through your fingers, my business is gone. I'll have to face the result. That, undoubtedly, affects you too. I don't think we both like the consequences."

"I understand, but patience is a virtue. I have given you my word and will not fail you. My men are right on her heels. She has had to change her looks a couple of times, and she is fast running out of options. I have kidnapped her only relative, and that I believe would force her to hand the parcel over to us."

"I suggest you stop preaching and move your ass!"

The caller's last words were harsh and jolting. Angered, she ended the call immediately and hurled the phone at the man, who caught it and scurried out of the room. Martina rose and walked to her cellar, which was tucked in the corner, reaching for bottles of vodka and vermouth. She took a glance and poured herself a martini which she sipped as she admired her cellar. She moved back to her seat and checked a cell phone on the table by it for missed calls. She had paid men to report to her the moment the SUV was sighted so she would go after it. The caller hadn't shown her respect, and that infuriated her. She had worked for him for years even though she hadn't met him in person before. As strange as that might sound to the level-headed, she had done him a lot of good. She smiled to herself as she sipped her martini.

"I'm going to get whoever has the parcel and keep it to myself. I will have him pay heavily for it. That will hopefully teach him a few lessons about manners," she said.

CHAPTER TWELVE

Steffie slowed down the vehicle until she found a safe place to stop. She had branched off the main roads and cart tracks to avoid the police and hold off the charge of interested parties. It explained why the SUV was spotted but later disappeared. A team assembled by Olga to get her had reported back to her that the vehicle had vanished from their radar. Steffie surveyed the area carefully and thoroughly, and then she got down and peed by the door. She was out of food but had a little water left in the plastic bottle by the gearshift. As she was about to sit in the vehicle, she heard voices coming towards her. She held her gun and took cover behind a tree. Two men she suspected might be farmers trudged past while they discussed the cost of living in the country, one suggesting he had shipped his family over the border to Poland, where the cost was lower. As they headed towards a shed she hadn't seen before parking, one looked back and saw the SUV. He nudged his colleague, who suggested they went to take a look at it. One took out a phone as they began towards the vehicle. Steffie knew he was calling to alert somebody. She fired a shot close to them. It did the trick. They turned and took off wildly past the shed where they were initially headed and faded away. She hurried into the vehicle and took off. The SUV sliced through coppices, passing a couple of tractors and farm trucks. Her hair was shaven bald now. She avoided drivers who waved or honked. The name 'Pitmann Farms' was on both sides of the vehicle.

Many wondered where the farm was. They hadn't heard of the name before. In that closely-knit farming area, every farmer knew their fellow farmers. Away from the barns and sheds, the vehicle crossed a cart track, according to the map on her lap, and plunged into another section, tires running over small boulders and stumps. It narrowly avoided a pond, throwing up huge splashes.

After driving for thirty minutes and avoiding herds of sheep she didn't expect to see, the vehicle suddenly descended into a clayey depression and almost got stuck in it if she hadn't employed skills she had picked up in military school. Out of the depression, she turned right onto a dirt track and drove for a short distance past a man riding a bicycle. The man waved, but she ignored him. Then, in the rearview mirror, she noticed the man had his phone out of his pocket. She wheeled the SUV around and raced to the man, who swerved the bike aside to avoid the vehicle. He held the phone in his hand and forced a smile, to which Steffie didn't respond. As he readied to speak, he noticed a gun was pointing at him.

"Give the phone to me," she said.

Shivering, the man hobbled forward and handed it to her.

"Hello? Hello? Hello?" a voice came alive on the device.

She looked at the man's face and then cut the call.

"Who were you calling?"

"Please don't kill me. I didn't even speak. Take the phone. It's yours, but don't harm me. I have a family."

"I said who were you calling?"

"I don't know their names. I received money and the phone and was told to inform them when I see you."

"Do you know me?"

The man nodded.

"Who am I?"

"You are a wanted person. You are a very dangerous person. You are a threat to national security and the whole of Europe. Somebody who must be killed at the slightest opportunity."

"Do you believe what you just said?"

"I don't know what to say, but I have seen your photos on TV and in newspapers. And I must say well done if all I have heard is true. I have seen top-notch criminals, but for a girl your age and the way you outsmart the authorities, I think you deserve applause."

"Thank you. I hope you understand one day why all these things are happening. How far is your house from here?"

"Six miles."

"Don't you have a car?"

"No. I depend on my bike. It takes me wherever I wish to go."

"I can give you a ride home if you don't mind."

"No, no, no. Thank you very much. I can manage with the bike."

"Scared?"

"Yes."

"Why?"

"You could harm my family."

"Then keep your mouth shut."

"Ok, but I have to tell you that you are surrounded in this farming area. There is no escape for you. There are many armed men posted around. It will be a miracle if you get out alive. I wish you well."

"Hmm. Like I said, if you open your mouth, your family is in trouble."

The man nodded profusely, mounted his bike, and rode away.

The SUV arrived at a farm fifteen minutes later and stopped under a tree. Steffie had come under fire from attackers shortly after she had parted with the bicycle rider. Still behind the wheel, she observed the farm for a while. The vehicle was conspicuous to anybody who would appear on the scene. She took a look at the phone she had taken from the man, it had only one number on it. She dialed it but got no response. As she tried again, the battery was low, and the call couldn't connect. The phone she had used to make calls earlier was also low on battery. She pocketed hers and dumped the man's under her seat. She heard a tractor and raised her eyes. She was right. A man sat on a tractor. Steffie started the SUV and backed it up quickly into the undergrowth, got out, and locked it. She ran her hand over her stomach to ensure the gun and envelope were in place. With her hat pulled down on her face, she kept the map in her pocket and started towards the tractor. The man on the equipment spotted her, stopped it, and dismounted to meet her. She looked to both sides of her and the farm, smiling broadly as they approached each other.

"Hello?" he said excitedly, stretching his hand.

"Hello."

"Gotze. Welcome to my farm."

"Thank you. You have a beautiful farm."

"Thank you,"

"Can I get a place to charge my cell phone?"

He glanced in the direction of the SUV and then focused on her face.

"Sure."

He took another look at the place where the vehicle was parked and then pointed to a farmhouse behind him.

"My wife's in there. Go tell her you've spoken to Gotze. She will allow you to charge your phone," he said excitedly.

She glanced past the short man at the cute farmhouse.

"Thank you."

He dipped his head gently to acknowledge while he scrutinized her face beneath the hat. Steffie departed in haste without looking back. He watched to see if she would look back at him. Steffie knew the man had seen the SUV. If that was the case, she was in the wrong place as its location instantly informed him it wasn't meant to be seen. That meant she was hiding something. The bicycle man had told her she was surrounded. She knew she was in for a long night, a very busy night. She didn't have a reason to doubt the man's information. Gotze got back to the tractor while he kept his eyes on Steffie.

She arrived at the front of the house and knocked on the door. The farmer's wife answered the door moments later to meet her.

While they spoke, the farmer retrieved a photo of Steffie from the breast pocket of his jacket and considered it. A short smile appeared on his face.

"I may not be an expert, but even with that big hat over your face, I still think you are the woman the world is looking for," he mouthed.

He looked at the two women in front of his house and reached for his cell phone. He made a quick call to inform somebody he had the target, reminding the person to honor his side of the bargain by bringing him the money promised. He put the phone back into his pocket, started the tractor, and continued working. He whistled loudly when he saw Steffie follow his wife into the house. The visitor would be in the house long enough for his contractor to catch up with her. It would also put money into his pocket.

She scanned the simply furnished lounge as she followed the woman past a desk that smelled like it had just been made. A curved couch enclosed a center table. An old TV set faced the couch while the dining furniture was by the wide window overlooking the farm. It helped them watch the farm and see anybody who appeared on it. The electrical socket was in the wall by a book shelf that served as a library. The woman stopped by it and pointed to the socket, which had a charger connected to it. Steffie smiled, took her phone from her pocket. She didn't have a charger, and the one connected wasn't right for her phone. She reached for the other phone, which fitted perfectly with the charger. Gotze's wife was a slender woman with deep-set eyes. She was slightly taller than her husband. Steffie still clutched the second phone. The woman got the message and hurried to get another charger from a room.

"Thank you very much," Steffie said as she received it from her.

She stooped by an extension board and connected the device. The woman looked on, glad to be of service to Steffie. When she was confident the phones were charging, Steffie rose and moved to the window as if watching Gotze, but her attention was on the farm and its environs. She knew people would come after her. She knew the area and how to get out. The map in her pocket told her that. She had to move, but with the whole area surrounded by police and the men after her, she had to be careful attempting to get out of the place. She must have a comprehensive plan and possibly, a contingency plan for getting out of Europe. If she made the wrong move, she was toast. At this point, nobody was after just the envelope she carried. They were after her life as well. If she got out of the area safely but didn't have a perfect plan of escape from the country, the pursuit would continue. She watched Gotze occasionally as she glanced at the SUV. She couldn't see it but knew it was there. He must have seen it parked, but she didn't think he would think of going near it. After all, she didn't keep anything valuable in it. Gotze's wife stole a glance at her as she tidied up the couch in which she had been knitting. Steffie noticed Gotze fixing the engine of the tractor and smiled. He must be a happy farmer, she thought.

"So, how long have you been living here?" Steffie asked as she turned from the window.

"Good question. I have been here all my life."

"Do you like it here?"

"Oh, yes, I do. I like it here. It is quiet. No one disturbs us."

She gestured to Steffie to sit after clearing her stuff from the couch. The phones were charging when Steffie inspected them. The woman moved to the kitchen and returned with a glass and orange juice. She poured her a glass full.

"Oh, no. I react badly to juices," she declined.

She was hungry and badly needed the drink, but she had to be alert. The drink could be drugged since she couldn't trust anybody. Randolph was right about trust.

"What about water?"

"I will have that later. Thanks anyway."

"So, how did you find us? I ask because we are very far from the nearest farm. And you don't look like somebody from around here."

"I'm a researcher. I had to send an important message to my boss. Then, I realized my battery was down."

"Married?"

Steffie wagged her head.

"I will be very soon."

Steffie glanced at the phones again.

"You may as well make yourself comfortable because it'll take time for the phones to charge."

"No, no, no. I need just about enough energy to help me contact my boss and answer any questions she might have. I don't need them fully charged."

"I have food for you."

Steffie smiled.

"Thank you very much. You are a good and kindhearted woman. You know, very few people in the world these days care for others."

Suddenly, Steffie spotted a woman watching the farmhouse from under the coppice beyond the farm. She rose quickly and moved to the window to take a good look at the woman. She couldn't see her face, but she had enough training to spot people like those. She couldn't tell if Gotze had seen the woman but knew she was there for a purpose. Moments later, a cab stopped by the woman. She barked a word at the driver. The cab moved on towards the farmhouse. Steffie spun around instantly, hoping her presence in this peaceful house hadn't brought trouble. They were coming for her. She backed off from the window slowly, holding her stomach as if in pain. Gotze's wife noticed her and rushed to hold her.

"What is the problem? Are you pregnant?"

"No, but I have to go to the toilet now," she replied as she grabbed her backpack.

"Let me call my husband to come and help you," the woman said as she dashed to the window.

"Oh, no. I don't think that will help me. Just show me where to find the toilet. I will be fine once I manage to get certain stuff out of my stomach. I think I have had too much food and drink. Usually, when I eat certain foods, I have an upset stomach."

The woman helped Steffie to the toilet, wondering why the stranger carried her backpack. She hoped she wasn't carrying any contraband. They were a happy family and liked it that way. They didn't want any trouble in their otherwise peaceful home. Once in the toilet, Steffie shut the door and locked it.

When the woman went back to the lounge, the cab was almost at the front of the house. She smiled, knowing who had alerted the men in the cab. She knew exactly why they were there.

Meanwhile, Steffie took out her gun and checked for rounds. She had to be sure she could rely on the weapon. Satisfied, she slapped the magazine back into place. Then, with her backpack firmly on her back, she opened the window, stepped on the sill, and hauled herself out of the toilet and up onto the roof. She lay immediately on the roof, her face watching the toilet window and the rear of the house while her gun was at the ready.

Two men in the cab sprang out with their weapons. The woman stepped out of the house to meet them, said a word to them, pointed to the house, and ran towards Gotze. The two men charged the house immediately. They had Steffie cornered, one thought. While one entered through the door, the other used a window.

"To the toilet," one said.

The first man located the toilet and stood in front of it as his colleague checked the other rooms. He opened fire on the door, riddling it with a hailstorm of bullets. Satisfied that whoever was behind the door was dead, he kicked the door open but found it empty. He moved to the window, opened it, and stuck his head through it. He looked to both sides but found nobody. He smiled to himself, knowing whoever was in the toilet might have escaped through the window.

"Have you finished her?" his colleague asked

Without saying a word, he gestured to his colleague to keep quiet. The man stepped on the bowl and then onto the sill. He held onto the roof and tried to haul himself up to take a look at it. As soon as his head emerged on the roofline, Steffie pummeled his face with the butt of her gun. He lost his grip and fell on the ground, the impact alerting his colleague. At the same time, she jumped off the roof to the ground. As he tried to rise to his feet, she kicked his face and broke his nose. He fell prostrate and began to crawl to his gun. At the same time, his colleague's frame emerged through the window to see what had fallen to the ground. Steffie spotted him and gunned his chest before he could act. The man leaned out of the window, with his hand flailing, the gun dangling. The man on the ground still reeled from the kick. She punched him in the face and dazed him. The man moaned and groped around for something; Steffie didn't know what. As he held the wall of the house to rise, she found a club by a tree a few yards from her. She looked around the rear of the house and the rear windows for signs of reinforcement. The man was almost standing now but still a little dazed. Partially conscious, he remembered he had a gun and tried to locate it. Steffie whacked his head powerfully. The man groaned and fell, rolling on the ground to his weapon. She hurried to kick it away from him, squatting by him.

"Where is she?"

"Where is who?"

She stamped his head to the ground, rivulets of blood appearing on his face. The man was in pain now as he held his face and restrained her from unleashing further punishment.

"The woman! Where's she? If you don't give me what I want, I will kill you. You are not here of your own volition. Someone must have sent you."

Three yards behind her, Olga stood. He saw Olga and gave a smile that baffled Steffie. She pointed the gun at his face.

"Behind you," he pointed as he burst into laughter.

Steffie spun around immediately, and there Olga stood in front of her with her rifle pointing at Steffie. The man suddenly found his steel and sprang to his feet.

Steffie remained frozen to the ground. He got behind Steffie. It was his opportunity to exact revenge. He waited for Olga's signal while he admired her behind.

"Let me have it," Olga asked, stretching her hand.

"Have what?"

"I won't ask again. I don't have the patience for that. Give it to me! Now! I see you have a gun; if you try anything, I will not waste a moment with my weapon. You are no use to me. I don't care whether you live or die."

"How many times do I have to explain this to you and in what language? I told you before, and I am saying it again, I haven't gone for it. Everybody is hunting me like I'm some terrorist. I don't have it. If I had anything, I wouldn't be here. And why are you pursuing me all of a sudden? I thought you were on the side of the man who died in my car?"

Olga took two paces towards her.

"At this distance, I can't miss. Drop your gun!"

Steffie obeyed as Olga motioned to her man to frisk Steffie. The man smiled and inched towards his target.

"Do it fast!"

As he started frisking Steffie from behind, she grabbed the man's arm with frightening speed and strength and flipped him over her shoulder onto the ground. The man rose immediately to show his employer he was equally up to the challenge, though he felt sharp pains in his back. Olga moved to shoot, but her man was in her way. At the same time, Steffie scooped up her gun, moved behind him, and vised her arm around his neck, her gun sticking into his spine. The man lifted both hands in a gesture of surrender.

"Drop your weapon, or he dies!" Steffie ordered.

"Who cares if he dies? I want the envelope now!"

Steffie smiled.

"You see, she used you. What you risked your life for hasn't been worth the effort after all. You should have been shagging bimbos in the brothel. She doesn't care if you live or die. All she thinks about is her life, future, and a parcel I don't even have."

The man was disappointed to hear Olga speak like that. He knew he could lose his life any time, but his employer had let him down. She didn't even respect him. Steffie moved the gun with lightning speed and shot Olga's hand. She dropped the gun instantly, a wave of fear and shock covering her face. She couldn't use her left hand, which meant she had to get away from Steffie. She had to live to fight another day. She also knew that where she had found Steffie could mean only one thing. She was headed to Austria. Once she was out of Germany, it would be very difficult to get the parcel. The man suddenly elbowed Steffie in the chest and sent her staggering to the ground. He turned around instantly and reached for his gun, but Steffie still had her gun. She made no mistake, firing twice into his chest. The bewildered man held his chest in disbelief, staggered back, and dropped to his knees. Steffie rose to her feet as Olga took off, rounding the corner with incredible speed. Steffie checked to ensure the envelope was intact. She looked at the man; he was still breathing. She fired another shot into his chest and took after Olga. He pitched face down, his hand clutching his gun. He managed to lift his head but gave up moments later.

As Steffie turned the corner, Olga, who had been bracing on the wall, hit her with a rod. Steffie fell to the ground. Olga lunged at her, and the two began to struggle, Olga on top. Two quick slaps from Olga caught Steffie on the face. She, in turn, used both legs to clutch Olga's neck and hurled her to the side. Steffie groped around and located the rod. She gripped it and hit Olga's mouth as she rose to her feet. Her lips burst, blood dripping from them while she reeled back. A tooth dropped from her mouth into her hand. She couldn't believe what was happening. Steffie hit her head with the rod, sending the woman down. Blood oozed from her nostrils and the wound to her head.

Gotze and his wife watched from behind the tractor. They were far from the action but could see every detail. The man watched in awe as Steffie walked to Olga, held her head, and pummeled her face. The woman was dazed. Steffie shoved her to the ground.

"Who are you working with? I know you can talk, so speak."

"Alone. Please don't kill me. You can go in peace. You've earned your freedom. I won't bother you again. And no one will know where you are. I promise you that."

Steffie scoffed at Olga's words. She took her gun and fired a shot into her head. Olga fell to her side, her eyes wide open in shock. She moved on into the house. Moments later, she came out, took Olga's rifle, and walked towards the tractor. The couple saw her and shared a worried look.

"We have done foolishly. We didn't think they would seek her life. Now she knows one of us might have informed the killers," Gotze lamented.

"We were given the impression she was a wanted person. We didn't know some people wanted her dead. Apologize to her when she arrives. She may show mercy to us," the wife advised.

The shivering Gotzes hid behind the tractor. Steffie aimed the rifle at the gas tank of the cab and fired until it caught fire and exploded. Over to her left, she spotted a sedan parked under the coppice. Olga's car, she thought. She did the same to it and moved on. The couple looked on and shared another look. Steffie spotted the Gotzes, who were holding each other's hands, the wife shivering violently. She waved them to rise and move. Hesitantly, they obliged, hobbling past her, both looking back at her. They feared she would shoot them from behind. She looked around the tractor and at the trees.

There was no one in sight. The SUV was in place, though she couldn't tell if everything was intact. She marched the couple into the house, surveying all sides for uninvited visitors. She took another look at the rear and sides of the house and then walked into the lounge. The couple sat on the couch, hand in hand, their eyes darting in her direction as she moved. Steffie's rifle pointed at them, a situation that made them uneasy. They were so scared they couldn't say a word. They hoped for the best, that she wouldn't kill them. It was late evening, and the room was getting dark. The couple held on firmly to each other as Steffi pulled a chair and sat across from them, the gun almost touching Gotze's forehead. She could see their lips vibrating.

"One of you made a phone call. Who did?"

The couple looked at each other and then at Steffie, wondering if they should answer the question.

"You should know my capabilities by now. Speak and live."

Gotze looked at his wife, pinching her to speak. The woman shook her head slightly and nudged Gotze to speak, reminding him in an undertone that he was the man. He pursed his lips, not sure what would happen if he came clean. Steffie repeated the question with growing anger.

"I did," admitted Gotze.

"Who did you call?"

"I don't know her name."

"Give me your phone."

Steffie dashed back to look out the window and then rejoined the couple. He removed the phone from his pocket and slid it across the short distance on the floor to her. Steffie picked it up and checked the dialed numbers. She instantly shot him an angry look.

"You just made another call. It was moments ago. You told another person where to find me? After this team failed, you called another team? I see you want me dead at all cost."

Steffie cocked the rifle and neared him. He nodded apologetically.

"What did you tell them?"

"That the woman and men are down. I said you killed them. That you are a pro."

"Are more men coming? How many are coming?"

"I don't know. They said you're a terrorist out here to bomb Germany and establish a cell to radicalize the youth against Europe. As a patriotic citizen, when you hear stories like that, you want that person arrested before damage is caused. I may not have behaved wisely, but I did what I did for Germany."

Steffie lowered the rifle, rose, and walked to the socket. She removed her phones and tucked them in the pockets of her shorts. She returned to her seat, holding the gaze of the couple.

"Relax. You did what you had to do. I don't blame you," Steffie said.

The couple was relieved. They knew now their lives were not in danger. At least not from Steffie, though if a shootout broke out, the story might be different.

"I think you should leave now if you're innocent."

"They'll come after you. These people don't give up."

Steffie looked at him and allowed herself a smile. The couple smiled too. She knew Gotze hadn't told her the entire truth. He knew how many were coming. Money had changed hands or been promised. Steffie yanked out a small flashlight and switched it on. Then she inspected a key and exited the house, wondering if her coming to the Gotze's farm had been helpful. If she had continued, she might have made it to the border with Austria. She might not have made it, given the people surrounding her or waiting for her to show up. As she made it to the vehicle, she hoped the couple wouldn't call another person and give away her position. She needed to get away from danger alive. The map had helped, but in the dark, she didn't know what awaited her. A quick glance around her told her it was safe to continue. There was no indication of a car or armed men following her.

She reached the SUV, opened the door, and sat down. She shifted the gear to neutral and got out. Then she pushed the SUV slowly from under the tree across the short width of the farm until it reached the coppice opposite her. Completely out of sight, she was ready to move on. Suddenly, she saw a flash and ducked to the ground, raising her head slowly to take a look at what it was. Now she could see more than one flash. There were many men headed to the house. She rose gradually and counted six men, their flashes crisscrossing the ground. They moved fast. Steffie had to protect the Gotzes. Her presence had drawn the men to the farm, and it would be in her interest to defend them. She rushed back to the house, grateful the lights were not on.

The men were now in a row formation. They were police officers. One was communicating on a walkie-talkie.

"Lion to Cub."

"Go ahead."

"Send reinforcements."

"How many more do you require?"

"I need air power."

"A chopper is almost there. Out."

The communication ended.

The house was still dark. Steffie had located the couple after hitting her leg against the chair she had sat on. Thankfully, it hadn't fallen to the floor, the impact of which could have given their position away. The couple had been so scared they hadn't moved since she left them. Her return worried them. They hoped she had returned in peace and not due to a change of mind. Gotze gave a muffled cough. His wife nudged him to behave himself.

"Are you alive?" Steffie consulted in a low tone.

"Yes," Gotze replied.

"Do you have a hiding place? I mean a place where no one will see or find you."

"Yes."

"Good. Go. Men ordered to shoot to kill are here."

The couple rose from the couch and padded away quickly. Steffie heard rapid footsteps, opening and shutting of a hatch. She dashed to the window and peeked out. The men were almost there, four in front and two behind. They were heavily armed. While she thought of how to handle them, suddenly, a man hurled tear gas into the room. Steffie took off towards the toilet. A flare was thrown into the room through a window, almost instantly providing illumination. They saw her fleeing towards the rear of the house.

"There! Don't let her get away!" a police officer barked as he pointed to the fleeing figure.

Four officers immediately opened fire on her. She crouched and lunged at the toilet door. Another fusillade of bullets filled the house, blowing out windows and chewing up everything in the room. Two officers got into the room through the window while two others rounded to the rear of the house. One stood behind the toilet window while the other monitored the roof. Both had their torches on. Steffie saw them. She crawled to the edge of the roof and dropped towards the man who was focused on the roof. She crashed onto him, sending him to the ground. At the same time, she fired a shot at the man watching the toilet window before he could react to the impact. The man lost his flashlight and gun and collapsed to the ground. She heard a groan behind her and spun around. The first officer was trying to rise. She kicked his face and followed up with another to his groin. The officer fell again, holding his groin and groaning. She dashed to the window and braced against the wall by it, tucking her gun in her shorts. An officer's face appeared in the window. In a sudden move, she grabbed his head and hauled him through the window, his head smashing in the ground. He lost his gun. While he tried to come to terms with what had hit him, the sound of a chopper dominated the air. She looked above her but couldn't find the chopper. A barrage was fired at her, taking her by surprise. She lunged to the ground and turned the corner, taking cover behind a tree. She knew it had come from the chopper. She reached for her gun and looked out, the tree branches hampering her vision. Moments later, the chopper shot into frame, its light sweeping across the house. She wondered how the shooter in the chopper knew where to find her in the dark. Then she remembered there were six men. Only three were down. While she contemplated her next move, an officer dropped from the tree behind her and wrapped his arms around her. She was startled by the man and began to struggle with him. She stepped heavily on his foot, but the man held on to her. She moved her head forward to head-butt him, but he read her and swerved his head to the side.

"How about this, honey? I got you, didn't I? Please tell me why I should let go of my grip on you when you smell so good? You haven't taken a bath in days, but you still smell good."

She struggled to break free, but the arms holding her were powerful. She elbowed his rib and stomach, but the firm grip on her arms diminished the effect.

"I got her! I got her!" he yelled.

Steffie heard footsteps as the chopper's light found her. With the light on her, she stood very little chance of escape. An idea struck her. She reached behind for his groin and squeezed the man's balls so hard, he screamed and let go of his grip on her. She retrieved her gun and fired on the advancing men, downing two. She took off towards the woods. The SUV was parked there. If she could reach it in time, she could get away and take the danger away from the Gotzes. The chopper shone its light on her again, which enabled the two officers to give chase while they fired at her. Her burst of speed through the farm was incredible. At the same time, a burst of gunfire from the chopper exploded the sand and grass around her. She had to take care of the chopper and prevent the light from following her. The light revealed a boulder up ahead. Steffie took cover behind it, aimed her weapon, and fired at the chopper's lights as it skimmed past above her, another burst of gunfire spitting the boulder. She immediately flung herself to the ground, rose, and ran until she reached the woods. With the chopper away for a while, she thought she would be fine, but she hadn't hit the light, which was her target.

Meanwhile, the men on foot were still shooting at her, even though they couldn't see her in the dark. A shot narrowly missed her elbow, forcing her to the ground. She crawled quickly towards the SUV, noticing the chopper was coming back. It did and hovered above the woods. She looked up at it. Its maneuver suggested it suspected she was under the trees. She opened the door of the SUV and slipped into the vehicle. The engine roared to life instantly, and she gunned it out of the farm.

The headlights came on as the SUV cut through the dense and undulating terrain at top speed. The men on foot couldn't keep up. The vehicle was out of shooting range when Steffie turned headlights on. One officer promptly took out his walkie-talkie.

"Lion to Cud One! Lion to Cud One!" he called.

"Go ahead," the pilot replied.

"She's getting away in an SUV! Follow her! She is going east!"

"Copy. Wilco."

"Don't lose her! Do not lose her!"

"Copy. Out."

The chopper pursued her as the officers detoured towards their car and departed the farm.

The Gotze house was quiet now. The couple shared a look in the dark hole, breathing heavily on each other. After waiting for a while and hearing nothing, Gotze opened the hatch and listened for voices and footsteps. He heard the receding car of the officers. He held his wife and pulled up the stairs to the ground floor. He moved to the window and looked out, checking the rear of the house and the sides. Everything was fine. His wife still shuddered. When the lights came on, the room was a mess. The Gotzes couldn't believe their eyes.

"Are they gone?" she asked, looking around her.

"I think so."

"You think so? I need a definite answer. Don't think so. What if they are still around?"

"Yes."

"Is anybody dead?"

"We have to put on the rear light to know."

She reached for a switch by her and flipped it on. He stuck his head through the window and saw bodies on the ground.

"I see three. There may be more around the house."

"I don't want to see them. I can't go out until they have been taken away from here. Call the police and tell them we didn't have anything to do with it."

He snatched the handset from the cradle on the wall and dialed.

CHAPTER THIRTEEN

The chopper kept pace with the SUV as it sliced through the trees. It missed the vehicle at times but located it moments later. It's doing a good job, Steffie thought. She hoped the Gotzes would be fine, regretting the trouble she had caused them. She had drawn unnecessary attention to the peaceful farming family and wished she hadn't gone there in the first place. She would have dealt decisively with the men but for the chopper's intervention. She looked up; the broad leaves gave the vehicle cover. She stopped the SUV, got out, and aimed at the lights of the chopper which hovered above her, waiting for the vehicle to resurface. Two shots in quick succession caught the light and blew it out. She heard the chopper moving away, but she knew it would come back. She got back in the vehicle and took off again. A couple of turns around boulders and hills followed, and then it plunged into a ditch and came out flying. It bounced off the ground a couple of times and crashed head-on into a tree, Steffie's chest hitting the wheel and her body bumping back into the seat.

The chopper noticed the vehicle had disappeared again, but the pilot knew it was beneath the chopper. So he took the radio from beside him while the shooter beside him loaded his automatic weapon.

"Cud 1 to Lion. Confirm present location," demanded the pilot.

"Cart track to join Route 6."

"Keep going. Target is headed in that direction. Out."

"Copy."

The pilot hung up and focused on the control panel as his colleague aimed at the vehicle. He had fired a couple of shots and missed. He wouldn't miss this time, he assured himself. He lifted a box behind them and opened it. A couple of lights lay wrapped in plastic and cork. He took two and connected wires to them. He held onto the door frame with one hand and, with the other hand, carefully attached the two lights under the chopper. He sat upright and gave the pilot thumbs up. He flipped on a switch, and powerful lights shot out onto the woods again. The shooter could see the vehicle as it raced through the bumpy scrub. He aimed his weapon, waiting for a clearer view. He could see the dent in the hood caused by the crash into the tree. A couple of holes on the trunk told the shooter he wasn't a bad shot. He just hadn't had any luck. He refused to credit Steffie for being good at what she did. He watched as the SUV cut fiercely through the thickets.

Steffie noted the lights from the chopper were back. She was frustrated. At the same time, she wondered if the people following her were indeed police officers. Surely, she expected more than what pursued her if they were. She had the inkling somebody was using a few of them to fight his dirty war. Or they were dressed in police uniforms but weren't police. The vehicle twisted around massive boulders, skidded menacingly on two wheels at one point, and sideswiped a tree, jolting her. The vehicle stopped. She shifted into gear and stabbed at the accelerator, jerking the SUV forward. The shooter fired a couple of shots that missed the target. Frustrated, he reached for an RPG launcher and fired. It missed the target by inches and exploded in a tree, breaking the trunk and felling it. Steffie saw the impact and knew what had been fired at her. She was in a war with the country of her birth. Another one came, missed the SUV, and exploded on the ground, splashing mud in the air. She was grateful to have escaped both grenades. The shooting ceased for a moment as the vehicle suddenly began to slow down. She thought it was out of gas. The fuel gauge said otherwise. Then why was it running slowly? She noticed the vehicle was beginning to sink and thought she was in a kind of depression. When she looked out the window, she realized the SUV was in a marshy area. It was sinking. She grabbed her stuff quickly and got out through the rear window. As she waded in the water away from danger, the vehicle's hood disappeared. The roof and upper part of the SUV still showed.

The chopper lost the target. It hovered above the swamp for a while. Then the shooter spotted the roof of the vehicle and alerted the pilot. It went down close to the surface. The men were convinced it was the SUV.

The police car barreled down the road at breakneck speed. The officers in it hadn't sighted the vehicle yet and hoped the chopper had dealt with it. The walkie-talkie crackled to life suddenly.

"Cud 1 to Lion," called the pilot.

The driver pressed a button, "Go ahead."

"The vehicle is stuck in the swamp."

The officer snatched it and placed it close to his mouth.

"Any sign of her?"

"Negative, but I believe she is still in the vicinity. I don't think she is in the vehicle."

"Keep watching. Out."

He shared a look with his colleague and focused on the road, admitting Steffie was good. If it turned out she was innocent, which was a possibility, she deserved a medal. Even if she were killed in this mission, she would have died a hero and deserved a Christian burial, he concluded.

Steffie watched from under a tree, her rifle at the ready. The chopper had banked and glided away. She didn't know what to expect next. She had checked for her valuables. Everything was intact. She looked around occasionally to ensure nothing was left to chance. She still had the map but couldn't use it in the dark. Route 6 was a little further beyond the woods. As she studied the fringes of the swamp, she saw through the trees in the distance a car racing very fast. Moments later, the police car swerved off the road towards the swamp, throwing dirt in the air. The chopper came back to the swamp, shining its lights on the hood of the vehicle. The other officer pointed to the roof of the SUV. The driver saw him, raced the car closer to the swamp, and halted. The officers got out quickly and hurried to the point where they could see the almost sunken SUV.

The shooter and pilot looked on at their two colleagues on the ground.

"What do you think?" the shooter asked.

The pilot looked at him, "Go for it."

At the pilot's signal, the ground officers pulled back as the shooter swung his machine gun towards the pool of water and started firing on the SUV, shattering the windshield. He kept firing at the windows until the engine caught fire and exploded. They watched to see the upper body of the vehicle burn. Steffie observed the proceedings, wondering what the explosion was meant to achieve. She had to get away from these two and the chopper, assuming they were the only ones following her now. If she didn't get away neatly, more officers and men would be coming after her. At this point in her life, she needed a perfectly thought-out plan. Any slip-up would spell doom for her. She didn't have a life in Germany and must find a new beginning in the US or any country where she would be safe. She had to be in a country where no one could identify her. It didn't matter where this country was located. She needed peace from all the people who were after her. She hoped the envelope would, in the end, serve a good purpose as promised by Randolph. She shook her head as she gazed at the officers arguing among themselves, hoping she hadn't been used for a dirty mission. She had a good and quiet life and was on course for a dream career. With that forfeited now, she needed a decent life for the rest of her life. She watched as the car's headlights came on, and one officer showed something she suspected might be a road map to his colleague. She overheard the other saying more officers were sweeping in on the farming community. She was surrounded, as the biker had said. They were bent on finding her.

One officer waved a hand towards the woods as he gazed at the chopper. It banked wildly towards the trees as the two consulted the map again.

"So, what do you think?" one asked.

"I don't know what you expect from me. She may have escaped. She may be dead even though we need proof if that is the case. She may be wounded somewhere given the number of bullets the vehicle took."

"I agree with you, but I also submit if she is still alive, she must be a genius. She must be a phenomenon. She must be quite a character."

"Extraordinary is the word. But, on a lighter note, I think I'm beginning to have a soft spot for her."

"So, you have the same feelings, huh?"

They shared a look and laughed.

"Without her body, our mission isn't accomplished. Our superiors will look at us as failures. So, we have to find the body. If she is in the vehicle, she must surely be dead with the shots and have drunk a lot of water. Let us call for a tow truck to get it out of the water, and if we don't see her body, we look elsewhere."

"That has to happen now."

One took his radio and made contact to request a tow truck as they turned towards the trees. The chopper was still overhead, shining its lights. It didn't yield much because of the canopy of leaves. Steffie observed the officers approaching her on foot and then glanced at the chopper. It was about sixty feet above the ground. It hovered for a while with its lights directed towards Steffie's hideout as if the pilot knew she hid there. She had to take action before the men on foot found her. Her head emerged from behind a tree; she aimed at the pilot and fired three shots in quick succession. The first two shattered the windshield, and the third hit the pilot in the eye. His hands let go of the controls as his body slumped to the side against the door. The chopper spun around, baffling the shooter, who didn't know what had happened to the pilot. He had heard shots but didn't know his man was hit. Suddenly, the chopper began to yaw menacingly, prompting him to glance at his colleague and ask why he did that. Then he noticed what had happened. He took a rifle, slung it around his neck, and jumped out as it spun forward towards the ground. Moments later, it crashed in the grass and exploded, sending the two men almost at the front of the woods running for their lives. The shooter joined them. As the officers ran towards her for safety, Steffie opened fire. One officer and the shooter died instantly as they took shots in their chest and throat. The other officer ducked for safety, wondering where the shots had come from. He knew they had come from the trees, but where specifically, he couldn't tell.

Panting heavily, he looked at the ground near him and saw his colleagues. He was a big target as long as he remained in the open. Whoever was shooting was looking at him. He crawled quickly to the edge, rose, and took off into the woods. Steffie observed him as he ran right in her direction. She stuck her leg out and tripped him. The officer fell and recovered immediately, his gun still in his hand. He didn't know what had tripped him. He looked around him. There was nobody in sight. As he readied to move on, he heard a crack behind him and froze. When he turned around, Steffie pointed her gun at his face. He knew now what had sent him crashing to the ground. He couldn't see her face but knew it was her. Who else would be in this part of the country at this time with a gun?

"Drop it. Drop your gun," she ordered.

He didn't move or drop his gun. He contemplated whether to fight back or surrender. If he fought and won, he would be a hero. If he didn't win, he was toast, just like his fallen colleagues.

"Drop your gun now. Don't make me lose my temper," she repeated.

He moved with incredible speed to shoot, but a shot from her hit his hand that held the gun. Then, as he dropped the gun and moaned, she whacked his chin with the butt of her rifle and sent him reeling back in horror and falling to the ground. She scooped up his gun and stowed it in her anorak; then, she beckoned him to rise. He obeyed this time.

"Turn around. Put your hands on your head now. If you try anything stupid, I will kill you."

He turned around slowly. She held his hand and wheeled him around, stamped viciously on the back of his knee, and forced him to his knees. A gun was tucked in his trousers at the back. She saw it, took it, and frisked his socks. She slung her rifle around her neck and buffeted his ears with both hands in a karate chop. The officer hunched forward face down. She reached for a flashlight, switched it on, and directed it at his face.

"How many more are coming?"

"I don't know. I hope you know what you're doing. You just attacked a police officer. You have already killed many."

"You better be telling the truth. I don't remember killing any officers, but I recall hitting their knees and legs, so they don't come after me when they don't know what they are doing. Many of you think you are working for Germany, but you are not. You are fighting somebody's little war. You are fighting somebody's dirty war for them."

"What? What did you just say?"

Steffie kicked his face so hard he screamed.

"There is no shame. You can scream some more. Make sure it is loud enough to grab the attention of the person or people who sent you. You don't get to ask questions at this point in your life. I do. Who's behind this insanity?"

He smiled.

"We obey orders. You won't get far. It's only a matter of time. But I must admit, we underrated you."

"And now what?"

"We've paid dearly for it. She'll come after you herself."

She instantly knew the man before her wasn't from the police. They had police cars and uniforms and even a chopper, but the police hadn't sent them. She was right about them fighting for somebody. Olga was gone unless she was mistaken. She fired a shot into his knee. He screamed like a child. Another shot found the other knee. Now he was crying and pleading for mercy. She took his cap, removed his shirt, put them on, and moved out. He scooted around and began to crawl out of the woods. He would get out and crawl towards the road. She found the police car and got in. The key was in the ignition. She started the car, departed onto Route 6, and moved on.

The man had said, "She will come after you herself." Steffie knew the person behind the attacks was a woman. Perhaps Olga had miraculously survived, or it might be somebody she didn't know. She stopped by the roadside, checked the map, and then barreled out of sight. A few minutes of rest wouldn't be a bad idea. She needed it if she was to stand a chance of escaping her pursuers. She would need another means of transport since she couldn't depend on the vehicle she drove now. It belonged to the police and would attract attention and make her an easy target. A signpost along the road indicated a gas station half a mile ahead. She sighed her relief. The car had gas. It branched into the quiet gas station and parked, its windows rolled up. She checked the glove compartment but found nothing of importance. She still had cookies and one soda. She uncapped it and sipped as she ate the cookies while she peered around. She hadn't killed the three men in the woods, and any one of them could radio the woman and inform her about the current situation.

More men would be sent after a girl in a police car. She didn't think the man would say his cap was also taken from him, but a police car would be mentioned. Steffie wondered who this woman might be if Olga was dead. That meant Olga worked for that woman or worked alone. She had sent men after Steffie at the Gotzes. The people after her had an army. She smiled to herself as she rechecked the map. Her eyes began to close slightly. She was tired and weak, but her vehicle was conspicuous to anybody who came into the gas station. On the other side of the station, two big trucks were parked. In the mart, only the manager was there, reading something she thought might be a newspaper. There was enough space between the trucks for a car. She started the car and moved across the pumps, coming to a halt between the trucks. The ideal situation would be to move on, but she was too tired to continue tonight. She was about to take a risk but hoped it would be worth it. With an effort, she finished her sparse meal, made sure the doors and windows were locked, and then she leaned her head on the wheel and slept.

CHAPTER FOURTEEN

San Diego

The old man sat in his lounge with his eyes wide open. His food was still on the dining table in his plush dining room that adjoined the lounge. The new nurse had come to remind him to eat, but he had dismissed her each time, assuring her he was fine. He didn't want her to be suspicious and had told her not to remind him again. That was Angela's mistake, and he didn't want the nurse to repeat it. It would trigger a response that wasn't desirable. The giant screen TV was on, but his attention seemed to be elsewhere. The two men he had dispatched to Germany hadn't yet arrived. One had called to inform him that the plane was low on fuel and was forced to land in London. The pilot had apologized to them and promised a refund of some sort to all the passengers. The computerized fueling system had been overridden, and the tank manually fueled. Apparently, the job hadn't been well done, and the plane had traveled on less fuel than it usually carried, but it had had to wait for a while in London until refueling was done.

The old man fumed as he lifted a bottle of wine on the table by him and hurled it at the wall. It crashed on impact and spilled its content, the shards falling to the floor and alerting the nurse. She hurried into the lounge and backed out immediately on seeing the mess. Moments later, she returned with a cleaning kit, cleaned up quickly, and scurried out without asking questions. The old man coughed twice, reached for a tissue from a box near him, and wiped his lips. He glanced at the food on the dining table. He admitted being hungry, as his usual eating time had passed. The last call he made to Martina wasn't replied to. She hadn't picked up and also hadn't called back even though he had left a message explicitly asking her to call back and give an update. He didn't have proof, but for her own sake and the safety of her family, he hoped she hadn't gotten greedy and now sought the parcel for herself. Surely she must be smart enough to know the consequences. He would send men after her and hunt her down within a day. Sweat broke out on his face, streaming down through his mustache to his lips. His reputation was at stake if he couldn't get back what had been taken from the museum. He would lose respect in the eyes of the churches he had donated to and continued to assist; universities and charities would also frown on him. The media would tear him apart in minutes. As if all these weren't enough, there would be criminal investigations into his dealings. There would only be one outcome. Jail. His frail frame rose with the help of a walking stick and hobbled to the dining table. He sat down and began to eat the food that was now cold. He enjoyed it anyway.

Munich

A tractor motored into the station to buy gas. The driver revved the engine so noisily, Steffie was jolted out of sleep. She opened her eyes and lifted her head. It was morning. She couldn't believe it. She had slept all night and never woke up. She could have been killed if any of the pursuers had located her or the car. She checked her valuables. A check around her revealed one of the trucks that gave her cover was gone. She stretched and yawned, rolled down the window, and glanced at the station mart. Big photos of her were posted on the windows. The cap she had taken from the man was on the floor of the vehicle. She looked at her face in the side mirror, quickly donned the sunglasses and cap, and stepped out. She closed the door and walked towards the store. She casually looked to both sides as she neared the door, her hand over her stomach. A woman came out of the mart as Steffie walked in and headed to the drinks shelf. The cashier, a plump man in his early forties, admired her legs. He smiled, licked his lips, and ran his hand over his balding head. He even whistled softly at some point, observing as she picked cookies and soda and walked to the register. While he ran the register, he admired her face, wondering how her skin would feel like in his arms. She looked forward at the large portrait of herself on the wall behind him. She paid for her shopping and headed out. The man still viewed those beautiful legs, wondering what her behind looked like, as the anorak didn't expose her back. As she opened the door and departed, her shoes caught his attention. The shoes were dirty. The excited face changed instantly. He maintained visual as she tore away towards the car. The shoes and shorts didn't match the shirt and cap. He wondered if she was a Girl Guide. He knew them and knew they didn't dress like Steffie.

"A police officer in shorts? That is new. I haven't seen anything like it before," he murmured.

Steffie opened the car and sat down. The man looked back at the poster behind him but couldn't make anything out of it. He was still suspicious anyway. He reached for his phone and dialed as the police car moved on. She had seen him lift the handset and knew he was calling the police or the woman.

Martina relaxed in bed, thinking about the call from California. Another message had been left on the machine asking her to call back, but she wouldn't call. She knew the implications of her actions, but she was willing to take her chances. She didn't have answers for the caller. Her life was in danger. She knew it. She had sent two men after Steffie but hadn't heard from them. Her world was about to crash on her. Her reputation was on the line, as was her career. If things didn't go her way and her cover was blown, she faced jail. This mission had to be tackled with the highest form of skill and finesse. She rose and sat on her bed, watching the stocky man through her window as he watered the flowers. He had been a good and loyal servant to her for years. She wondered if he could be trusted to play an active role in the mission. The phone on the bureau rang. Another one under her pillow rang moments later. She yanked the one under her pillow and flipped it open.

"Somebody came here moments ago. She was dressed like a police officer, but her shoes didn't look like those worn by the police. She also wore shorts. She just left in a police car," the cashier from the gas station informed her.

"Did you get the registration?" Martina asked as she got out of bed and moved to the window.

"No, but I know the car is headed to Route 6."

"Thank you."

She hung up and made a call, waving at the stocky man. She dialed the number again.

Two men sat in the green sedan, which was parked on the shoulder of the road that joined Route 6. A phone rang. One of the men answered.

"I am listening."

"The target has been seen driving a police car. She left a gas station towards Route 6 moments ago. Go!" declared the unmistakable voice of Martina.

"We are moving right away. She can't get through the security checks we have mounted ahead."

He clicked the phone shut, started the car, and rocketed out of sight.

Steffie was in a bookshop. She had seen the roadblocks on Route 6 and avoided them by detouring through the countryside, past small farming towns, and taking a bypass to a street that boasted two schools and a clinic.

"I need it now," she said.

"Give it to me," replied the elderly man who ran the bookshop.

"Let me handle the photocopy while you deal with the envelope. It will be faster that way. What do you think?"

The man nodded as she took the black envelope from her bra. She opened it and took out the list, handing the envelope to the elderly man. He departed into an inner room while she focused on the list. She looked around her. The two people in the store scanned some of the books on display. She covered the first three names on the list with a book and ran a copy of the list on the photocopier. The elderly man came out two minutes later with a black envelope in each hand. He handed one to her.

"This is the original."

She took it, studied it briefly, and put the original list in it. She sealed it and tucked it back in her bra. Then she took the other one and put the photocopy in it. Finally, she paid him and sealed the envelope.

"Thank you,' she said

She walked briskly out of the shop.

The two men from California emerged through the exit doors of the airport. They wore sportswear, each carrying a bag. Tom hailed a cab, they got in and departed. Their trip had been delayed, but finally, they were in Munich. That was all that mattered to Frank. The airline had refunded part of their fares to compensate for the delay. Some of the passengers had refused to accept it as they threatened lawsuits. These were business people who lost serious money whenever their flights were delayed. They missed out on important meetings and conferences that cost their companies a lot of money. Frank had been tasked to watch his colleague at all times. The old man trusted him well enough to give him that assignment, and he was determined to do it well. The driver stole a glance at them occasionally as he drove. They looked forward, no word passing between them. Whenever the cab reached an intersection, the driver typed into a cell phone tucked between his seat and the door. He sent a message informing the person on the other end that he had picked up the two men from California.

Martina had received a message that the old man was sending two men to Germany. She knew they were coming for a two-fold assignment. They were to find the parcel and also kill her. She had to take precautions. She had liaised with Immigration for the identities of the men and posted one of her men at the airport to collect them. She had also tasked somebody to monitor their movements while in Munich.

CHAPTER FIFTEEN

The blue car pulled into the car park of the supermarket. Steffie had painted the part that showed it was a police car with blue paint she had bought in a hardware shop. A girl had seen her paint the police inscription and alerted her parents. They had come out to challenge her, threatening to call the police. She had had to move on quickly. The car wouldn't help her now. She couldn't leave it at the gas station as people could be out there waiting for her. The only place she could think of was the supermarket. The police wouldn't suspect she would go among crowds. They would consider her to be in hiding or go to places where there were few people. An elderly man spotted her and dialed on his phone while he watched her. Steffie opened the door and stepped out, shutting it. She wore a long blond wig, polo shirt over jeans, and sunglasses. She pulled down on her blue baseball cap as she walked away from the car. Male shoppers admired her as she strode past them. She flagged down a cab and hopped in. The cab moved on.

Moments later, the green sedan pulled over by the curb. The passenger got down and dashed to the car. He returned instantly to the sedan with the police cap and shirt that now looked blue. She had used it during the painting.

"Gone!"

"This chick is sleek and smart."

The elderly man knew they had responded to his call and approached them.

"Where did she go?" the man asked.

"I didn't see her leave. Sorry," he replied.

"You called our boss and didn't know where the target went?"

"That is what I'm saying. A shopper needed directions, and by the time I finished with her, the lady was gone."

The elderly man departed, leaving the men disappointed. The driver banged on the steering wheel in frustration. The other man dumped the stuff in his hand on the backseat and got in the sedan. The sedan moved on, the driver wondering if the elderly man had told them the truth. He hadn't sounded convincing.

While the Chief spoke to an officer about young applicants who wanted to join the police force, the analyst burst in. The Chief looked up at him.

"What have you got for me, bursting in like this?"

"She was last seen at a supermarket. She caught a cab moments later and disappeared."

"I see."

A female officer joined them.

"That was minutes ago, but what I have is fresh from the barrel. She was spotted at a bus terminal a few moments ago."

"Which one?" the analyst said.

"I mean the one near the supermarket."

The Chief couldn't believe his ears, but he was hearing right.

"She must be really smart, but where is she going with all this fuss?" He asked as he got on his phone.

He snapped his finger at the two informants and gave them a wink, indicating he appreciated their effort—the call connected at the third ring.

"She is at the bus terminal! Go! If you don't find her there, try searching the area. Cafes, bars, and hotels! Search wherever you think a criminal will be likely to hide! Be careful not to fall for any beautiful girl. You might go to bed with our suspect without knowing. The way I see her, even the Chancellor can make a mistake and welcome a nun to his office without knowing a criminal was seated in front of him. And guess what? I can easily be fooled by her as a clown at the circus. I like the circus."

They laughed.

"I got it, Chief."

The cab taking the two men stopped by a payphone in the business district of Munich. Tom got down and hurried into it. He reached for change in his pocket and dialed a number. A response came immediately.

"Yes?" enquired a booming voice.

"Ti Heights?"

There was a haughty laugh on the line, prompting Tom to also laugh.

"Long time no see, no hear. Where the hell have you been? I have been asking after you for some time now, and no one from the group seems to know shit about your whereabouts."

"Yeah, I know. Once in a while, I have to snatch myself away from the public and resurface later. We will talk about it later. As of now, though, I need information. What about this cadet punk giving the German police hell?"

"She was last seen at a bus terminal. Oh, wait a minute, she was last seen on a bus. Where she is headed, I don't know, but if what I hear about her is true, she is probably headed to the train station. This just came in."

"Thanks."

"Hey, Ti Heights, you know the drill? Come on, don't make me talk too much as if I'm some monster always fleecing folks. Come on, man."

"I know. I will get in touch with you with your pay in my hand before the day ends."

"Promise?"

"Come on, man, don't you trust me? Have I failed you before?"

He hung up and got out into the cab, which moved on quickly. He debriefed his colleague about what he had picked up from his snitch. Frank was impressed with the informer's accurate information.

Chapter Sixteen

Steffie sat by the window of the bus. She looked forward but out the window at times. The elderly man who had seen her and phoned hadn't seen her leave. She made sure of that. While the man spoke, she had hurried through the shoppers and slipped away. A young man seated next to her was eating a sandwich. He offered her the sandwich. She declined with a hand wave and turned her eyes away from him. Up above her on the window was her poster. There was another on the windshield staring right in the eyes of the driver. She had seen her photos on all the buses and vans en route to the bus terminal. All the images were not the same. They showed her in her various disguises and some from the military school. Pressure mounted on her to get out before she was caught. She might have a chance of a fair trial if caught by the police, but if she were captured by the bad people headed by the woman she hadn't met yet and posing as the police, they would kill her. If she knew exactly what to do with the list, she could defend herself if arrested. The driver looked at the passengers through the rearview mirror. A second look drew his attention to the boy eating a sandwich. He reminded the driver of his son, who drowned in the Rhine years ago. They looked alike. He studied the boy's face for a while, and then his gaze swerved to Steffie. Her beauty struck him.

"What a beautiful girl," he thought.

While he drove, he considered the poster on the windshield. Then it occurred to him the photo bore semblance to Steffie. He compared the photo to Steffie's face in the mirror. As the bus stopped for passengers to board and alight, he took time looking at the target. The bus moved on again. He kept comparing the face and the photo. He didn't want to make the mistake of accusing the wrong person. Finally, he was satisfied he had the right suspect in his bus and abruptly slammed on the brakes. The bus stopped instantly, throwing passengers off their seats. The boy's sandwich fell out of his hand to the wet floor while a sleeping woman was jolted out of sleep. An old woman reading her Bible jerked forward and dropped her Bible on the floor. All eyes fell on the driver, some passengers wanting to know why he did that.

"Hey, what is the matter with you?" an angry passenger asked.

"Are you drunk?" queried the old woman.

"Speak! What have you got to say for yourself? You got to apologize to Grandma now!" charged a man.

The driver got up and started towards Steffie without saying a word. Passengers were angry that he hadn't bothered to say sorry for his reckless driving. Eyes turned to look at him. Steffie looked up, saw him, and made her move. She threw her backpack through the window.

"Hey, you!" the driver pointed.

All eyes turned now to look at Steffie. The driver reached her and held her hand as she attempted to escape through the window. She broke his hold. He tackled her again. She turned around and punched his mouth. He let go of his grip and reeled back, wiping blood off his lips. Passengers around them moved to the other side to avoid getting in the way of the brawlers; many were shocked how Steffie dealt with the driver. She lunged out of the bus through the window. The driver hurried back to his seat, took his phone, and made a call.

"Will you please move the bus? I'm going to a funeral. You are not that strong; why did you get in a fight with her? Now you are bleeding all over," the old woman fumed.

The passengers laughed.

"Yes, man! Get the fucking bus moving, will you?" a boy yelled.

Passengers rained insults on the driver.

Meanwhile, Steffie picked up her backpack, crossed the street, and melted in the milling crowd of shoppers and passengers. Many of the passengers on the bus hailed her. They didn't know her or why the driver charged her. The driver heard their murmurings and understood their anger. He turned and faced them, rendering an unqualified apology to them, and then he pointed to the poster on the windshield. When they saw it, they understood why he had done what he did. Their mouths opened in shock. The old woman was still not impressed. She couldn't be bothered by a suspect wanted by the police. She felt it was a matter for the police and not the driver to effect an arrest.

Moments later, the green sedan halted next to the bus. The two men stepped out and boarded the bus. The driver pointed in the direction of the crowd on the other side of the road.

The cab carrying Tom and Frank stood behind the bus. Tom got out and observed the men on the bus as they consulted with the driver. They got off the bus and charged after Steffie across the street. He beckoned Frank to join him, which he did, carrying their backpacks. They crossed the street and took after the men. They hadn't seen Steffie, but following the two men would definitely lead them to the target. The cab driver, meanwhile, quickly made a call and moved the cab on.

Steffie walked very fast, shouldering the backs and chests of people. She looked back and saw the two men on her heels. They hurled everybody in front of them out of the way to reach their target. She took off, collided with a newspaper vendor, and shoved him off her path. The vendor smashed into a parked car and dropped his newspapers. As she wedged her way through the crowd, the driver aimed his gun and fired a shot, missed, and hit a man in the arm. Frightened strollers and shoppers screamed and took to their heels. Tom and Frank gave chase as the two men broke into a run after Steffie. A man, running because he saw others running, crashed into the second man as he aimed to shoot. The shot rang out but hit the side of an ambulance. Its driver stopped the ambulance in the middle of the street, got out, and took off. The two medics in the back also got out and hurried out of sight. Moments later, a pregnant woman looked out with a baby's head showing between her thighs. The result was chaos as passengers, shoppers, and motorists got caught up in the madness, some taking photos of the pregnant woman.

Steffie turned into a clothing store, startling a couple just about to exit. The men burst in after her, clutching their weapons. Moments later, the other two also entered, guns in their hands.

The store manager was alerted by a salesgirl. He came out of his office and saw the confusion in his store. He went for his phone to call the police but took a shot in the head instantly from Tom. He fell like a log, causing sales assistants to flee the store. Shoppers screamed and shrieked, mothers running around and shouting for their stray children. Steffie got on the crowded escalator. The driver spotted her and fired a shot at her. She ducked at the sound of the shot, the bullet hitting a man in the back. The man tumbled down the escalator. She doubled up the escalator to the first floor and took refuge in the jeans aisle, her gun at the ready. She melted into the racks of jeans, panting heavily. She looked out for the shooter while she observed fleeing shoppers struggle for supremacy to escape. The result was a stampede at the exit door. The sight of the manager's body made her feel sorry. Her presence in the store had killed him. She hoped the pursuit would be over soon, so no more collateral damage was done.

She noticed some of the shoppers and employees still remained in the store. These were trapped by the gunfire and couldn't afford to risk their lives to escape. They took cover behind clothing shelves and stands. An abandoned little girl screamed loudly and broke into a series of cries. An elderly woman beckoned her to come to her. Out of fear, the girl refused to go to her. The driver reached the first floor and approached the jeans section. His colleague followed him and took the other section, forming a two-pronged attack. Tom and Frank caught up moments later and took cover behind concrete columns, observing.

Steffie saw the two men but not the men from California. She looked behind her. There was a window, and the restroom was a few feet from it. Her sudden movement alerted Tom, who signaled Frank. Both saw her for the first time. When she looked to her right, she saw them and knew now she had four pursuers. While she considered how to get into the restroom without being shot, the driver's head popped up in front of her. They made eye contact and studied each other for a while. He aimed his gun and was about to shoot when she hurled a couple of pairs of jeans at him and ducked diagonally to the floor at the same time. She shot him in his groin before he could get the clothes off his face. He fell on the clothing rack to his side, firing indiscriminately into the clothes on display. When she pulled the trigger again, she was out of ammo. A couple came out of hiding and took off. A boy screamed after them, tripping over a mop and falling. He recovered quickly and burst out of sight. Steffie had a second gun to use, but the two men behind the columns were watching her. Frank aimed his weapon and was about to shoot when a hand clamped his shoulder. When he lifted his eyes. It was Tom.

"Why?" he asked, surprised.

"This is not the right time."

Frank lowered his gun.

Steffie heard a click behind her and turned around instantly. The second man in the green sedan pointed his gun at her, a big smile on his face. She froze briefly, contemplating her next move. He smiled as he considered his colleague lying on the clothes on the floor.

"Nice try," he said, extending his hand.

She began to flinch towards a rack as he inched closer to her.

"Give it to me and walk, lady. Give it to me. I will let you go. It doesn't have to be like this. People always don't have to die in order to get a problem solved."

"I don't have anything."

"Then why is everybody chasing after you? There must be a reason why. Give it up and stop the madness. Everything around you is spinning, and the result isn't good."

"They think I have it, but I don't."

"Don't fuck with me, lady!"

She removed her backpack slowly and hurled it at him, "Take it and search it."

At the same time, she lunged at him. The man caught the backpack but found himself falling backward. The two crashed to the floor. Tom and Frank shared a surprised look. They enjoyed the drama.

The combatants recovered, the man clutching the backpack in his left hand and the gun in his right hand. As he readied to shoot, a sudden kick from Steffie moved his hand. A shot rang out in the wrong direction, missing her. She kicked his groin powerfully as he aimed again to fire; the man held his groin. Instantly, she spun and kicked his face with the other foot. The kick was so powerful it knocked him out. He staggered and fell backward as he tried to rise, losing his gun. The gun skittered across the floor and hit her foot. She scooped it up and aimed at his head.

"Throw it back to me," she ordered.

The man shook his head and held on tightly to the backpack. Frank glanced at Tom, wondering why he didn't want them to intervene. He still wanted to shoot, but his colleague shook his head to indicate otherwise. Steffie fired a shot into the man's knee. She neared him as he edged away from her. She fired another shot into the other knee. The man groaned and threw the backpack at her immediately. They heard sirens blaring in the distance, getting louder. She picked up the backpack. Suddenly, police officers invaded the ground shopping floor. Steffie slung on her backpack and took off towards the restroom. The other two men saw her and took after her, firing at her. She ducked for the door, crawling quickly into the restroom as bullets whipped past. The police officers had difficulty climbing the escalator as relieved shoppers on the first floor rushed down towards the ground floor.

The restroom had six toilets, each with a window that overlooked the street behind the store and four urinals to the side. She locked the door behind her, rushed through a toilet, and tugged at the window. It was shut tight and wouldn't budge. She got out quickly and tried the next window. The story was the same. The men began to pound on the door after they had tried it and found it locked. She glanced at the urinals, hurried to one, and with a huge effort yanked it off the wall. She carried it to the toilet and flung it at the window. It shattered the pane. She scraped through it quickly before the men knocked down the door and burst in. Tom stuck his head out through the window and looked out. He didn't see Steffie. He decided to push his upper body through it to get a better view.

Steffie braced against the wall by the window; her feet firmly fixed on the narrow concrete hood above a ground floor window. She punched his face powerfully, followed by another to his mouth, bursting a lip. Tom withdrew from the window immediately, holding his lips. Frank moved past him to the window, pushed his gun through, and sprayed a volley of bullets. Steffie held her place on the hood. Below her was a fence around the store, and beyond it was another street that teemed with motorists, shoppers, and pedestrians. When the shooting stopped for a moment, she lunged off the hood and held onto the fence.

Tom's face appeared in the window again. This time he could see her. Quickly, he aimed his gun and began to shoot at her. She scaled the fence rapidly onto the street and took off, shouldering aside a beggar receiving alms from a donor to the pavement. Moments later, the two men also scaled the fence onto the street and took after her. A backward look revealed they were there. She turned a corner into a narrow alley flanked by stores, running fast through the rather crowded space. The armed men after her gained on her as strollers and shoppers swerved out harm's way, screaming at the sight of their weapons. Tom fired two quick shots at her; she darted to the right. The shots missed her and hit the wall, shattering concrete. Another bullet shattered a window, the store owner taking cover behind a van. She leaped over a couple of boxes blocking the way, landed on the cobble-stoned pavement, rose up quickly, and took off again. All the stores were now closed, and no shoppers were around. They hid in stores and recesses in the wall. Frank aimed his gun and fired two shots in quick succession, one hitting Steffie in the shoulder. She slowed down, holding the affected shoulder as she reached the end of the alley. She turned the corner and took a look at her pursuers. They didn't seem to be giving up, and their speed was still good despite running for a while. She had thought they would slow down a bit. She took off again onto a quiet lane, feeling for her valuables and her gun. She had killed people she didn't intend to kill. Another glance behind told her the men were far back. She was tired and needed rest. She had to find a safe place to rest, but where was safe in this situation? The men wouldn't give up. She kept going.

Tom, meanwhile, had an argument with his colleague, who was absolutely livid with the way the mission had gone.

"I had her. I had the bitch and could have taken her down, but you restrained me. Now see what we have on our hands. The police are after us. This was a case we could so easily have handled without the police coming in. How are we going to get the girl now? Huh? Talk to me, Tom."

"Hey, take it easy. I'm the one in charge of this mission. And you have to do what I tell you. We are not here to kill her. We want something she has or doesn't. So, if she has it but isn't carrying it on her now and we kill her, what do we get? If she knows where the parcel is stashed and we kill her, what do we get? Nothing! So we have to have her cornered and get it from her and kill her afterward if there is the need for that. You just don't kill people when you need them. We need information that will lead us to the parcel and this we can only have if we catch her. That is what I have in mind. If you have better ideas than what I have just said, let me hear it, pal."

"Even then, I could have maimed her. I could have shot her leg or knee to immobilize her. What are we going to tell the old man if she gets away? He has paid a lot to get us here, and we have to make sure the work is done."

They were at the end of the alley now.

"If you persist in your funny ideas, shoot her when you have the opportunity but keep this in mind that if you end up killing her, I will personally put my gun in your mouth and blow your fucking brain out. That's a promise."

At the end of the quiet lane, two police officers stood by a barricade with their backs to her. There were no people there. The whole of Munich had many of these barricades and roadblocks now. Steffie could hear the officers chattering. Her pursuers were still some way behind her. She looked to both sides of the lane. The setting of the buildings had been set alternatively in offsets, creating recesses. She dashed into one and braced against the wall. The officers still chatted. She heard one braying into his radio moments later, telling the caller they hadn't spotted Steffie. She smiled to herself as the two armed men appeared. They stood for a while surveying the lane that looked empty but for the officers at the end whose backs were to them. Tom pointed to the recesses. Frank agreed. They started checking them one at a time. They knew she would be hiding in one of them. There was no way she could have gone past the barricade at the end of the lane without being seen by the officers. Frank spotted her as she popped out her head to check the lane but noticed her gun trained on him.

"Shit. She got us," Frank said undertones.

"Where is she?" inquired Tom as he turned around.

Frank pointed to Steffie's position. She fired a well-aimed shot at Frank and downed him. Tom responded with a sudden burst of gunfire. Steffi ducked and returned fire. The officers heard the shots and turned around with their weapons ready. Then they discovered the shots weren't meant for them. Steffie ran out of ammo, dumped her gun, and yanked out the second. Tom was also out of ammo and had to duck to Frank to get his. She rose and ran closer to him so she wouldn't miss at short range. As he rose and turned around to fire, she lunged onto the sidewalk, firing at his legs. The shots caught his knees and chest. Tom danced and twisted, finally collapsing to his knees. She heard footsteps behind her, turned, and looked back. The police officers were running towards her, one speaking into his radio. Steffie took another look at Tom. He wouldn't make it. She took off, back towards the alley. It was the only way that guaranteed safety. There were shots behind her.

"Shit!" she exclaimed as she hurried around the corner.

The officers were also shooting to kill. Now the whole world was shooting to kill her. That meant she had to shoot to kill as well if she was to stay alive. She couldn't believe she was fighting the country of her birth. She didn't have dual nationality. Germany was her country and the only country she knew. Until she could get out with her life, she remained a German.

She arrived on the street behind the store she had escaped from, amazed at how fast she could run with a wounded shoulder. The officers who had abandoned the barricades were still not in sight. She looked around her. Some shoppers still remembered seeing her a few minutes ago. Others weren't bothered; they shopped and did business as usual. She darted to the middle of the street when a cab came along, waving both hands to stop it. The cab halted; she hurried to the driver's door and pointed her gun at the driver. He remained still behind the wheel.

"Get out now and don't challenge me," she said quietly.

He didn't move. Steffie forced him out of the cab after hitting his face with the butt of the gun. He tried to fight back. She punched his face, held his hand, and tugged him across the pavement. The driver staggered and fell on the sidewalk. Steffie sat in the cab, took the wheel, and drove off. The rotund cab driver ran after the cab, swearing angrily. The police officers arrived moments later. The driver looked on as his cab zigzagged through the traffic and disappeared. He looked at the advancing police officers, fuming.

"Where were you when I needed you most?" he asked, flinging his hands at them.

"Take it easy, pal. What is the problem?"

"She just took my cab from me," he pointed.

"We'll get it back for you."

"Take it easy? We'll get it back for you? That's all you've got to say? That's my daily bread. It is gone, while lousy police officers look on! What do you get paid for?"

"Hey, watch it! Watch what you say!" the second officer warned, "We just got here. We'll get it back for you, my colleague said. Give us the registration number."

The angry driver gave it but spat at the officer's foot nearest him and departed, kicking a trash can on the sidewalk in frustration. He wasn't convinced he would have his cab back intact. It was the second time this had happened to him, and when he got his cab back in the first instance, some of the fittings were gone, as well as the rear seat. Meanwhile, one of the officers radioed for the cab to be impounded when it was found.

CHAPTER SEVENTEEN

The cab halted in front of a clinic. Steffie got out, removed the registration plates, and hid them under the front seat. She locked the doors and hurried to the entrance of the clinic. She looked to both sides, her left shoulder drenched in blood. Cars raced past the one-way street. She walked in. The bone hadn't been affected. She knew that from experience; only the flesh was torn. Nurses and patients parted in front of her as she neared the reception. She was alert for anyone who might make or receive a call. The person might be calling the police or the woman. A glance at the notice board revealed what she feared. Her poster was conspicuously posted. Anybody who saw her would instantly identify her. The people looked at her as she reached the desk, the nurse shivering slightly. Steffie noted she was scared.

"Fear not. I'm not here to harm anybody unless I'm forced to."

The nurse nodded as another one emerged from a room with files in her hand. She identified Steffie the moment she made eye contact with her and glanced at the poster. She dropped the files on the desk, reached for her phone, and was about to make a call. Steffie yanked out her gun and pointed it at her, shaking her head gently. The nurse got the message and pocketed the phone. Steffie removed her anorak and waved for the nurse who had the files to fix her wound. She nodded and hurried to get a first aid kit. The nurse at the desk and the patients around held their noses because of the foul smell of her anorak. Steffie couldn't get her wound fixed in the dressing room as she had to keep her eyes on the main door.

"I'm sorry for the inconvenience. I know I smell like hell but indulge me for a while. I will be out of here, and then you can breathe fresh and clean air devoid of bad odors," Steffie assured.

The nurse took time fixing the wound as Steffie studied every move the people around her made. She held her gun towards the entrance door and the people.

They knew better and remained calm. No one attempted to incur her wrath. When the nurse finished and had applied bandages over the wound, Steffie took out some money and thrust it in her hand. The nurse received it with mixed feelings. She wasn't sure whether to keep it or give it back to her. She consulted with her colleague at the desk. She shrugged and looked at Steffie, who scanned the faces of the people in the waiting room.

"Step forward," she ordered, pointing to a woman in a blue blouse.

The woman obeyed, shivering and hoping Steffie wouldn't harm her. The nurses shared a concerned look.

"Fear not. Relax. Remove your blouse," Steffie ordered.

"What?" the patient asked.

"You heard me."

The woman realized the gun was pointing at her face.

"Now!"

The woman removed her blouse and gave it to Steffie. Steffie slipped on the blouse quickly and smashed the phone on the reception desk, startling the nurses. She asked them to place their cell phones on the desk. They did. She took all the cell phones and headed to the restroom. When she came out, her long hair was red, and she had no backpack. She headed for the entrance door with the phones tied in her anorak.

"Thank you for fixing my wound and for your cooperation."

She exited.

Back on the street, she looked to both sides of the street and turned right on the busy lane. A couple of yards down the lane, she spotted a trash bin outside what appeared to her like a café. She walked to it, untied the anorak and dumped the cell phones in it, shut it, and continued down the lane. She still had the sunglasses on. Her strides were normal though slightly faster. She didn't feel pain in her shoulder, and that was refreshing. The nurse had done an excellent job. They would find a way of contacting the police, especially with her new look. There might be phones in the other rooms or offices at the clinic. Her attire would be described to the police. They would come after her any moment now. She turned the corner into another narrow alley at the sound of a siren. The siren grew much louder now behind her; it was an ambulance responding to a distress call, perhaps. She removed the blouse and turned it inside out. It assumed a different color. She put it on, tied her long hair into a ponytail, and put on a scarf. She hurried to the end of the alley and turned left onto another busy street. Cars raced past. People walked past her, none paying her any attention. She was encouraged, as none identified her. She was armed but knew the gun had a maximum of two bullets. She still had some but had forgotten to load it when she was in the toilet at the clinic. She spotted a signpost that announced a train station ahead. She pressed forward confidently. Sixty yards from the entrance of the train station, she spotted a couple of police officers. They scrutinized passengers as they went in and came out. This was her only way out of Munich, and she had to plan it well. She couldn't get into the station without being seen. A phone booth was to her right. The officers asked some passengers for identification, while others were interrogated, which she could see from where she stood in the phone booth as she pretended to be making a phone call. She studied the officers for a while, and at the same time, she scanned the area around her. As she weighed her options, a woman with two young kids appeared on the walks, approaching the station. Steffie hung up and stepped out of the booth instantly. She bounded towards the woman with a big smile that baffled the woman. It was as though she knew the woman, who wondered what would make a stranger behave like that.

"Are you headed to the train station?" Steffie asked excitedly in her well-rehearsed German with a Danish accent.

The woman nodded, drawing her kids to her.

"Let me help you with one of them, so you don't miss your train."

The news excited the woman.

"Ok. That's refreshing because I have had a rough ride to this place; carrying the two of them has always been a challenge."

Steffie lifted the younger one in her arms and walked the woman towards the station entrance, talking about a football match between two teams that never met at the weekend. The woman was confused about the topic but kept quiet. She was an ardent supporter of Bayern München, and the Bundesliga was on recess. Steffie kept her small talk going while she observed the officers. They did their work well, making sure all the passengers were checked for identification. Steffie knew she had to come up with something extraordinary to beat them.

On the other hand, it was possible also to beat them at their own game with a simple trick or finesse. Sometimes the most sophisticated security networks were outsmarted with little fuss. She didn't have to worry, she assured herself, hoping the woman whose kid she carried wouldn't betray her. That was a possibility that could prove costly if she did. Steffie would have no option but to defend herself when shot at, or she would have to fight her way out of the station. She glanced at the woman and forced a smile at the kid in her arms. Two tourists arguing in a language Steffie couldn't make out suddenly began a fight at the entrance, bringing proceedings there to a standstill as police tried to normalize the situation. Steffie considered the circumstances, wondering if it was better to set the kid down and force her way into the station. While she thought about it, she noticed more officers run to the scene from a room across the street. Three other men also chanting words in that language joined the fight, two women following. All passengers entering the station were advised to wait outside for a while until the situation was contained. When Steffie looked back, there were six heavily-armed police officers waiting in a squad truck. She was surrounded, but she decided to keep calm as they hadn't noticed her. They would have swooped down on her if they had. At the entrance, the situation was getting worse by the minute, leaving passengers frustrated.

Martina stood by the pool in her residence with her phone to her ear. She had avoided the caller for some time now by not taking his calls. Somehow the caller had found out the number to a phone she hadn't used before to call him and had called her on it. The caller's identity was local, and Martina had assumed it was a call from one of her men after Steffie. The caller had taken her by surprise.

"I paid you one million dollars to ensure the safety of this information! What the hell have you done for me! Talk to me! What makes you think I should let you enjoy that money? Do you deserve it? Talk to me! I can't hear you; I said talk to me!"

"I will if you calm down."

"Calm down? Calm down? Is that all you have got to say? Calm down, my ass! I am not gonna calm down until I have some fucking answers!"

"You won't have them until you learn to show me respect. You paid me a hefty sum, and I haven't made any attempt to deny that, have I? If you think you can handle it better, why don't you come here and deal with it so we all know you can do it. Until then, I suggest you relax and let me handle the situation. I am in charge, and I say relax. There is no cause for alarm. You worry and fume over trivia. You make a calm situation look like an emergency and get people running helter-skelter when all you should do is critically access the situation and devise the right response to it. Sometimes your best option is to remain calm and let the situation resolve itself."

"Watch your tongue, woman. I made you whoever you are."

"Don't talk shit to my ass. I had a job, a very good job before we started talking business, so don't talk as if I was jobless. I'm still gainfully working, and I am a happy woman. I suggest you keep quiet and listen to me when I speak. Every operation has its setbacks."

"Ok, go ahead and talk to me."

"Now that you are calm, I've information that might be of interest to you."

"What is it? I don't need any information apart from the fact that the parcel has been retrieved and brought to me."

"Well, I don't care what you deem important, but I suggest you find a Johann Steinberg. I understand he is somewhere in Silicon Valley. It will be in your interest to strike a deal with him or kill him. The information I have is authentic, and

I have to warn you that if he gets the parcel, you are going down. There will be no redemption for you. Not even God can save you."

"The name rings a bell. I will look into it, but I will be expecting a call from you concerning the girl and the parcel."

"I will make sure to keep you posted. She can't get out of Germany without me having the parcel. I assure you."

She ended the call and smiled.

"Bitch," she mouthed.

She was glad to have given the caller a telling-off. She had suffered many harsh words from him, and today it was her turn to exact revenge. The man couldn't come to Germany. He could only stay in California and talk big. She was in charge and was doing her bit to get the work done, but he wouldn't let her. Martina had received a message about the death of the two men sent from California. Whatever they came for hadn't materialized, and she was certain they had come to get the parcel because the caller didn't have confidence in her and also to kill her once they succeeded. Once the caller hadn't heard from them, he knew they were dead and had gotten in touch with her. The stocky man approached her with his phone. Another caller was on the line. She took it from him and listened while he took a couple of paces from her and waited. She ended the call and handed the phone back to him. He bowed and scurried out of sight. Smiling broadly, she hurried into the house through a side door. She had received information on Steffie that could prove crucial in her mission to retrieve the envelope. She planned to reward the informant handsomely if she was able to retrieve the parcel. Once she succeeded, she would blackmail the caller in California for a record sum of money. It would make her rich for the rest of her life. As a matter of fact, her descendants would never go broke for a century. And if they played their cards well, she was looking at two centuries. She stormed out of the house, beaming proudly. She knew where Steffie was headed. She had been spotted at the train station.

CHAPTER EIGHTEEN

The situation at the entrance to the train station was normal now. The brawlers had been whisked away in the squad truck, and passengers moved in and out of the station after going through the checks. Steffie and her newfound friends approached the entrance, where an officer stopped them. He studied their faces as Steffie looked at the kid in her arms and pointed jokingly at the officer. She kissed the boy as the officer focused on her face. She beamed proudly at the officer, who was stunned by her beauty. She could see her poster right behind the officer and hoped the woman by her didn't see it. Another officer was talking to her. Steffie prayed the interrogation kept her eyes away from the poster. If she saw it, she would become suspicious and raise the alarm. The boy began to pull Steffie's hair. She brushed his hand off gently, kissed him as she looked at him, and considered the officer.

"Stop it, honey. You're hurting Mom," she said loud enough for the officer to hear.

The officer still looked at her face. Somehow something didn't feel right with him. He knew there was something wrong with the lady in front of him, but he didn't know or wasn't sure what it was. Sweat broke out on his face as Steffie forced a smile at him. The boy pulled her hair again.

"Kids," she said jokingly while she looked at the officer in the face, still smiling.

The officer looked at the kid and then at Steffie's face.

"You have a fine son. What is his name?"

"Philip. After my father," she said softly.

"Nice name. Go in."

He waved them on into the train station.

"Thank you," she said as she hurried past.

The boy's mother and sister were waiting for them.

The station was crammed with a lot of passengers. It was the beginning of the new academic year, and many of the passengers were students, both local and international, coming to the university in Munich. Others used the station as a transit point to other cities. Steffie walked the woman to the information desk and set the boy down. She looked at the woman with a smile and shook hands with her.

"Thank you very much. You have been most helpful," the woman said.

"It was nothing. Take care."

The woman nodded and attended to her kids. Steffie rounded a group of black girls, rehearsing basic lessons they had learned in German.

"As soon as I master this language, I'm getting a job," one said.

"I will find me a nice German man and settle down," another contributed.

She smiled at their comments as she passed behind a security officer to the departure hall. She didn't think the students were in Munich to learn. They had come for some other reason. So far, she had had a quiet and easy way around the station by avoiding security and police officers. Passing them and avoiding looking into cameras made her movements easier. She needed information but couldn't approach anybody, so the information board would have to do. She was also hungry and thirsty. She had money but had to be careful. The woman would have helped her if she had remembered to ask for her help to buy soda and a sandwich.

Steffie hurried past an officer with a sniffer dog, wondering what the dog was meant for. Was it there to catch people carrying drugs, or was it there to help catch her? At the information board, she checked the departure time for the next train to Austria.

"1508. Fifteen minutes," Steffie muttered to herself.

A man collided with her as she turned to move, almost shaking her red wig off her head. She held it in place immediately as though she was scratching her head. She had to be careful not to raise her voice and draw attention to herself.

"Hey, are you blind?" she asked softly but angrily.

"I'm so sorry, ma'am. Can I buy you a drink to make up for the little disturbance?"

"Beat it."

She departed the board and took her place behind a group of men and women who were chatting while they waited for their train. She held a phone to her ear as if making a call while she scanned the departure hall.

In the corner of the big hall by a security officer, Martina stood searching for Steffie. Her eyes kept moving across the hall, scrutinizing every face. She scanned both sexes. Steffie could dress as a man and slip through her fingers, and Martina couldn't allow that to happen. Her informant had told her Steffie had been spotted in the clinic and then heading towards the train station moments after leaving the clinic. She had driven to the place immediately and hoped the information was accurate and that Steffie indeed was somewhere in the hall. If that were the case, she was on a winner. She had sent men after Steffie, and all had failed; she couldn't tell if some of them were in hiding or dead. She hadn't been able to locate the driver of the second SUV, which was found later in the pond along Route 6. Subsequently, she had decided to go after the target herself. If she failed, it was her fault.

Steffie walked briskly past the numerous passengers purchasing tickets. She was headed towards the restroom, walking past a male janitor. She looked back at him and gave a smile as she reached the door. The man was absorbed in his job and didn't pay her any mind. She opened the door and entered. Martina's eyes swept the lobby in front of the restroom, catching sight of the back of Steffie. She wasn't sure it was her but suspected it might be. A photo of Steffie she had received on her fax machine from a trusted colleague showed her back and hairstyle. Moving confidently, Martina took after her, shoving passengers out of her way.

Steffie had seen her as her eyes swept the hall but didn't know her. She knew Martina was there for her. She locked the door behind her and checked her looks in the mirror. Satisfied, she moved to the toilet window, opened it, and let herself out of the restroom through it. She shut it carefully after her. She couldn't afford to buy a ticket at the ticket booth. Anybody could spot her and alert the police. Even the woman whose son she had carried could identify her and betray her.

There was pounding on the door to the restroom. It went on for a while without a reply. Moments later, the door crashed open, and in came Martina and the janitor. She looked in every toilet stall for Steffie but didn't find her. She looked up and saw the window in the first toilet. She walked to it and tried it. It opened easily. Martina shook her head and smiled. She understood what had happened. She was right about the figure she had seen. It was Steffie. She couldn't tell if she was out in the tracks or used the train station as a decoy to prompt her pursuers into thinking she was in the station while she bolted in a different direction by another mode. If a car was waiting for her, for instance, she could be miles away by the time authorities realized they had been fooled. Martina walked out of the restroom, refusing to answer the janitor's question about why he was made to break down the door. He threatened to report her to the station manager so she would be charged for the repairs. She turned around and pointed a hidden gun at him. When the janitor saw the barrel showing in her coat, he kept quiet and lifted his hand in a sign of surrender. Martina moved on. She knew what she had to do. She didn't know Steffie's plans, but she would monitor the tracks while a phone call would help her men watch the streets, cafes, stores, and buses. She marveled at how Steffie could run around town with confidence, and no one picked her out. She was always a step ahead of the authorities. Martina smiled when she considered how the girl had managed to enter the station with all the police officers manning the entrance. She reached for her phone when she was away from the waiting passengers and made a call.

Steffie padded gently behind the offices. She heard computers and people communicating on phones and radios. They discussed trains, passengers, and signals.

She dropped to a crouch whenever she reached a window. At the end of the offices, the building was reduced to a shed. She heard voices and stopped by the wall of the last office. She braced on the wall and peered out. Two employees and an officer were chatting. She looked behind her and saw a tree whose branches almost touched the roof of the shed. She looked around and saw she was alone, but the men could easily see her if she made a dash for the tree. She observed them briefly and hurried to the back of the tree trunk. She waited for a while to be sure she hadn't been seen. Then she grabbed the trunk and gradually hauled herself up onto a bough. She carefully hurried to the upper branch and let herself down on the roof of the shed. A wall started from the shed for another fifty yards. She could see the tracks and a train departing. She waited for a while and then noticed the men under the shed were leaving. Moments later, she was certain they were gone. When she decided to jump down, a huge gantry across the tracks caught her attention. She changed her mind, let herself down on the wall, and walked close enough to access it. She observed it briefly and, with great effort, lunged at it, her hand catching the top frame. She hauled herself up and lay on it. She knew it was almost time for her train to start moving. Hanging on the gantry across the rail lines, she watched the tracks for signs of officers or dogs. No one seemed to have picked her out. She knew if Martina were there to arrest her, she would come after her in the restroom, and if she found it locked, she would raise the alarm or get men to search the tracks. Steffie jumped down and dropped to a crouch behind a car. She moved quickly across the cars, looking at the display at the top of the cars until she found the 1508 train.

The engine was running, indicating it was about to depart. Three police officers suddenly appeared in the tracks with dogs. They patrolled the rail lines. The dogs began to bark. Steffie observed the officers. They hadn't seen her, but the dogs had. It was time to change her position lest the dogs lead their masters to her. Then, she heard an announcement on the PA system that the train was about to move and that all passengers must board. She lurched under the car and quickly crawled away from the dogs. At the same time, she was careful not to go near the boarding platform where passengers could see her. The train had fifteen cars. Still holding onto the undercarriage, she watched the passengers for signs of Martina. The officers patrolled past, but to her surprise, the dogs were quiet. She heaved a sigh of relief as she dropped to the rail. She would need strength in her shoulders and arms for the journey and must conserve energy for now. The announcement came again on the PA system, informing passengers the train bound for Austria was about to move. While she observed the platform, she spotted Martina walking to the edge of it and holding the door of a car. She looked to both sides of the platform. Steffie knew the woman was looking for her.

A security officer alerted Martina to board if she was a passenger. Hesitantly, she got on the car as the doors shut. Moments later, the klaxon honked, and the train began to move. Steffie held onto the undercarriage. Suddenly, the dogs began to bark furiously at Steffie, bewildering the officers. She hadn't seen that another group of patrol officers was on the tracks. She looked in the eyes of the beasts as the train passed them. One broke loose from its holder and took after the train, still barking and trying to get under the train. She picked up a stone and hurled it at the head of the dog. It stopped but continued barking until the train began to gather pace.

The train passed farmlands and buildings, many of which were farmhouses. Hanging on the undercarriage was difficult. She couldn't hold on for much longer. She searched around her and saw a couple of steel corbels running from her head to the other end. They formed supporting brackets for something – she didn't know what. She could rest her feet on them, but she had to find a way of supporting her hands. She began to feel pain in her shoulder. The train plunged into a long, dark tunnel. Moments later, it emerged from the tunnel and cut through dense terrain. Steffie held onto the supports and turned gradually but carefully to face the rails. Then she placed each foot on the bracket, used one hand to hold onto the support while the other searched her pocket for her valuables. The packet was firmly buttoned. There was no way its contents would fall out. Her gun was also intact. The best place for her was the roof of the car, where she could relax in peace. She had to find a way of getting from where she was now and make her way up to the roof without being seen. Martina would be looking for her in all the cars. She knew that. And if she didn't find Steffie, she would probably ask her men to search the roof and undercarriage unless she was acting alone. Steffie looked ahead to see how best to move toward the coupling between the cars. That was her best chance of getting up the roof.

Meanwhile, a few passengers drank and played cards in the buffet car. Many didn't really enjoy the card game but didn't have much choice. In times past, there had been more games on the train to neighboring countries, but passengers turned it into a casino, betting and gambling big time. It had resulted in shootings and deaths. The practice had been terminated, and even when they played cards, conductors occasionally visited the car unannounced to check on activities, so it didn't violate regulations. Others read newspapers and magazines, some of which they found boring. One passenger questioned why they didn't show movies in the buffet car. He was told folks brought pornographic materials, slotted them in the tape deck, and watched them. The bartender told them once a man wanted to have sex with his girlfriend in the car while they watched porn. Two ladies walked into the car hand-in-hand past two men at a table. One man alerted his friend, who turned around and saw them. He reached out and spanked the buttocks of one of the ladies. She turned suddenly and slapped him on the face, attracting other passengers' attention. The guy's head hit the table, prompting laughter around him.

"If you think me a whore, you're mistaken! I'm old enough to be your mama."

The other passengers burst into laughter as her friend held her hand and snatched her away, leaving the man confused. The man, who couldn't stand the ridicule, rose suddenly and charged the lady. Her friend saw him, whipped past her, and stood in the way of the charging man. She dummied with a hand and slapped the face of the man as he took the bait. He still wouldn't give up. He shot a foot forward, and she stamped his knee while at the same time she palmed his chest so hard the man reeled and fell on the table behind him. Now he looked like a clown. The customers began to clap for the girl as more passengers barged in to see what was happening. The man's friend was embarrassed by his friend's failure. He rose and held him.

"I'm sorry for my friend's behavior. Please forgive him. He has had too many beers and liquor and doesn't know what he is doing."

"Oh, I think he knows what he is doing," replied the lady.

"I suggest you collect him and leave now before I call security," the bartender cautioned.

The man obeyed and departed with his friend as passengers mocked and called him names.

In the corner, Martina sat at a table, smoking. She had been sitting there for a while now as she thought Steffie might come for a bottle of water or food if she needed it. She was talking into her cell phone.

"I didn't count many. Eighteen, maybe twenty. Twenty minutes. Swift and clean. Don't spare. I may be wrong about the number. Whatever the case, this is one mission we can't afford to fail. You know where we are headed. If this slips through our fingers, we have lost everything," she said softly in a language that sounded Russian or Romanian.

"Got it."

She held the phone to her chest as a man took the seat across from her. He smiled at her. She ignored him and placed the phone back to her ear.

"Be very careful. She is smart," she advised.

She clicked the phone shut, stubbed out her cigarette, and rose. As she made for the door, the man grabbed her hand. She shoved him back into his seat, but he held onto her hand. A man seated at the next table stepped in and broke his grip, setting Martina free. She departed, smiling a thank you to the man. However, the man whose grip was broken was angry with the man who did it and started a quarrel with him. Soon, it turned into a fight that left bruises on their faces, while the angry man also had a broken nose that bled profusely.

Martina, meanwhile, began to search every car from the last to the first. She did it thoroughly, scanning all the female passengers in each car. She was certain Steffie was headed to Austria if she still had the envelope. With her posters everywhere across the nation, she couldn't stay in Germany. Her first option would be to depart the country and find a way of getting to a safe haven which was likely to be California, if the information she had received about Johann Steinberg was accurate. Once Steffie made it out of Germany, the chances of getting the parcel were lost, and Martina would have to find a place to hide. She was fully aware of this. More men would be sent from California, or locals would be hired to finish her off overnight. She had a team behind her, but that couldn't match the might of the caller's team. It occurred to her that Steffie could be hiding under the train, but this option she discarded on the grounds that she would get tired at some point and would need to move up to the roof or into one of the cars. Equally likely was the possibility of Steffie now on the run to Switzerland or Denmark on a bus or in a hired car. The girl was smart and capable of anything.

The clerk at the hotel had told Martina that Steffie was headed to Switzerland through Stuttgart. Martina couldn't believe she was en route to Austria because of Steffie. The girl didn't know Martina but had been smart enough to locate her in the train station and locked the restroom after her, knowing the woman would go after her. While she tried to get the door open, the girl had maneuvered out through the window and escaped. Martina shook her head as she exited a car and entered another. She wondered if it was possible that the girl who had beaten the man in the buffet car could have been Steffie. The possibility was there, but she doubted it. At least she got a good look at her. What about the other girl and the bartender? She stood for a while, contemplating whether to go back to the buffet car and check again. She decided to go for it. By the time she got there, the car was empty, and the bartender was dozing behind a pair of steel-rimmed spectacles she didn't wear earlier. She studied her face carefully and concluded she wasn't the target.

CHAPTER NINETEEN

The red VW van screeched to a halt. The driver had binoculars in his hand with which he observed the rail line. The few farms around were a quarter of a mile away. He checked his map and pointed to a particular section of the track.

"This is the spot. I received information from her that this is the right spot. Gentlemen, let's go for it."

"We hear you," replied a group of five men in dirty green coveralls.

The section gang of six got out of the van with tools in their hands and walked towards the track. Their business was to disrupt the rail lines.

"Remember this, gents…" they looked at him, "…the reward that awaits us is huge. Let us do a good job."

They took their places on the track and removed two sections out of the line. The lines looked normal from afar but were out of alignment nonetheless. It was good enough to derail any train that went over it. They did it quickly while looking to both sides for signs of human activity. Finally, an armed man rose up from the meadow and whistled to the section gang. The gang saw him and dashed to join him. The driver moved the van out of sight while they waited for the train's arrival. He was pleased with what Martina had arranged. A backup team to her mission waited in the brush. The man had been working for her for two years now and knew her well. She was determined not to fail. The police, fire service, ambulance and company that managed the rail would be called to deal with any derailment, but she needed her men on the scene to handle the mission before the police arrived.

Steffie wove slowly towards the coupling, panting heavily as she reached it. The train still moved at top speed. She came out from the undercarriage, clambered onto the coupling, and peered out at the two cars connected to it. Martina reached the door of the car, but as she was about to open it, she saw Steffie. She drew herself back and gently braced against the wall without alerting the other passengers. Steffie held the ladder at the edge of the car and began to climb. She did it quickly to avoid being seen. Martina peered out, waiting for her to reach the roof, and then she came out of the car. She checked her gun for rounds, placed it in her jacket pocket, held the ladder, and began to climb after her. She could have shot her, but she would need information if Steffie didn't have the envelope. If Martina shot and killed her but made a mess of it in the process and drew attention, she couldn't search her for the envelope. This was one opportunity she couldn't afford to blow. It might not come again if she missed her on this train. She smiled to herself as her head reached the roof. She would spring a surprise on Steffie since she wasn't expecting her, Martina thought. She raised her head slowly and peered out, her hand clutching her gun. Steffie relaxed on the roof, her hand also holding her weapon. Martina observed her for a while and then inched up a rung, her head appearing on the roof. She made another move up and leaned on the roof while she looked behind her. They were the only ones on the roof, although Martina couldn't tell if Steffie had an accomplice or hired men to back her up. She didn't know if there were other parties on the train who were also interested in the envelope. Steffie prostrated herself on the roof as Martina withdrew her head quickly from her position. Steffie's eyes roamed ahead on the roof, certain she was alone. Martina climbed up again and took a quick peek. The target remained prostrate. It was Martina's opportunity. She climbed up quickly onto the roof to within two yards of her target, cocking her weapon noisily. Steffie froze initially and turned over slowly. She saw Martina and remembered her instantly. The woman's presence on the roof stunned her. Martina smiled at her while her gun pointed at her face.

"Slide the gun to me!" Martina commanded.

Steffie obeyed her command while she studied her face. She didn't know what would happen to her. Although she smelled death in the woman's eyes, Steffie was also aware the woman couldn't kill her since she needed the envelope. Steffie was stable as she sat on the roof, but Martina battled the strong cold wind and struggled to steady herself.

"Give it to me! I mean the envelope!"

Steffie sat still but didn't move. Martina inched closer and pointed the gun at her face.

"That will be now! Many people have died because of your stupidity!"

"Really? I didn't know that! The last I checked, I didn't kill anyone, so if many have died as you say means you must be behind the deaths! Looking at you, I don't think you are from the police! That means you are working for yourself or somebody! Therefore, you are not a good person!"

"Don't fuck with me, young lady! Don't make me talk a lot! Don't let me lose my temper!"

Steffie reached into her bra, removed the fake black envelope, and stretched it towards Martina. She reached forward and snatched it from Steffie. Observing her closely, Martina opened it. She moved closer to her and stepped on Steffie's gun. Then she took out the list and opened it to read it. She looked at the list and shot Steffie an angry look. Now the train was slicing through more dense terrain, the trees passing in a blur. Martina struggled to hold the paper against the strong wind. She managed to take a look at the list while her gun pointed at Steffie.

"This is not the original! This is not the real thing! I want the real thing! And I want it now!"

"Really? What you have is all I received! If you think that is not the real thing, then you tracked me to this train for nothing! I suggest you go back and leave me alone!"

"Don't fuck with me, girlie! Hand it over, or you die! I am not joking! I don't joke! I don't laugh!"

"I don't care about your emotions! Whether you laugh or not has nothing to do with anything! I don't have what you want, and that's the truth!"

The train was fast approaching a big tree branch that hung across the rail in the distance. Martina's back was to it. Steffie saw it and smiled at Martina. The woman inched forward a bit and pointed the gun at Steffie's face.

"Go ahead and shoot me! If you think that will get you what you want, then do it! Otherwise, I suggest you pocket your weapon and check your notes before you attack people!"

The woman couldn't believe her ears. She had a gun pointing at the girl's face, but the girl wasn't afraid to die. She knew Martina couldn't kill her as long as she had cause to believe Steffie had the original. Martina had to be careful how she dealt with her. She needed the original first, and then she would decide whether to kill her or maim her. Steffie still smiled at her attacker, who hadn't bothered to look back. Steffie burst into a haughty laugh as the train neared the hanging branch. Steffie was certain the branch would hit the armed woman. She knew the impact would be great given the speed of the train. Moments later, Martina's back smashed against the branch with such force, she dropped her gun, the letter and fell on Steffie. Steffie shoved her off onto the roof, grabbed the gun and crawled quickly towards the edge, and caught the fake list, which was being blown away by the wind. She turned around and aimed the gun at Martina, who was trying to rise to her feet, still unsure what hit her. Steffie pocketed the list, aimed her weapon, and fired a shot into the woman's knee. Another bullet lodged firmly into the other knee. Martina slumped onto the roof; her wide eyes fastened on Steffie. She groaned and writhed in pain as Steffie lunged from the car onto the roof of the next car. Martina held her knees, reaching for her phone. She was grateful Steffie didn't kill her. At least she could make a call and still get the job done. Her men were in place, armed and ready for the task ahead. The girl might be dangerous and sleek but might not be a killer after all. Martina dialed a number while she crawled to the end of the car, telling somebody to kill the target without fail. A scream wouldn't help in the circumstances due to the noise made by the train's wheels, but a hand wave could alert somebody and get her help. She was fully aware of the arduous task of explaining to authorities and passengers how she ended up on the roof of the train with gunshot wounds to her knees. The train entered another tunnel and came out moments later. It skirted a chain of hills, over viaducts and descended gently into the meadows. She lay on the roof, showing her face to the door of the next car while she figured out what to say to the person who found her. On second thought, she withdrew from her position. She preferred her men ahead to find her instead and rescue her. Her life would be safer with them than in the hands of the police or any other person on the train.

The train driver, a slender, stern-looking man, gorged himself on a sandwich and listened to music at high volume. He made slight bodily movements at times. By all indications, he enjoyed his work – a job he had done for over twenty-five years. He looked ahead as he washed down the sandwich with soda. He liked such trips, which offered him the opportunity to see his twin girls, which he had with a Polish nun in Austria. His Ghanaian wife didn't know about it, and that was refreshing. He had kept it a secret for six years and made sure the family in Austria never contacted him at home on his cell phone or landline phone.

When the train hit a straight stretch, he whirled around and clapped his hands, wriggling his body like a snake. Ahead in the distance, the disrupted rails lay. He danced to the music while he finished his sandwich, his back to the tracks. He usually paid attention when the train neared a curve, tunnel, or went over a bridge. As he spun around slowly, he saw the mess ahead. It didn't mean much to him at first because the lines looked straight. On second thought, he decided to check to be sure as one of the lines didn't look straight. He reached for binoculars on a shelf behind him and looked out. The lines were out, slightly out of both vertical and horizontal alignment. He checked again, concluding he wasn't dreaming. The lines were out of alignment. He dumped the binoculars. The train was fast approaching the mess. He donned his spectacles that he yanked from a small case and checked again. It was real. The threat of derailment was there. It was imminent. He applied the brakes immediately, the wheels responding with a loud screech and sparks resulting from friction between the wheels and rails.

The application of the brakes jerked the passengers off their seats, causing them to crash into one another. Those who had been sleeping were jarred awake. They looked outside but found nothing. A few screamed, many wondering why the driver would do something like that.

Martina was forced off the roof onto the grass with such force she screamed on impact, rolling several times down the gentle slope into a ravine.

Steffie, meanwhile, slid off the roof but clung onto the window frame of a carriage. Her body dangled as the train slowed. She wasn't sure what the problem was but suspected something was wrong. She hadn't killed Martina and knew she could arrange for people to cause trouble if she had a means of contacting her team. She was capable of anything. All she had to do was make a phone call, and the work would be done.

The train was well patronized by both local and foreign passengers. It was always full of passengers to and from Austria. The company made sure competent drivers with long-standing experience handled the trip. Two men decided to contact the conductors to enquire about the incident. The train was still screeching, and they knew something was wrong with it; either the driver or the tracks. As they left the middle car, more passengers in other cars began to murmur, wanting to know what the problem was. A few shrieked and banged on the windows.

Steffie rammed her knee into the windowpane of the cabin and shattered it. She steadied herself and slipped in. She discovered to her amazement, a couple in bed, sitting upright with their eyes wide open. They clung to each other, wondering why Steffie had invaded their privacy. She smiled at them, noting they were not fully dressed. She didn't know why they chose to make love on the train. The cabin didn't look like one that was official. Somebody with authority on the train had been tipped off to allow this development. The couple looked like a boss and his secretary or a married man with his girlfriend. She stared at them. They stared back at her.

"Oh, I'm so sorry," Steffie offered.

The woman noticed Steffie's gun and the blood oozing from her shoulder. She nudged her man, who had also seen it. They held on firmly to each other, scared that Steffie might harm them. They knew she was dangerous by her looks.

"Please enjoy yourselves, but I'd rather you slip into your clothes because we might be in for a surprise."

"What?" asked the surprised woman.

"Have you taken over the train?" the man asked as he looked out the shattered window.

They heard screams as feet thumped past in the corridor. Steffie could tell passengers didn't know the makeshift cabin existed. She wondered why they were able to make love in the midst of chaos. They didn't seem distracted by the screech of the wheels. The man repeated his question as they began to dress.

"No, but the situation doesn't look good," Steffie replied as she moved to the window with her gun poised.

The frightened couple began to shudder, the woman advising that they hide under the bed. The man disagreed, opting instead to join the passengers running in the corridor.

The train was still moving but at a slower speed now, its wheels still screeching eerily with sparks. It was only yards away from the mess on the tracks, and the driver who had been trying very hard to stop the train and avoid derailment had given up. He had done his bit, but it hadn't been enough. With his mouth wide open in shock and fear, he opened the door and lunged out of the cabin. He landed with his head against a tree as the train derailed and impacted the ground. A couple of cars decoupled and crashed into one another, throwing passengers through smashed windows. Others were trapped by the mangled cars, blood and flesh littering the seats. The seriously wounded remained in place; a few who were mobile crawled to safety. There were screams everywhere.

Suddenly, the section gang sprang out from the grass with weapons. On the other side of the railroad, another group of armed men charged the cars. About twenty-five armed men surrounded the cars. They had received the message from Martina and knew exactly what to do.

"There are only twenty on aboard! Kill! Don't spare! Let's go! I said only twenty girls on board. Not men! Women!" the section commander reminded.

A man leaped out through a window. They ignored him, but when a woman did, they shot her. Men dashed out and got away through the brush. Another woman disembarked; the gang leader shot her in the head instantly.

The couple in the makeshift cabin heard the gunshots and screams. The woman moved to the window and saw the armed men as they gunned down the women. She turned to look at her man.

"They are killing women!" she yelled.

"Why would they do that? Quick, let's get out of here!"

"No, I don't want to die. If we get out, they will kill me on sight. Can you defend me without a gun? Even if you had one, they are many. You can't take them on. Let's stay here. The police will come to our rescue."

As they argued and contemplated what to do, Steffie burst in, dressed like a man. She wore a beard and mustache. No wig. The couple froze immediately at the sight of her gun and flinched into the corner. They smelled death in the room. What they feared had found them.

"Shh!" Steffie said.

She dashed to the window and peered out. An armed man stared at her. She aimed her gun and fired a shot into the arm that held the gun before he could act. He fell to the ground, his gun over his chest. She held the window and peered out again to ensure it was safe to go out. She leaped out through the window quickly and lay down in the grass. The couple moved to the window and saw her. She beckoned the woman to join her, assuring her she would be protected. The woman knew it was her only chance to survive. If the maniacs killing women got her, she was finished. Her man helped her to the sill of the window and pushed her off. She fell clumsily to the grass, rolling a couple of times to a small boulder. Steffie crawled to her and dragged her to safety behind a tree. The man hurried out through the window, landing in a thud. He rose immediately and took after the woman, making a big fuss that infuriated Steffie, as the woman had been skillful in her movements, but he had behaved in a silly way, drawing a shooter's attention.

The man raised his weapon and aimed, whistling to a colleague to shoot, so they didn't miss the woman. Steffie rose with frightening speed and gunned him down. She spun around quickly and hit the other shooter in the shoulder before he could do any damage. She hadn't acted with the intent of killing, but where she wasn't able to hit an arm or shoulder, death resulted. Steffie rose and observed as passengers ran. She was the target of the attack. Initially, she thought the driver had tried to avoid a rail block, but now she realized the truth. While she crawled towards a mound, she looked out for a crawling woman. She looked for Martina. She might have been knocked off the roof when the train derailed. If that was the case, she could be dead or alive. Steffie hadn't killed her because she didn't want many people hurt because of what she carried, but when she considered the likelihood of Martina calling her men to invade the train and kill women, she now wanted her dead.

She heard sirens in the distance. The police were en route to the scene. She heaved a sigh of relief, but she was still a wanted woman and had to get out of the area. She noticed the armed men were now shooting anybody on sight. The couple was out of danger. She could see their backs and was satisfied that she'd saved their lives. As she rose to escape from the police, a slap from behind caught her ear and sent her to the ground, losing her gun. Partially dazed, she turned over and looked up at her attacker. It was the section commander, and his gun was pointed at her face.

"Are you the target?" he asked.

Steffie didn't respond. She was disguised as a man, but somehow the man had seen her. Her features had betrayed her. The man kicked her rib. She felt the pain but didn't scream.

"Are you the reason why people are dying? Huh?"

She shook her head. Now the sirens were closer and louder. As the man looked over his shoulder momentarily to check how many officers were at the scene, Steffie reached for her gun and aimed at him. As he moved to shoot her, she fired right through his arm. The man dropped his weapon as another shot caught his knee. He fell towards her; she rolled out of his way. He fell to the ground as she crawled away from danger. When she spun around, the man had another gun which he intended to fire. She downed him with a shot to his face. Her shoulder ached again due to her little adventure and needed fixing. Anyone who saw the blood would instantly become suspicious of her and want to know what happened to her. Anything that exposed her had to be avoided. She crouched in the grass while she checked her valuables. She stopped occasionally and looked back. Ten police cars arrived at the scene from both directions. Armed officers sprang out of the cars, going immediately into action, gunning down eight attackers within moments. Excited by the work done by the officers, she decided to check if Martina was still alive. She hadn't had the opportunity to find out from the section leader whether he worked for her. The man would have killed her if she had wasted a moment. Another quick scan around convinced her the woman was dead.

While she observed the action, an idea struck her. She could do with one of the police cars. She still had her map and could make it to Austria, as the present location was close to the border. She studied one car carefully and began to crouch towards it. All the officers were busy dealing with the chaos. A couple of ambulances arrived on the scene. She looked to both sides of the car. No one watched her. Then she crawled to it, opened the door, and got in behind the wheel. As she started the car, two officers saw her and charged the car. She threw the gear into reverse, stabbed at the accelerator, and backed up. She lurched the car to the left and took off with a screech, spraying the pursuing officers with mud and grass. One took out his radio and made a call immediately. Steffie meanwhile motored the car through a marsh, thus slowing it down. She swerved the car out of the marsh onto dry ground, the undercarriage scraping stones and stumps. She reached for bread in her trouser pocket. It was compressed almost like a chapatti. During

the chaos, she had visited the buffet car and picked up two pieces of bread, ate one
and drank soda, and kept the other in her pocket.

As the car cut through the meadowland, a police chopper raked the sky above
her. She didn't have to kill the pilot or attack the chopper. It might be the opportunity she needed to get into Austria. She looked out the window and spotted the
pilot. He was alone. Surprisingly, the chopper hadn't attacked her. She knew why.
The officer who had alerted the chopper hadn't identified her. He had probably
said a passenger was running away in a police car. That meant the chopper was to
keep track of the car until a ground team impounded it. There were officers posted
ahead of her somewhere in the bush. She had to avoid them. She looked out again
at the chopper. It lurched close to the car, the pilot studying her face. He wouldn't
know the driver was a female. Steffie's disguise was still firmly in place. The chopper banked across the car to the driver's side. Now he could see the driver, but
Steffi hid her face. She slammed on the brakes suddenly and halted the car as the
chopper tried to cross to the other side. She got out quickly through the window
as the chopper was directly overhead. She leaped and grabbed the skids of the
chopper. The pilot, who was unaware Steffie was hanging underneath his chopper,
hovered above the car, waiting for the driver's next move. He waited to see what
the driver would do. He radioed to inform a team the target was cornered and that
the car was stuck in a marshy area and couldn't move. He said the driver remained
in the car and that the team should move in quickly and arrest the driver.

Meanwhile, Steffie hauled herself up slowly to the passenger door. She held the
handle, opened the door suddenly, and clambered onto the chopper. The pilot was
stunned by her sudden intrusion. He had grossly misjudged the situation and conveyed the wrong message to the ground team. It was a colossal blunder that could
cost him his job and create problems for the police. The two stared at each other
like lovers who had found themselves hours after a shipwreck. Steffie gave a thin
smile. The pilot didn't respond. He had thought of the driver as a man, but now
he saw a woman. He focused on the panel, knowing who was in his chopper. The
unmistakable face of Steffie was staring him in the face. Even in her disguise, he

could still make her out. She jolted him with a sharp object prompting him to take a look. A gun was sticking in his ribs. Surprised, he moved to press a button. She moved the gun to his face, shaking her head slowly. The man got the message as he banked the chopper.

"I want you to stop the chopper! Don't move it away from here!" she ordered.

The pilot ignored her. She hit his chest with the butt of her gun.

"I don't want to harm you! Don't force me to do otherwise!"

The man obeyed and hovered the chopper over a bare patch of ground. She reached for her road map and opened it. Staring at him with the gun to his face, she consulted with the map intermittently. She observed the path she had outlined with ink. The pilot made a move for his weapon with one hand; Steffie noticed him and put the gun to his nose.

"One wrong move, and you die! I told you I don't want to kill you! Do what I tell you to do and live!"

The man nodded.

"Turn around!"

"What?" the pilot asked angrily.

"You heard me! I said, turn the chopper around! Do it now!"

She sat by the pilot with the gun to his head.

"Where to? Where do you think my turning around will take us?"

"It will take us over the border into Austria! Take me to the nearest airstrip!"

"Hey, do you know what you're doing? You are getting us into trouble!"

"Shut up and move it!"

The chopper banked and knifed through the air.

"Look, before I can land anywhere in Austria, I need permission! Immigration is very tight there! Why don't you get off now somewhere in the quiet villages down there and melt among the people! I don't think they know you! You will be fine there! I will make sure not to tell anyone!"

"Don't tell me what to do! If you need permission to land, I suggest you get it now before we get there! I don't want to get there and be kept waiting! Do it now!"

"I have to state my business in Austria! What do I tell them?"

She stuck the gun under his sunglasses, very angry.

"Stop bothering me and get on with it!"

"I just don't want to get arrested! That's all! I have to do what the law says!"

She hit his chin with the butt of the gun. The pilot felt the pain and focused. He could be killed if he continued challenging her. He got on the mike and initiated contact with the nearest Austrian airstrip. She pressed the gun further to his face. The pilot knew he had to do a good job. He had to comply fully to save his life. He wouldn't lose anything if he could alert the police immediately after dropping Steffie. She would be picked up in Austria within minutes.

CHAPTER TWENTY

The control office of the airstrip was crammed with computers and monitors. Printers and copiers hummed and churned out papers with maps and charts while fax machines spewed out faxes from Austria and beyond. Air traffic control operatives sat behind an array of consoles and monitored images of flights while others busied themselves scrambling orders into phones. A young, suited female stood by a screen, fidgeting with a pencil in her hand. The other hand held a handset to her ear.

"I cannot grant it," she advised.

"It's an emergency! I repeat, it's an emergency!" a male voice insisted.

"We are talking space here. If there is no space, where are you going to land?"

"Thank you for the permission! I thought you would understand."

The line went dead before she could say another word, leaving her surprised. She hadn't granted permission, yet the caller had assumed she had and hung up on her. She set the phone on a desk and moved to the window to see which plane wanted to land on her strip.

Steffie looked through the windshield, her gun still trained on the pilot. The chopper rumbled on over trees. Occasionally, it skimmed past the roofs of farmhouses and barns. The pilot was calm now. He was at ease. Steffie wouldn't kill him. He had sought permission from Steffie to radio back his team to ignore his earlier message about the car being stuck in the marshy grassland. The team had been angry about the prank call, threatening to report his conduct to their superior. He would have questions to answer when he got back. Asked to state his current location, he had told them he was following the suspect who was running on foot and that he would get in touch with them when the time was right. A small airfield shot into view, drawing a thin smile on Steffie's face. She could see light planes arrayed side by side. They saw the control tower and a couple of structures.

"That is the border!" the pilot pointed.

Steffie ignored him. Beyond the border lay dense woods.

"We are now in Austria! Happy?"

"Shut up and focus! I have spared your life, and I think you should be grateful!"

"I am, actually! I just felt the urge to inform you!"

Steffie looked at the pilot.

"Now what?" he asked.

"We don't have to land on the strip! Just drop me in the woods! I will be fine there!"

The chopper skimmed just above the land and hovered briefly, trying to find a safe place to drop her.

"Remember, I have spared your life!"

"I know, and I will not alert the authorities either!"

She nodded, tucked her gun in her trousers as the chopper went close to the ground. Then, she jumped off the chopper into a clearing.

The pilot was relieved. He reached for his radio and called his team. He had a perfect explanation for what had happened. The chopper banked and skimmed away as Steffie recovered from her fall.

Steffie knelt by a tree and consulted her map. She looked around her and rose, walking down a path towards the control tower. The pilot had given her his word, but that was no guarantee that he would keep quiet. He had to explain to his team what had happened. A good explanation was needed as to why the suspect disappeared without a trace. When pressed, he would speak and tell them where to find her. She stopped for a while, watching the tower. She was headed in the wrong direction. The pilot could have alerted the tower to look out for her. If Martina survived and found out her body wasn't among the dead, she would know she had made it to Austria. She wouldn't give up until Steffie was dead. While she contemplated which direction to go, a cab raced past her to the landing strip. She observed a passenger alight and walk into an office. Up in the control tower, she could see the suited young woman. She watched Steffie with binoculars, and Steffie knew instantly the woman had seen her jump off the chopper. She had to avoid the tower and get out of the place. If she didn't know her or hadn't heard about her, there was no cause for alarm. The woman would probably look on her as an illegal immigrant from Eastern Europe or South America. Some traffickers ferried their people in choppers across borders and dropped them in the villages of the target destination. The cab returned towards her. She looked down to avoid the driver's face. At the same time, she monitored the strip for signs of security officers coming after her. She wouldn't be standing there if she didn't work there. A check on her gun satisfied her. She would get to a town where she could access the internet and book a flight out of Austria. Then she would call her cousin to check on her. The cab neared her. She removed the beard and mustache, flagged down the cab, and got in.

The driver looked at her in the rearview mirror. She looked forward and then out the window.

"Are you new in town?"

"Hell no. What makes you think of me as a stranger or tourist? This is where I come from. I have been away for years in Graz helping my family farm."

"Good to hear that. Where do I drop you?"

"The nearest place I can get access to the Internet."

The driver nodded, smiling as he swerved the cab onto a street that joined a major road. He knew where to take her and how to get there quickly. Traffic usually wasn't heavy at this time of the day. Steffie still looked out while her hand relaxed on her gun hidden beneath her shirt.

The cut-rate shop that sold used books and office equipment stood alone by the street that linked all the farming communities in this part of Austria. A plump man sat behind the counter watching TV, a small bucket of popcorn on his lap. Steffie got out of the cab, crossed the street, and walked in. She spotted the man, walked to the counter, and said a word to him. He put the popcorn aside, went into an inner room, and backed out instantly with a laptop. He set it on a desk in the corner and beckoned Steffie to use it.

The cab waited for her, the driver relaxing behind the wheel with a newspaper. He didn't like sports but forced himself to read them. Business wasn't good these days. He would wait for this customer from Graz.

Steffie set to business immediately as the man attended to a customer. She browsed the website of an airline and booked a flight, took out the credit card Randolph had given her, and entered the details. Soon, she had completed her transaction, snatched a pen from the tankard on the desk, and scribbled something on the back of a business card. She put the card into her pocket and closed the website, deleting the history of websites visited in the last hour. She didn't want to leave traces that could lead anybody to the airline and her. She walked to the counter, paid for the service, and turned to leave.

"Your change," reminded the man.

"Keep it. Thank you for the service."

"Thank you."

The excited plump man admired her as she departed the shop. Then, she remembered something and returned to the man. She asked him if she could use the restroom. The man pointed to a tiny corridor to his right, winking at her. She hurried into the restroom. A minute later, she opened the door and peered out at the man. Three customers stood in front of him. It was the right time for her to move. She stepped out and backed out of the shop with short black hair, wearing her sunglasses. The man didn't have to see her new look. She knew how to deal with the driver when she got to her destination.

The ride through town felt good. No one had bothered to confront her. The information hadn't gotten to Austria, or the security authorities here were relaxed and couldn't be bothered by a German girl on the loose in Munich with a deadly weapon. They minded their business, having their own problems to deal with. Workers in the health sector had embarked on industrial action, complaining about the massive influx of foreign doctors from Eastern Europe and Cuba who were prepared to work even more hours per day for less salary than Austrian doctors and nurses. The industrial workers union also complained about cuts in the risk allowance they received. Steffie noticed the driver stole a glance at her.

"Nice hair," he said without looking at her.

"Thank you."

"Why black and not red or blue? I think you would have looked your best in blue."

"I'm glad to hear that, but I prefer black because my boyfriend has been cheating on me with a friend of mine. So he will be expecting a girl with brown hair. If I suddenly appear with black hair, I will catch them by surprise. What do you think? Blue hair, as you suggest, will give me away easily. The moment he sees blue, he will want to know who is wearing it."

"I agree with you."

The cab went past the airport. She looked back suddenly at a café, attracting the driver's attention.

"Bingo! Can you please stop the cab?" she asked.

"What is the problem? Have you spotted him?"

"Yes. I have seen him with a girl I suspect might be his new girl. He should be at work by now, so I don't know what he is doing here. Please stop the cab."

"Wait, let me find the right place to stop; otherwise, a traffic warden will slap a fine on me."

"Thank you very much. You may have saved my relationship," she said as she got out of the cab.

The driver watched her run to a huge store and brace against its wall. She peered out in a direction and withdrew her head. The driver shook his head, turned the cab, and headed back in the opposite direction. He waved at Steffie, who put her index finger over her mouth to indicate he should keep quiet. The cab moved on. Steffie waited for a while and then dashed behind the next column. After two minutes, when she was certain the driver was gone, she stepped out from behind the column and stretched her neck as if looking for somebody. She dashed back to the point where she was dropped by the cab and waited by a store, her back to the street. She gave money to a small girl to buy her cookies and candies. She would wait here for a while and then rush into the airport. She didn't want the driver to know she was flying out of the country and had to make it look like she was tail-gating her boyfriend. The girl brought her shopping. She took the small plastic bag and gave the change to her. The happy little girl pranced away. Behind her, across the street, a huge wall clock hung on the wall of a housing complex. She checked the time. She was on time. It would be better for her to go into the airport and wait, but if she waited for a long time, security could become suspicious and want to know who she was and why she had been sitting there for that long. She began to eat her candies and cookies. She had to fill every space in her stomach as she didn't want to talk to anybody on the flight. She wouldn't want to eat whatever was served on the flight and therefore not speak to any cabin crew member. She read notices on a board attached to the side of the store as she ate. She heard voices behind her but didn't turn to look back. Two men were discussing her.

"Who cares about a cadet freak on the run?" one said.

"If it's not important, why would the German authorities bother to alert us?"

"I don't care what they think. It's not important to us. Just forget about it. I have a case to answer in court concerning battery."

"Oh shit! That case? You know I expected your wife to take it easy and settle it out of court."

"That was my expectation too, but it didn't happen. As you can see, I couldn't be bothered about the German shit. Let the girl or whoever she is walk around town. I will grant her refuge if I see her. Who knows, she could become my next wife."

They laughed as they turned the corner. Steffie glanced at them. They were police officers. Her photos must be at the airport. She smiled as she took a bite of her cookie. She would definitely find a way of getting on the flight. Once she had made it out of Germany, there was no turning back. She knew that for certain.

Chapter Twenty-One

San Diego

The huge aircraft touched down on the runway and began to taxi, the speed reducing gradually. Moments later, Steffie dropped from the landing gear onto the tarmac. She fell heavily and rolled a couple of times, rose to her feet, and began to move. She staggered a bit for a while, and then she regained full consciousness. Behind her, a refueling truck raced towards a shed. She waited for it to reach her. Then she ran after it, grabbed a ladder at the rear, and hauled herself onto the wing above it. As the truck moved, she noticed a fence to her left. Other structures were scattered around that part of the airport. She jumped off the truck when it turned towards a workshop she suspected might be the point where it drew fuel to refuel aircraft. Security had still not picked her up. That unsettled her in a sense as it could be a trap to lure her to a place where she would be arrested. She rose to her feet after rolling a couple of times on the tarmac. She held onto the fence, surprised it didn't raise the alarm anywhere in the airport, scaled it to the other side, and disappeared from the scene.

Steffie got out of a cab. She had bought a baseball cap and new clothes from a store along the way from the airport. She would be safe now once she got in touch with Johann. As she headed for the payphone, she admired the city of San Diego. She reached for the card as she entered the booth. She began to dial the number on the card.

Johanne was a short, slender man with a heavy mustache. He was reading a newspaper in his lounge when his cell phone rang. He took it from his pocket, flipped it open, and placed it to his ear.

"Hello?" he asked.

"Johann Steinberg?"

"Who are you?"

"Comb."

Johann beamed proudly and rose to his feet immediately.

"Ass! Welcome home! Shall I come and get you? Or should I send somebody to collect you?"

The call ended suddenly, to his surprise.

"Hello! Hello! Hello!"

He dumped the newspaper and leaped for joy. He checked the caller's identity and called back the number, but no one responded. He tried again, with the same result. He knew the call came from a payphone. The caller would definitely call again. He had heard of the heist at the museum and followed carefully all that happened afterward. All hope disappeared when he heard two of the three men he had sent were dead. He had harbored, without proof, the impression that the third man had disappeared with the envelope. He had also heard about Steffie but didn't think highly of her as he didn't believe everything he heard about her. The code mentioned by the caller told him the parcel had arrived in California. He couldn't explain how the caller had pulled it off and wouldn't bother to attempt an explanation. It could have been given to her by Randolph. The only way Johann's real name could have been known by the caller was through Randolph. He knew Randolph might have died, but the caller knew something, which was why she had made contact. He looked out the rear window of his kitchen, hands on his waist. He didn't care if Randolph was alive. He would get in touch with the caller and hear what she had for him.

"Jeurgen, here I come. You thought you could sink me, but you were wrong. I have survived, and hopefully, I will have the list. But, once I lay hands on it, you are in trouble. You are in serious trouble. I will make sure you go way down and never rise again. I will send you to the bottom of hell. There, you can have dinner with the devil, but out here in San Diego, there is no place for scumbags like you," he said as he leaned on the wall by the window, laughing.

He made coffee and sipped while he waited for the caller to make contact again.

Outside his house, a white sedan with two men in it waited on the street. It had arrived there two minutes before the call came through and had been standing there since. The men, who were both armed, had earpieces in their ears and had been listening in to Johann's conversation with Steffie. One had an electronic device in his hand, which he studied while the other watched Johann's house.

"Got the location?"

"Yeah. It came from a payphone on the boulevard south of the airport."

The driver took out his phone and dialed. A response came instantly.

"Speak."

"She's out! She eluded immigration. God knows how she did it. Comb Ass is the code. Boulevard, south of the airport."

"You got it."

He snapped the phone shut and glanced at his colleague.

"What about him? What do we do with him?"

"We are not here to kill him unless he does the unthinkable. We will let him live for now."

While they discussed, a biker emerged from the rear of Johann's residence onto the end of the street and rocketed out of sight. The men shared a look, wondering if that was Johann. Had he communicated again with the caller without they hearing? They started the sedan and took after the biker. By the time the sedan reached the junction, the bike was gone. The men shared a worried look, but there was no cause for alarm. They knew where it was headed, and their men would be waiting for him, assuming he was going to meet the caller. The passenger took the driver's phone and dialed.

"Speak," the voice said.

"A motorbike is en route. Stay alert."

"You got it."

Steffie plodded down the boulevard. She felt tired and weak. She looked back anytime she heard a car, hoping it would be a cab, but none came along. A plane flew above her, reminding her of her trip to California. She had walked boldly to the boarding gate wearing her hat over the short black wig and shown her boarding documents. Airport and airline security were simply not concerned about a girl on the run from Germany. She had boarded the flight without being asked questions and slept for most of the trip after telling the hostess not to disturb her with food and drinks. She had told them she was full and wouldn't need anything. When the pilot had announced they were about to land, she had visited the toilet briefly and made her way to the pantry when the crew members were all busy attending to passengers. She had used the elevator to get to the cargo hold from where she had worked her way to the landing gear as it came out from the underbelly of the plane. She smiled to herself, wondering how this story would look in a novel. She couldn't believe she managed to pull it off.

Suddenly, a motorcycle spun from an inlet onto her path and stopped, startling her. She stepped back and stared at the rider. The rider briefly looked at her portrait in his hand and considered her face. Satisfied she was the target, he dismounted and neared her. She remained calm and studied his face as he approached. She was ready for any surprises. She didn't have her gun but had purchased a hunter's knife on her way from the airport.

"Johann sent me to fetch you," the rider said.

"What else did he tell you?"

"He gave me the code. He doesn't know you, but he has your photo."

"Show it to me."

The rider showed it to her. She stared at him suspiciously, knowing anybody could have tapped their conversation and gotten the code.

"Ass," she said.

"Comb."

The man mounted his bike, Steffie sat behind him. He started the bike and revved it.

"Ready?" he asked.

"Yup."

"Alright. Let's go."

Suddenly, a truck spun out of control onto the street and sideswiped a parked sedan. As soon as the truck drew close enough to see Steffie's face, the men in the truck opened fire on them. The bike jerked forward and took off. The truck gave chase, still firing at the two. Ahead of the boulevard, a biker emerged from a feeder road and started firing at the two. The rider returned fire at the biker with one hand while the other held the handlebars. Steffie hid her face behind the rider, hoping she wasn't hit. At the same time, she wished she had a gun. Now the bikes were close. The rider shot the biker in the chest while the biker's shot hit the rider in the eye. The biker fell off his bike, which skidded into the path of the truck. The truck swerved to the side to avoid it but ran over the biker. At the same time, the rider lost control and headed for a parked car. He held his eye, trying to contain the blood loss. Steffie saw the danger and lunged off before it impacted the car's trunk, throwing the rider over its hood. He flew a few more yards and smashed into a tree, falling to the ground on his back. When Steffie turned, the armed men in the truck were right behind her. They all pointed their guns at her. She studied their faces and then glanced at the rider on the ground. People knew she was in California and were prepared for her. She couldn't tell if her phone call to Johann had triggered it. Somehow, she suspected somebody might have paid for her to have easy access to California so they might have what she carried. Her escape from Austria to the States had been far too easy. The leader of the men in the truck waved her to move into the truck. She stood watching them briefly. Two men inched closer to her, held her by the arms, and dragged her towards the truck. She took another look at the rider's body, wondering which of the two teams was genuine. Hesitantly, she climbed into the back of the truck. They flanked her on a bench as the truck moved on. She stole a glance at the men at times, blaming herself for not checking a few more details before mentioning the code on the phone. She still had her knife, but without a gun, she couldn't handle the men. She was outnumbered. She looked at the leader, resisting the temptation to ask where she was being taken. If they came from Johann's camp, then there was no need to worry about anything.

On the other hand, if they came from different quarters, then she could be killed after they had gotten from her what they wanted. Randolph had said some-body wanted to cover his ass, and Johann was the only person who could identify him. She knew there were two parties interested in the envelope she was carrying. There could be others perhaps that she might not be aware of. Anything was pos-sible.

The team leader glanced at her face and smiled. She ignored him. He held her chin gently, caressing it. She parried his hand away immediately. The men laughed.

"You're a phenomenon, lady. I give you that. I mean, you are quite a character. Anybody who hears your story would salute you."

She ignored his comments. The man considered his men.

"What do you say to her story, guys?"

"We agree with you, boss. She is smart and a phenomenon. Your words are correct."

He held Steffie's hand. She snatched her hand from his.

"You actually outsmarted the German authorities? And then you taught US immigration a lesson to get this far? You are a genius. Can you please tell me how you did it? With you in town, who is safe in San Diego? My wife's genitals can disappear, for instance, without her knowing. The president of the United States can disappear while delivering the State of the Union address."

The men laughed again as the truck hit a beach road.

"I've lost faith in US Immigration," a man lamented.

Steffie pursed her lips as she studied the guns the men held.

"You see, what I don't understand is this. You did all that great stuff in Germany, and God knows where else only to fall into my arms. This is much ado about nothing. Tell me something, what's next for you, little flower? What did you achieve with all the ingenuity? It was just a waste of time, effort, and taxpayer's money. You have gained something, though. And that is, you have succeeded in exposing serious flaws in German police and immigration. That could be beneficial to robbers and drug barons. I wouldn't be surprised to hear of rampant robberies in Germany."

"That affects us too. She walked into our yard without knocking, and none of us heard it. The next thing we knew, she was having lunch in our kitchen," another man said.

She still didn't respond. The men laughed themselves silly as the truck turned into a residential street. It made a series of turns and ended up on a road by a river. Steffie looked out and saw a small dock. On the other side lay grassland interspersed with stunted trees. She had checked her pockets; everything was intact. She was surprised the men hadn't frisked her to take anything from her. Whoever they worked for must have issued a stern warning that she wasn't to be touched. She hadn't come to San Diego to fight. The killing couldn't continue. Already, too many had perished in Germany. If the madness persisted here, it would draw attention to the authorities and possibly lead to her arrest. This had always been her guide, but if they forced her, she knew what to do.

The truck pulled up by the dock. The men got down and hauled Steffie out towards an inflatable equipped with an outboard motor. A muscular man in combat fatigues started the engine as the men shoved Steffie onto the inflatable. The man turned to see her, smiling shyly at her. She looked at the man's height and biceps, her heart pounding within her chest. Then, the man yanked a rifle from a bag near her, pointed it at the men, and gunned them down. Steffie was shocked as the men fell one after the other. The truck driver backed up immediately and barreled out of sight. The man considered Steffie again. He glanced at Steffie, still smiling.

"You look surprised. Why is that? This is familiar terrain to you, isn't it? So don't give me that funny look."

"Where are you taking me?"

"I'm taking you to my house. I'm going to have fun with you. It's been a while since I had a woman of your type. Since I got off the Marine payroll, I haven't had good women. I have sex only with women in uniform. Marines. Army. Navy. Air force. Police. Coast Guard. Immigration. Customs. Name it. Hahaha! Would you like to know what they are like in bed?"

"I haven't been in any of them, so why choose me? And no, I don't want to hear about the styles they prefer."

"I know you haven't been in any of the services I mentioned, but you are worth more than the entire team I have mentioned. You have done what millions cannot do. One night with you in bed is worth sleeping with all the women in the world. And that is what I want. What do you think? I just want to know what you taste like in bed. I know how good you are with guns. I know how smart you are with the German authorities. Today, history will be made. I will have a German genius in my room. I can't believe this is happening to me."

The man laughed as the inflatable lurched forward.

The inflatable cruised very fast on the river. She had to do something to stop him from taking her to his house, as he said. She hoped it was just talk and that he worked for somebody. She couldn't take him on unless she was sure of victory. Whatever she did had to be carefully thought through.

Meanwhile, in the grasses at the bank, the truck driver had the crosshairs of his rifle on the muscular man. He had given him the impression he was scared and taken off. He had turned around and moved back to the same spot where they had left Steffie when the inflatable departed. He fired a shot that missed the target. He aimed again, fired, and missed. The inflatable was tearing away from him. He reloaded quickly, aimed, and fired a third shot. The bullet hit the head of the muscular man. Steffie watched as the man tumbled over into the water. She knew he had been shot by somebody on the river bank. When she turned, she saw it was the truck driver. His rifle was on her now. She ducked and scooped up the muscled man's rifle. She jerked her head up and fired a barrage at the driver before he could shoot. The driver dropped to the ground and returned fire. She ducked, crawled to the outboard motor, and killed the engine, stilling the raft. The man reloaded as she spun the inflatable around and started the motor. As the raft gunned for the bank, she opened fire on the man. A bullet caught the man in the chest, a second hitting his shoulder as he returned fire. He dropped his weapon and reeled back in horror. Moments later, the inflatable reached the bank; she jumped off onto the bank and approached the driver. She held his arm and turned him over, but he was gone. She dumped her rifle. A search on him returned nothing of importance. She lifted him, staved in his face, and shoved him to the ground. Scooping up his weapon, she located the truck and got in. The key was still in the ignition. She started it and moved on. While she drove, she paid attention to both sides of the road. She didn't know the place well but had a rough idea of how they got there. She could work her way back to the boulevard. From there, she could reach where she wanted to go. She knew Johann's residential address. That was her next destination. Men were dead again, and possibly more would follow. She shook her head. She had done everything she could to avoid it but fate preferred otherwise. She hoped Johann was a man of his word, a man of integrity. If he turned out to be another man, a man contrary to the impression Randolph had given, she would be drawn into another battle of survival. A battle whose outcome could be anything from one death to many. That would be one unwarranted situation too many. She hoped to make the US her new home. That meant keeping a low profile for the rest of her life. If her past kept chasing her and people kept pursuing her for the envelope, she would have no option but to defend and protect herself. Anything that would draw the attention of the authorities had to be avoided.

The truck pulled up next to a small commercial area with shops that sold hardware, gardening and outdoor furniture, and DIY stuff. A man in front of a barbering salon admired Steffie as she got out of the truck. She ignored his smiles as she approached a phone booth. A short, slender woman walking two big dogs came her way. Steffie stopped, glancing at her. When the woman drew near, she took the card that contained Johann's residential address.

"Excuse me?" Steffie said.

The woman paid attention as she sized her up and then glanced at the truck. The dogs began to pull the woman. She fought to control them.

"Do you know the way to this address?" Steffie showed the address to her.

The woman studied it briefly and nodded gently, "Sure. Go down the freeway and take the third exit. There are a couple of residential developments there. You will find it there. You can't miss it."

"Thank you."

The woman moved on as the dogs jolted her with a sudden coordinated pull. Steffie hurried into the phone booth, surprised the woman kept such dogs when she wasn't strong enough to control them. They could easily topple her to the ground. While she dialed, she glanced at the front of the salon and noticed the man was no longer there. As she waited for a response, her eyes strayed to the truck and spotted the man by the passenger window, looking into the truck. She hung up instantly and stepped out of the booth, dropping to a crouch. She hurried to the trunk and peered around the tailgate at the man. He took out his cell phone and was about to make a call. She rose and dashed to the man, who spotted her and turned a gun on her. At the same time, she parried the hand that held the gun away from her with frightening speed. A shot rang out immediately as a struggle for control of the weapon began. The man elbowed her chest; she jammed her fingers into his eyes. The man reeled for a moment as he tried to focus. She followed up with a powerful punch to his face, felling him. As he tried to rise, she kicked his face and broke his nose. The man dropped the gun and held his face. She took the gun and hurled it into the truck, grabbed the man's foot, and twisted it so violently, the man screamed.

"Who the hell are you, and what were you looking for in my truck?"

"That isn't your truck, is it?" he pointed.

"Well, you may be right, but it is mine now. Now answer my question."

"I don't have a name. My business is to find the parcel. I have to be honest with you that I don't even know what the so-called parcel is or looks like."

"So you just acted because somebody said to find the parcel?"

"That is correct. I take orders. I follow instructions. They said find the parcel, but I don't know what to look for. I was actually looking for anything unusual. A bag or briefcase, a box or an envelope, say."

She kicked the man's face again and caught his lips.

"Get out of here! And tell whoever sent you that I don't have anything. If he thinks I have the parcel, he should come and get it himself, whoever he or she is. I will not kill you. I don't go about killing people. Get out of here!" she dismissed him.

The man, who was bleeding in the mouth and nose, staggered to his feet and took off.

"Thank you!" he offered as he turned the corner.

She hurried back into the phone booth.

CHAPTER TWENTY-TWO

Johann sat on his balcony with the cell phone in his hand. He had received news about the death of the man he sent to collect Steffie. The abduction or disappearance of Steffie unsettled him. He couldn't tell who was behind it, but Jeurgen came to mind. He was the only one who was fighting to keep his identity secret. It was possible that somebody in Germany who knew the significance of the envelope's contents had become an interested party. Johann worked with the CIA for five years before being released on compassionate grounds. He still had friends at the agency. Perhaps a call to one of them might help him locate the caller. As he moved to make the call, the cell phone rang suddenly, startling him. He flipped it open.

"Ass."

"Comb. I was wondering when you would call again," he beamed.

"I'm coming in."

"There are men. They are armed. They are in a white sedan. Be careful," he warned in perfect German.

"Thanks for alerting me," she acknowledged in German.

He smiled and licked his lips, punching the air in delight as the call ended. He looked up at the ceiling and walked to the window. He parted the curtain slightly and peered out at the white sedan. He knew they were there to monitor his activities. They had parked the car some distance from the entrance to his house and pretended to be waiting for somebody. Sometimes, they got out to buy snacks and cigarettes. They made calls and smiled at passers-by. He hadn't bothered to confront them because they had every right to be there since they weren't a threat to the street and the neighbors. That was the law, but frankly, they were a threat to him. He returned to his seat. Hopefully, Steffie would come in with the parcel. He couldn't wait for the moment when it would land in his hands. He had been praying for years for this moment, and finally, it was here. Someway, somehow, his dream was about to become a reality. Steffie had turned out to be the savior, the hero of the exciting adventure story. He regretted the death of the three he had sent to Germany but took consolation in the fact that the trip hadn't been in vain. It had yielded the desired result. Somebody was en route to his home with the parcel, and that was all that mattered to him. He considered Jeurgen and the night he and his uncle Gerhard invaded their home. He remembered his parents and the way they died. He recalled what happened to his two sisters and how the little money and the treasure that had been in the family for years were taken away by the invaders. Johann shook his head, fighting tears from his eyes. Sometimes, he dropped into depression when he recalled that night. He had been adopted by a philanthropist and brought to the US, but the man had abused him since he was six until he got fed up, mustered his courage, and reported him to a neighbor. The adoptive parent was investigated and sent to jail. The neighbor had offered to take care of Johann and seen him through his education. He had spotted Jeurgen at a fundraising party in Boise, Idaho, and identified him. He had threatened to expose him, but the man whose new status he knew little about sent him to jail on framed charges. A move Johann regretted to this date. He hadn't been smart and skillful in his approach and handling of his quest to get revenge and send Jeurgen to jail. Today, he had a perfect opportunity, and he knew better. He was fully aware of who he was dealing with. Jeurgen was powerful and connected, and only evidence with a very high value could pull that off. Steffie was the provider. He burst into laughter, wondering how she would come in.

"The sucker is coming home to roost," the man behind the wheel of the white sedan said as he stubbed out his cigar.

His colleague glanced at him, wondering why Johann hadn't bothered to leave his house.

"Yes. I heard that in the conversation. I'm worried though about the behavior of the man in the house."

"What about him? He knows we are here. He is scared, and that is why he can't go out. Is that what your worry is about?"

"I think he is up to something."

"Something like what? The man is cornered, and there is no hope for him. He may as well remain indoors and spend the last few days of his life with his pets. You worry about nothing. You worry about trivia."

"The last communication was confusing. Did you catch a thing of what was said?"

"No."

The men shared worried looks with each other like lost tourists.

"I know what you are thinking, but don't worry about it. We can handle whatever comes our way. That girl might have been smart in Germany, but this is the US, the greatest and strongest country in the world. We will show her we are the busters in California."

They burst into laughter.

Suddenly, they became aware of a figure by the passenger window and angled their eyes to see who it was. A black woman in a big hat stood watching them. They were expecting a white young lady. Baffled by her presence, they froze in their seats while their frightened eyes stared at her face and then fixated on the rifle in her hands.

"Wow, wow, wow. I think there is a mistake here, sister. We are not the people you are looking for. I suggest you check your facts well. We are here to pick up a friend to go to town. He will join us very soon. He lives in that house," the driver pointed.

She wagged her head to indicate she was at the right place and had the right people. Steffie cocked the rifle in their faces and pointed at them. They knew she was there to deal with them but couldn't tell who had sent her. They shared a look, exchanging winks. Then, in a synchronized move, they went for their guns but were beaten to it. She shot their hands before they could shoot. The driver fell on the wheel while his colleague slumped on the door, both dropping their guns. They were grateful she didn't kill them. As a matter of fact, they knew she didn't come to kill. She could have done it if that was the motive.

Johann watched the action through the window in his lounge. He watched as she snatched the earpieces from their ears and started for the front door to his house. He was confused about the black woman heading to his house. He had expected a young white woman; the girl he had heard of wasn't black. He started towards the door to answer once the knock came. Was the woman there on somebody's assignment? Was she there for Jeurgen? Was she Steffie in disguise? Who was he about to let into his house? The woman had just shot two men. What was the guarantee she would let him live?

The knock came on the door. Johann darted to the door handle and opened it, beaming. She studied his face carefully for a while and then walked in. He took a glance at the street and shut the door. The two studied each other briefly, neither saying a word. He stretched his arms towards her, still smiling. She gave a short smile that radiated menace at the same time. Johann noted that. Gradually but cautiously, they moved towards each other and finally hugged, stepping back almost immediately. She gave the card to him. He looked at it. It was genuine. It was what he had given to Randolph. He dashed to the kitchen and came back with a glass of juice, which he offered her. She declined the offer. She didn't know who the man in front of her was and therefore had no business accepting a drink from him. Disappointed, he set the glass in a tray on a table.

"I understand perfectly. You're welcome."

She dipped her head slightly, still clutching the rifle and watching every move he made. He knew if he made one wrong move, he was dead.

"Please, put the weapon away. We've to leave this place before they reorganize and strike again. The people who sent the men in the car will hear what has happened and send more men."

"Ok. Then let's leave now. Hurry!"

Johann hurried to get his car keys, relieved that he had the right woman in his house. Steffie's accent told him he was dealing with the target. They left via the back door into his car, which was parked at the rear of the house.

As the vehicle zoomed out of the area, the two wounded men in the white sedan sighed their relief. Each had two gunshots in their hands and feared the black girl would come back and kill them.

"What do you suggest we do?" the driver asked.

"I suggest we go back to our families and stop working for the boss. The woman saved our lives. It is a sign that we have to change our ways. Let us stop this work. We can find jobs elsewhere. The pay may not be that good, but it may be decent."

"I agree with you."

While the car raced down the freeway, Johann looked at her face and smiled, shaking his head.

"You're amazing! Very amazing! How's life back in Germany anyway?"

"Good."

"Will you be kind enough to tell me how you met the men I sent? I mean, what specifically happened during the mission? I know they all died, but how?"

"I can't help you with that. I didn't kill them."

"Oh no, I didn't mean you had anything to do with their deaths. I just want to know what specifically went wrong."

She looked out the window as he focused on the road. It didn't look like she was in the mood to discuss the issue.

"Where are we going, by the way?"

"You'll find out soon. You have the envelope with you, right?"

She nodded. He smiled to himself. Fifteen minutes later, the car pulled up in front of a condo in a quiet neighborhood. They got down and entered the condo, the door shutting behind them.

As soon as they took a couple of paces into the condo, a man grabbed Steffie's neck from behind, his large hands squeezing her neck. She began to choke. She lost her gun, her legs flailing as she struggled to break the man's hold. Johann thrust his hand into her jacket and yanked out the fake envelope. He looked at the man holding her and then tapped his massive arm.

"Kill her." He ordered.

Johann opened the door and exited towards his car as the man tightened his grip on her neck. Steffie's effort to free herself amounted to nothing. She bit the man's arm, but he wouldn't let go. Still choking and struggling to breathe, Steffie yanked out the hunter's knife and swung it viciously over her shoulder. The blade caught the man in the eye. He released her instantly as she pulled the weapon out. Holding his eye and groaning, she thrust the knife into his chest and yanked it out. The man fell to the floor, holding his chest. Steffie neared him and stabbed his right knee repeatedly until the man surrendered. She rechecked her pockets. The original envelope and her wallet were in place.

Johann sat in his car, opened the envelope, and checked the list. He discovered to his shock, he didn't have the right document. What he had was a fake. He glanced at the door to the condo, pursing his lips and clenching his fists. He had been fooled.

Steffie, meanwhile, opened the door a crack and observed as Johann got out of the car with a gun in his hand. He approached the front door, looking at the two adjoining windows to the door. He wondered if his man had finished the job. She crossed to the wall by the door, waiting for him.

The door swung wide open, a hand holding a gun appearing moments later. She slammed the door on the hand so hard, Johann moaned and dropped the gun. She held onto the hand at the same time and forcibly hauled him into the condo. She kicked the door shut. Johann rolled a couple of times and hit his head on the wall.

"You didn't think I was going to give the original to you, did you?" she asked.

The bewildered man looked at the man on the floor, holding his eye and then at Steffie. He rose and charged her. She hurled the knife at his head and, at the same time, scooped up his gun. The knife pierced his shoulder. He held his shoulder as he wobbled closer. She aimed and fired at his knee. She shot the other knee. Johann was now on the floor, crippled. She picked up her hat and donned it.

"You ordered me killed, but I am sparing your life and that of your friend here," she pointed.

Johann crawled towards the corner. She knew there was something he was being drawn to. She watched as his shaking hand moved towards his back. She aimed her gun at his face.

"Stop whatever you are about to do. If you push me, I will kill you," she warned, taking paces towards him.

The man's hand moved forward with a pistol; she shot the hand instantly. Then she kicked his face. Johann dropped the gun, which she took and emptied of bullets. Finally, she fired two more shots into his knees.

"Maybe this will make you humble. I just told you I didn't come to kill. Stupid fool! Your friend here appreciates what I have done for him, but you don't," she pointed.

She dragged the two men by the legs into a room at the back of the house. There was a phone on a desk. She checked to ensure it had a dial tone.

"You can call for an ambulance or the police using this phone. I see it is working perfectly," she said.

She hurried out and locked the door, throwing the key on the floor. She located a phone directory by the landline phone in the corridor. A quick check gave her Jeurgen's phone number. She lifted the handset and dialed. She dialed again after the first attempt failed.

CHAPTER TWENTY-THREE

Jeurgen relaxed in his rocking chair on the lawn when his phone rang on the small table next to him. He reached for it and checked the caller's identity. He didn't know the number and decided not to take it. The phone kept ringing. He stopped it. All his calls to Germany hadn't been successful. He hadn't heard from Martina or the two agents he had sent. Everything he had invested into the mission had failed woefully. He knew the game was up. He could only wait to see what would happen next. The phone rang again. He unwrapped a gum and placed it in his mouth. On careful consideration, he decided to take the call. He pressed the receive key.

"Hello?"

"Jeurgen Reuter?"

He sat up suddenly, wondering who the female voice was. The name had jolted him. The caller knew him. The caller knew his real name. Then it occurred to him the caller might be Steffie. His checks had revealed the girl on the loose hadn't been nabbed. Reports said she was hiding somewhere in the southern part of Germany, but he knew she might have escaped the country with the envelope. The caller repeated her question.

"I've been waiting for your call. I'm glad you made it. I applaud you."

"I don't need that. I know everything, and I don't think we should go over anything. There is no time for that, and frankly, there is no need for it. So drop $20m into the trash bin under the big tree at the park. Come alone. Otherwise, your business is gone, as will be your reputation. And guess what? A long vacation awaits you in jail."

There was a brief moment of silence. He coughed a couple of times.

"Is that all you want for the parcel?"

"I'll come after you if you fail to deliver. You make one wrong move, and I will go to the FBI. 1400 hours prompt. Remember to carry your phone with you."

"You got it. Thank you for getting in touch."

He got up quickly with the help of his walking stick and headed to the house. He was relieved by the call, admitting if Martina and his men were dead, Steffie must be very good at what she did. However, there was no guarantee he had spoken to the right person. Anybody could have called him if the person knew his background. Johann could be behind the call, but he didn't think he was still alive, given his men's attack on him on the golf course months ago. Could the caller be Martina? He smiled as he entered the corridor and shut the door. It was in his interest to meet the caller even though he wouldn't meet her demands. Since he didn't know if she had the parcel as promised, it didn't make sense to give her what she had asked for. He would carry some money to the park, though.

All the benches in the park were occupied. There were many people in the park, some of who played games, read books, and ate. Others simply enjoyed the warm weather by lying on the ground with their faces gazing at the sky. Two RVs parked side by side did business, serving coffee, soft drinks, hotdogs, sandwich, and candy. A Bentley pulled not far from the trash bin located yards from the second RV. The driver didn't get out but waited as he scanned the park. After a couple of minutes, a hooded man got out and walked to the trunk. He opened it, took out two black bags, and walked very slowly to the trash bin. He opened the bin and dropped the bags in. He went back for two more bags, dropped them in the bin, and stood waiting. His eyes darted around the park, searching for the caller. When his phone rang, he yanked it quickly from his pocket.

Up in the tree a couple of yards from him, Steffie watched the hooded man as he looked around him.

"Remove the hood and spin around slowly," Steffie demanded.

"I don't think that will be a good idea."

"Do as I ask."

He obeyed her order with difficulty and then quickly pulled the hood over his head again.

"The envelope is under the bin."

He smiled at the statement as he turned around towards the bin.

"How do I know it's not a fake?"

"You have my word."

He reached the bin with some difficulty as he walked without his walking stick. He bent gently and looked beneath the bin. A black envelope was there. He picked it up, turned around carefully, and walked back to his Bentley.

He looked around but found no one he suspected might be the caller. He opened the envelope, took out the folded paper, and unfolded it. He took out his reading glasses and put them on. As he studied the list, he discovered that his name was off the list. He got on the phone immediately, retrieving the caller's number so he could call. He felt something on the nape of his neck and froze. When he looked in the rearview mirror, Steffie's gun was sticking in his neck. He began to shake. He couldn't tell if the real Steffie was with him or an imposter. He had expected a young white lady with an accent. Now he was confronted with a black lady with an American accent. She spoke like an African-American.

"Relax. There is only me. No one else is with me. I came alone as promised. Once it's just the two of us, don't you think we should have fun in here? Please keep the phone in your pocket. You don't have to contact me. I'm here, Grandpa. I am right here with you."

"This is not the right list."

Steffie stole a glance at the trash bin every now and then to ensure that no one tampered with the bags.

"Oh? That's what he gave me before he died."

"The paper is not of the correct period. I am smart enough to know that. This is a fake."

She frisked him for weapons. The man was clean.

"How much did you put in the bin? If you lie to me, I will shoot you in the head. I'm sure you know what I can do."

"$2m. I was going to add the difference after I'd checked the authenticity of the list."

"Get out to the bin and bring all the money. Now!"

He got out and wobbled to the bin, opened it, and took out the first two bags. He brought them to Steffie and then went back for the other two as she scanned the park for signs of gunmen. There was no sign of gunmen or suspicious characters. The man had come alone as agreed in the phone conversation. She ordered him to sit behind the wheel. He sat weightily in his seat. She took a cursory look at the contents of the bags, opened the door, and was set to get out. The old man was worried about the transaction. He had been short-changed.

"When do I get the original?" he asked warily.

"As far as I know, that's it, but if I find the original, we'll have another transaction. So don't worry about anything, Grandpa. I stick to my word, and I don't cheat in anything I do, but if you don't mind, I would like to ask a question."

"What is it?"

"What is special about the names in the list? Who are the people on the list?"

"I don't think you need to know that. You told me earlier you know everything, so why ask?"

"I know parts of it."

"I suggest you hold on to that. I feel cheated and betrayed."

"I have done my bit, Grandpa. I have given you what I received. If what you are holding isn't what you expected, then the fault must have come from the man who gave the list to me. Maybe that was all he also got, or maybe he didn't believe me well enough to give everything to me. Come on, be fair to me. I can't be blamed in a situation like that. Can I?"

She reached out and took his cell phone, got out with the bags, and kicked the door shut. He slammed the wheel as he glanced back at the receding figure of the girl who had just shafted him. He thrust his hand underneath his seat and took out a gun. He took another look at her and wished he had the strength to use it. Then, shaking his head in disbelief, he started the Bentley and moved on.

"Shit!" he exclaimed.

The car eased forward slowly past kissing couples to a side street, turned right, and disappeared. He had taken a good look at Steffie but couldn't have her killed. Where would any killer he sent look in the US for her? The accent of the lady he had dealt with confused him. He couldn't tell if he had spoken to a black girl or somebody disguised as such.

The truck raced on the highway while Steffie listened to the radio. She wore a blue baseball cap. She had stopped by a store and shopped for a month. Everything she would need was in the trunk. She had money to live a peaceful, quiet life anywhere in the world apart from Europe. She opened the bags, admired the money, and re-tied the bags. An apartment had been arranged already before coming to the park. It was located in a quiet neighborhood in San Diego. She didn't need more than a one-bed apartment where no one would suspect and come after her. That felt good, but with the original list secured, she was safe now. If identified and arrested, she would present that in any court of competent jurisdiction. She would be acquitted immediately. She wouldn't tell the court she knew what it contained. Germany would then go after anybody who helped to keep the list in the museum. Anybody who protected it would be in trouble for protecting a Nazi war criminal. She was home free. She had called her cousin to inform her everything was fine and that she would receive remittance in due course. The elated cousin had screamed for joy. She had also been promised a visit to the US. She said she couldn't wait for the moment when they would meet again. Steffie looked back at her shopping and smiled. She was back to a normal life again. She liked steak and pork loin. She couldn't wait to get home and start cooking.

The lounge was typical of houses for low-income earners. The furniture was of high quality. A framed photo showing Randolph, Roger, and Calvin in military uniforms hung on the wall. It was evident to any visitor that the three were bud-dies. Steffie sat quietly, watching the three women. She had seen the other men who died in the photo. Locating the house had been a struggle, but she hoped it would be worth the effort. After all, she had given Randolph her word to look for them. These were the widows of the three men who had died in Munich. She had a plastic bag by her feet. The widows were all in their mid-30s. They sat opposite her on the long couch while their kids looked on. They didn't know the visitor sitting in front of them but were prepared to hear what she had to say.

"My name is Naomi Bruce. I am British. I believe you saw the pictures on TV concerning the three men who died in Munich, Germany?"

The women nodded as they exchanged anxious glances.

"What about it?" asked Mrs. Sith.

"Mr. Sith said I should give this to you."

She gave the bag to Mrs. Sith.

The women shared concerned and surprised looks. They wondered who this woman was.

"Really?"

Steffie nodded, "He said it must be shared equally among you."

The women rose to their feet as Mrs. Sith reached for the bag and opened it. Her mouth sprang open at the sight of the contents. The other two joined her and gasped.

"How much is it?" Mrs. Travers asked as she glanced at Steffie.

"$480,000."

"Oh my God!" they chorused.

"Jesus!" Mrs. Palmer yelled in excitement, "…how much do me and my kids get from that obscene amount?"

"$160,000 each."

They moved closer to her and shook hands with her, tears flooding their eyes. Their world had suddenly changed by the gift they had received from the toil and sacrifice of their husbands. They hadn't expected to receive anything. Nobody told them anything about why they went to Germany. They had heard rumors but didn't know which version to believe.

"I thought it was all lost. The kids, you know. Education, bills, stuff like that," Mrs. Sith said.

"Yeah," replied Mrs. Palmer and Mrs. Travers.

"Thank you," the women acknowledged.

Steffie rose to leave, "I think I'd better get going."

"How about a contact number, we'd like to call you someday?" Mrs. Palmer asked.

"That's very kind of you, but I'll call you once I get back to England. I will call you. Take care of yourselves."

"Ok."

"Excuse me, madam?" Mrs. Travers said.

Steffie granted her audience.

"Do you know who sent them there? And how they died?"

"No. I also read in the newspaper, but I met Randolph through his lawyer in England, and he asked me to travel this far to give this to you. The next thing I heard, he was dead. That is all I can tell you. His lawyer and I went to the same school. He asked me to do it because he trusted me with the money. Generally speaking, women are more loyal when it comes to money. That was his belief when I asked Randolph why he chose to give the money to me and not his lawyer. Please don't ask me where he got the money because I don't have an answer to that question. I have done what he asked me to do. I have to catch a flight back to England to see my family."

"Thank you. We were fortunate to have their bodies shipped to us for burial. We didn't have much but managed to bury them anyway. Thank you."

She exited the house and got into her truck which was sprayed in a different color. She noticed the women and their children had followed her. She smiled as she started the truck. They waved amid broad smiles. She honked and zoomed the truck away.

Florida

Steffie sat at a table with a glass of orange juice in her hand. The table stood by the window of her one-bed apartment. She was reading brochures from universities in Florida and planned to get a degree in electrical engineering. Then she would get a master's in the same field and teach. She had already spoken to three universities, all of which had promised to make her stay on campus a memorable one and her studies quite an experience. She had contacted Jeurgen again through one of his companies and given him a one-week ultimatum to report himself to the German authorities, outlining everything he had done. Furthermore, he was to exonerate Steffie by his confession. If he failed to act within the given time frame, she would go to the FBI with her evidence. Johann was still alive, and she knew he would be willing to testify against him. She had returned half of the old man's money to him, explaining why she had kept one. She needed money to start a new life since she had lost everything. The man had promised to tell everything to the authorities, adding that his life was almost spent and he didn't have anything to lose. He had children who were all filthy rich and would continue with his various businesses even if most of his assets were frozen. Jeurgen, in turn, had given back the one million dollars to Steffie for fighting for what was good. He had learned that Johann was still alive and recuperating at home. That made his options to resist Steffie's proposal limited. With Johann alive, he couldn't lie about his past and what he had done. Steffie had lied to Jeurgen; her conversations with him both on the phone and in his Bentley were recorded and would be presented in court if he lied about anything.

HISTRIA
BOOKS

Addison & Highsmith

Other fine works of fiction available from Addison & Highsmith Publishers:

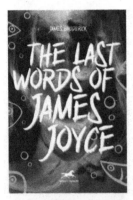

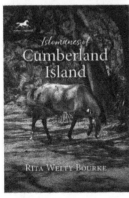
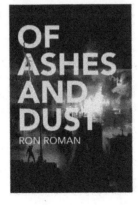

For these and many other great books visit
HistriaBooks.com